THE SANDALWOOD PRINCESS

"I realize flirting is practically an addiction with you, Mr. Brentick, but you must try to show it who is master. If I were a man you wouldn't try to flirt with me, would you? Why not just pretend I'm a man."

He gazed at her for a moment, then laughed. "The task you propose, Miss Cavencourt, is quite impossible."

"Then you shall have to flirt all by yourself."

"You don't know you're provocative, do you?" he asked, his voice low, puzzled.

Alarmed, Amanda swung round sharply. That was a mistake. She came up short mere inches from his chest. Her glance flew to his face. "What are you doing?" she demanded.

"Flirting. All by myself. I'm trying to pretend you're a man." His face bent closer. "I'm trying to remember my place." His hands clamped down on the rail on either side of her. "It's not working," he whispered, his breath warm on her face as his mouth descended to hers.

Winner of the
Romance Writer's of America Award
for Best Regency of 1990

THE
SANDALWOOD
PRINCESS

LORETTA CHASE

AVON BOOKS ◆ NEW YORK

All characters and events portrayed in this work are fictitious.

AVON BOOKS
A division of
The Hearst Corporation
1350 Avenue of the Americas
New York, New York 10019

First Avon Books Printing: November 1991

AVON TRADEMARK REG. U.S. PAT. OFF. AND IN OTHER COUNTRIES, MARCA REGISTRADA, HECHO EN U.S.A.

Printed in the U.S.A.

RA   10   9   8   7   6   5   4   3   2   1

To my husband, Walter

Prologue

1811

THOUGH THE HOUSE Hemu had so nervously entered was finer than any he could aspire to, it seemed at first far too modest for the powerful woman who dwelt here. Yet perhaps her secluded abode did suit the Rani Simhi. She was the princess of secrets. Even her true name was no longer spoken. The great Lioness, the most dangerous woman in all India, might live precisely where and as she chose. So her humble messenger Hemu meditated as he stood, head bowed, patiently awaiting her pleasure.

Moments passed. The fan her large manservant held swayed languorously over her head, and the smoke of her hookah curled and shuddered in the lazy current.

At last she spoke. "You bring me news, Hemu."

"Yes, princess."

She gestured to him to speak.

"My master but two days ago composed a letter to his friend in England," Hemu said. "My master expressed his sorrow that the friend's wife is no more."

The rani raised her index finger a fraction of an inch. Instantly, every servant vanished from the room, except for the great, hulking man who continued dragging the fan back and forth in the heavy air.

"Is it the name I gave you?" she asked Hemu.

He produced a piece of paper on which he'd painstakingly copied the English letters: Hedgrave.

The princess glanced at the paper, then up at her servant.

1

"This is an intelligent man, Padji," she said. "We will give him five hundred rupees."

Hemu's jaw dropped.

"You see the advantages of literacy," she told the messenger. "You are a rich man now. I advise you to leave your master."

As she spoke, the fan stopped moving. Padji drew out a bag of coins and gave it to the stunned Hemu.

Hemu left, showering hysterical blessings upon the wise and generous rani whose life, he prayed, would continue a thousand thousand years. When his footsteps died away, the rani rose.

"Padji," she said, "we go to Calcutta."

1814

In England, in the richly furnished study of Hedgrave House, the Marquess of Hedgrave trembled with fury. "It is incomprehensible to me," he raged. "At last the she-devil comes out of hiding, and you tell me we can't touch her."

"Politically, her timing was perfect, as usual," Lord Danbridge answered. "Ranjit Singh is bound to capitulate, sooner or later, and he's not above selling his supposed allies. She had sense enough to move before he did. She knew Bengal would be a deal safer than the Punjab for her, especially with the Company's protection. Rightly so, I must say. Whatever you think of her, the Rani Simhi's invaluable. The Ministry could do with a few more minds like that. Why, her spies—"

"I know. The whole damned subcontinent's infested with them." Lord Hedgrave stood up and stalked to the fireplace. Glaring into the flames, he said, half to himself, "I had them offer her twenty-five thousand. It's *mine*, curse her, but I was willing to pay. I might have known that wouldn't work. She knew who wanted it. Who else knows she's got it but the man she stole it from?"

Hedgrave had always had a bee in his bonnet about the Indian woman, his friend thought. In the years since Lady Hedgrave's death, however, the thing had grown into an obsession. Masking his concern, Lord Danbridge said gently, "Maybe she hasn't got it any longer. It's been a long time."

"Then what's she hiding?" his host snapped. "You sent the news yourself. Six different agents assigned. Three now incapacitated, two mysteriously vanished, one dead."

"India can be a dangerous place."

"Precisely." Lord Hedgrave turned back to his guest. "That is why I want you to contact the Falcon."

As Danbridge opened his mouth to protest, the marquess shook his head. "I know what you're going to say, Danbridge. Don't waste your breath. I happen to know he's working for us."

"I merely wished to point out that this is not the sort of enterprise he's accustomed to undertake."

"He'll undertake anything, provided the reward is high enough. You may offer him fifty thousand pounds—in addition, of course, to expenses. He'll get his money as soon as he puts the object into my hands."

"Here?" Danbridge asked incredulously. "You want him to come to England?"

"Into my hands. We're a long way from Calcutta, and the woman's fiendishly clever. Too much could go wrong along the way. I won't have him passing it on to anyone. He is to get it—I don't care how—and put it into my hands," he repeated, as though it were an incantation. His blue eyes glittered with an odd light.

Lord Danbridge looked away uneasily as he considered his friend's demand. Certainly, Hedgrave had, when required, moved mountains. Dealing with India—which was to say, the East India Company—was generally a case of moving mountains: Board of Control, Secret Committee, Directors, Council, Governor-General, and General Secretariat, not to mention Parliament itself. A lot of stubborn men, precious few of whom truly considered the well-being of the vast subcontinent England now reluctantly managed, thanks to Clive and Wellesley and their ilk.

Except in this one disturbing matter, Hedgrave at least acted disinterestedly. He was one of the few who truly grasped the difficulties of overseeing India's internal affairs and strove to accommodate the contradictory demands of the British and the many differing cultures of India.

Considering Hedgrave's unstinting political labours, one could hardly begrudge him a favour in return.

The Indian woman had apparently stolen from him an object of considerable value. Now that she was out of hiding, Hedgrave wanted it back. Given the previous failures, the Falcon was their only hope. In any case, he was the only man Danbridge could rely on not to get killed in the attempt.

Lord Danbridge met the feverish blue gaze. "I'll contact him," he said, "but it will take some time."

"I've waited thirty years," was the taut answer. "I can wait."

=1=

1816

THERE WERE WORSE places to live in Calcutta, and better. Here in the crowded quarter, as elsewhere, the streets flooded in the monsoon season and the price of a palanquin soared in consequence. Fever, too, struck here, just as it did in the great palaces of Garden Reach and in the meanest slums.

The place stank, as all Calcutta stank. Indoors, the odour of ghee blended sickeningly with the reek of bug flies. Out of doors, the stench of death overpowered even that of animals and refuse, as the smoke of funeral pyres on the Hooghly riverbank thickened the broiling atmosphere. Incense only added to the miasma. In the near one-hundred-degree heat of midday, the noisome compound curdled and churned like some foul sorcerer's brew. All the perfumes of Arabia would not sweeten this place and make it fresh again, had it ever been.

All of India was not like Calcutta, Philip knew. Places existed where the breezes blew sweet and pure. He had long since learned, however, to close his senses to what could not be mended or amended. Fifteen years in India had taught him, if not an Oriental patience, then a sufficient Occidental stoicism. The climate, the stench, were beyond his control. Thus he simply accepted them. As to the neighbourhood—admittedly, one might have lived more luxuriously, but then, not so anonymously.

His rented stucco cottage suited his current role as a hookah merchant. In this busy quarter, his comings and goings aroused little interest. His command of the language was flawless, as was his grasp of etiquette. The fierce Indian sun had darkened his complexion, and an application of nut oil did the same for his fair hair. Even the blue of his eyes did not betray him. Eurasians were scarcely rare in this place.

Calcutta's founder, an Englishman named Job Charnock, had married a Brahmin lady. Like Job, the British who came in earlier times mingled freely with the natives. One found their progeny not only throughout the subcontinent, but at Eton and Oxford as well.

Thus Philip Astonley, youngest son of the Viscount Felkoner—blue-blooded and unequivocally British—easily passed in India as a mongrel. This was no great transformation, in Philip's opinion. In the process of ejecting his youngest son from the family, his lordship had called the eighteen-year-old an ungrateful cur. Philip perceived small difference between Nameless and Anonymous. In any case, if he ceased at present to be anonymous, he would very likely cease to live.

The thought was not an idle one. As he turned the corner into the narrow street, his finely tuned instincts stirred in warning. The street was deserted, as it usually was in the sweltering afternoon, when most of Calcutta slept. Yet he'd caught a movement, a glancing shadow at the opposite end of the street. His steps quickened.

He had the house key in his hand when he reached the door. Before he opened it, Philip glanced about once more. The street lay empty and still. In the next instant, he'd slipped through the door and locked it behind him. The small house, shuttered against the glaring sun, was dark, but not altogether quiet. From the room beyond came a strangled moan. Silence. Then another moan, higher pitched.

Philip drew out his knife and crept noiselessly to the bedroom. A wail of agony tore through the stillness, and he saw a man on the floor beside the bed jerk convulsively. Muttering an oath, Philip hurried forward, and dropped to his knees beside his servant's knotted body.

His face was hot and soaked with sweat, his pulse frenetic. As soon as Philip touched him, Jessup jerked spasmodically and began to babble. The words, half English and half Hindustani, spilled in a steady, chattering stream, punctuated by strangled cries of anguish. It looked like fever, but it wasn't.

"Damn you," Philip growled. "Don't you die on me, soldier."

Grasping the servant under the shoulders, Philip hauled him onto the bed. The body twisted and trembled, then knotted up once more in pain. The hysterical litany—of scorpions, cobras, bits of the Book of Common Prayer, fragments of battles, women's names, oaths—was broken only by choked wails of agony.

The poison evidently acted slowly, bringing hallucinations as well as pain. Without knowing exactly what sort of poison, Philip dared give his servant nothing, not even water.

He squeezed Jessup's hand. "I'll have to leave you for a minute, old man," he whispered. "I'm going for help. Just hang on, will you? Just *hang on*."

The old woman Philip sought lived across the way. Silently praying she'd be home, he threw open the door.

He found her waiting on his doorstep.

He was not altogether surprised. The aged Sharda was the local midwife and doctor. She could probably smell illness and death.

"My servant, mother—" he began.

"I know," she said. "You have great trouble, Dilip sahib."

Sahib? Though Philip bowed his head respectfully as she entered, his eyes narrowed with suspicion.

"Jasu—" he began again.

She gestured him to be silent. "I know," she said.

In the room beyond, Jessup screamed, then subsided again into demented babbling. The latter was worse than the screams. Philip gritted his teeth. It was all he could do to keep from dragging the old woman to the sickbed. She had her own ways, however.

He felt her gaze upon him.

"I will go to him," she said. "Have patience."

She studied the small space which served as kitchen, living room, and dining room. A plate of pastries sat upon the table. She took one, broke it in half, stared at the fruit center, then sniffed it.

"Figs, you see," she said, pointing to the dark paste. "To add another sort of seed is not difficult, and the flour, I think, was tainted. He has terrible visions?"

"Yes," Philip said tightly, "and pain. Yet I hesitated to give him anything."

"Opium we can give him for the pain," she said. "The other must run its course, I fear."

Her examination confirmed the preliminary diagnosis. Accordingly, she measured out a dose of the laudanum Philip handed her. After what seemed an eternity, Jessup began to quiet somewhat. He still babbled, but more like a drunken man, and the spasms and strangled cries ceased. Perhaps he would sleep, Sharda told Philip. At any rate, the servant would not die, though he may wish it. His recovery would be very long and very painful.

"A fiendish mixture it is, to bring both madness and maddening pain," Sharda said as they left the sickroom, "and no relief of death. But it was not meant to kill him." She patted his arm in a sad, kindly way. "Only to cause great suffering, so that you would heed the warning."

He had known, hadn't he? He'd felt it as he'd entered the street, and seen it in the vanishing shadow.

While the old woman was examining Jessup, Philip had put on water to boil. Now he courteously offered tea, and made himself wait until she was ready to enlighten him.

She sipped and nodded her approval. Then she looked at him.

"A little while before, a man brought me a message," she said. "I must tell the blue-eyed merchant he is known, as is his intention. And so, he will die if he does not depart Calcutta before another day passes."

Not only known, but his mission known as well. Gad, the woman was incredible. "And this, I take it," Philip said calmly, nodding towards the sickroom, "is what I might expect?"

"You know of whom we speak. Your death will come slowly, only after many times Jasu's sufferings. Go away, as you are told, and *live*."

Philip Astonley was not a reckless man. He never underestimated his adversaries. If the Rani Simhi said she'd kill him, she'd do it, and, naturally, in the ghastliest way her evil imagination could devise. He'd known she'd penetrate his disguise sooner or later. He had not, however, dreamt this would occur quite so soon. What had it been? Less than forty-eight hours. Still, he should have been prepared. It was his fault Jessup lay in the room beyond, mad with pain and hallucination.

He met Sharda's anxious gaze. "I will heed the warning," he said.

Minutes after, her grandson, Hari, set off with a message to Fort William. Two hours later, Hari returned with the Honourable Randall Groves. A trio of servants and a pair of palanquins followed them.

Every window and door in the street promptly filled with curious onlookers. This was perfectly satisfactory. The rani would speedily receive word the merchant was departing.

Philip was already packed when Groves entered, looking exceedingly put out. He grew even more put out when

Philip led him into his own room and quietly explained what was expected of him.

"Confound it," Randall snapped. "This is your specialty, ain't it? How the devil do you expect me—"

"However you can," Philip said. "Bribe, lie—I don't care. The *Evelina* is scheduled to sail tomorrow, and Jessup and I have to be on board." He thrust a packet of papers into Randall's hands. "Don't use them unless you have to. I'd rather not bring his lordship into this, and he'd rather I didn't as well, for obvious reasons."

"Philip, the ship's loaded to the limit, and Blayton don't even want the passengers he's got. The Bullerhams, Cavencourt's sister, Monty Larchmere, and all their servants. You expect me to throw a couple of 'em overboard?"

"If you must. I'd talk to Monty first. He's a greedy devil. For a hefty bribe, he'll probably agree to wait through the monsoon season for another ship." While he spoke, Philip was winding a turban about his head.

Randall stared at the turban a moment. Then a horrified understanding widened his eyes. "Good grief," he said. "*That's* why you sent for me. You're still meaning to do it, ain't you? For God's sake, Philip, the curst woman knows who you are!"

"Exactly. As I so carefully explained, she means to kill me if I'm not gone by tomorrow, so I'd better work fast, hadn't I?"

Philip slipped his knife into its sheath and fastened it to the sash he wore under his long muslin *kurta*. With the loose shirt he wore muslin trousers. For the evening's endeavour, these would be less encumbering than the *dhoti*'s complicated draping. His toilette complete, Philip returned his attention to the now grim Randall.

"Don't mope, Randy," he said. "I don't plan to get killed. The lady wants me gone, and I'll oblige her. But I'm damned if I'm leaving without it. I've never failed yet, and a man must consider his reputation."

"You're mad," said Randall.

The blue eyes flashed. "Have a glance in the other room, my lad," Philip said in a low voice. "Have a look at what the witch's done to Jessup. I can't pay her back as I'd like, because the curst female's too precious to our superiors. But I'll repay her as I *can*, that I swear."

The Rani Simhi resided in a vast mansion on the banks of the Hooghly at Garden Reach. Though the English had built these Palladian palaces exclusively for themselves, the Indian princess was an exceptional case. The Governor-General, Lord Moira, had personally overseen the previous resident's eviction, in order to provide the enigmatic Indian woman a domicile befitting both her status and her usefulness to His Majesty's government.

This night, she celebrated her fifty-fifth birthday. The palace was packed with guests both British and Indian. She appeared briefly, to receive the company's good wishes, then, according to her custom, retired to her private rooms. Though in so many ways unlike other native women, she chose to imitate them in leaving the responsibilities of hosting to her sons.

Since the party was held in her honour, she might have lingered if she chose. This night, however, she had one visitor whose company she wished to enjoy privately. So she explained to Amanda Cavencourt when the latter voiced regret about keeping the princess from her guests.

"You leave tomorrow for England," said the rani. "We may never meet again. Besides, they are all idiots, and tiresome." She made a slight gesture with her hand, and a large, jewel-encrusted hookah was brought forward.

"Your brother, for instance," she went on, as she examined the mouthpiece. "Generally not a stupid man, but he has married foolishly an ignorant woman. If she were not so ignorant, she would love you. Instead, she hates you, and drives you away. I detest her."

"Two women cannot rule one house," Amanda said

calmly. "My presence is a constant irritant. Or perhaps embarrassment is more like it. My ways aren't hers and never will be, so there's always friction. You understand," she added.

The rani studied the silken-clad woman who sat cross-legged opposite her. "I understand she would fly into a rage, could she see you now. I am told she considers the sari indecent."

Amanda grinned as she took up her mouthpiece. "She'd certainly drop into five fits if she saw me smoking this." She gave a defiant shrug, and drew on the hookah with practised ease.

She knew her erratic attention to deportment merely aggravated her sister-in-law's dislike. In time, Eustacia might have nagged her wayward relation into more acceptable behaviour. Unfortunately, no lessons, no reminders, however regular, could change Amanda's appearance.

Her light complexion resembled too closely the mellow ivory lightness of the natives of the northern Ganges. Glossy dark brown hair, rippling in thick waves, framed the oval of her face. Thick black lashes fringed large eyes of a peculiarly light, changeable brown. The bones of her countenance strongly defined, the nose straight and well-modeled, the mouth wide and overfull, Amanda's face was far too exotic for European beauty. More mortifying to Lady Cavencourt, both Europeans and natives regularly mistook Amanda for an Indian.

"I comprehend well enough," the older woman answered, "but I object. We will speak no more of her. She is tiresome. I have a story for you, much more interesting than your foolish new sister."

Nothing could be so pleasurable as this, Amanda thought. How she would miss the sultry Calcutta evenings spent with the fascinating princess . . . the languorous clouds of smoke and incense that filled the room with shifting spirit-shadows . . . the rani's clear voice, smooth as a running river, coiling through the twists and turns of ancient legends. Amanda forced back the tears filling her eyes.

The rani smoked silently for a moment. Then she raised a finger. All the servants scurried from the room, save the large Padji, who stood still as a statue by the door. When the rest were gone, she began:

"Tonight, I tell you of the goddess Anumati, she from whom the childless women of my native kingdom besought sons and daughters. When she answered their prayers, the women would bring her gifts, as rich as their means permitted. But whether rich or poor, the new mother must always bring as well a carved figure."

From the cushion beside her, the rani picked up a small wooden statue. Amanda had seen it before. Normally it stood upon a shelf, along with other statues and talismans in the rani's vast collection. It was about ten inches tall, a beautifully carved sandalwood figure of a smiling woman whose belly was swollen with child.

"Many lifetimes ago," the rani continued, "such figures filled Anumati's temple, and precious stones adorned her magnificent statue. In her forehead was set a large ruby, and in her right hand an immense pearl in the shape of a tear. These were the gifts of a prince and princess of ancient times. The ruby, from the prince, symbolized the blood of new life: the son Anumati had given the previously childless couple. The pearl, his wife's gift, represented the tears of happiness she'd shed at her son's birth. This stone, more rare than even the ruby, was called the Tear of Joy."

By the doorway, Padji shifted slightly, and threw his mistress a glance. Her eyes upon the statue, the rani went on.

"Many lifetimes later, marauders came and ransacked the rich temple. The chief of them must have the greatest jewels, of course. With difficulty, he removed the ruby. The pearl, however, was more deeply set. To get at it, he must break the hand from the statue. He beat upon it with an altar stone and at last the arm began to crack. At that same moment came a great rumbling. The temple walls shuddered and the ground beneath trembled. His terrified companions fled, some dropping their loot in their haste. He remained, still struggling for the pearl. Just as he broke the hand away, the temple roof collapsed."

"Anumati was very angry," Amanda murmured. "I don't blame her."

"Her revenge was greater than that. Mere hours after the temple's collapse, several of the marauders returned. The new leader, as greedy as his predecessor, determined to have the two great stones. They dug through the rubble—a tremendous task—and at last, by the next day, found the chief's crushed body. The ruby lay in his hand. The pearl was gone."

She looked at Amanda. "What do you make of that?"

"The logical explanation is that the pearl was crushed to powder," Amanda said thoughtfully. "Yet Anumati's worshippers would probably conclude she took away her treasure because, instead of Life and Love, death and destruction filled her temple."

The princess nodded. "It was said Anumati had abandoned the defiled place and taken all joy with her. The temple grounds were considered accursed. My people followed the advice of their priests, and did not attempt to restore either the temple or their ravaged town. Instead, they built new houses a safe distance away."

Gently she stroked the figure's forehead. After a moment she said, "Now I come to my own lifetime."

From the doorway came a long, drawn-out sigh. The princess affected not to hear it.

"I was many years younger than you when a Punjab prince conquered my father's kingdom," she said. "When this conqueror investigated his new domain, he made two discoveries. One was myself. To strengthen his political position, he took me as his wife. He also discovered the temple ruins. His greed being far greater than his fear of curses, he ordered the temple excavated. Thus he unearthed all the treasure the robbers had left behind in their terror. Also, he found the skull of the chieftain, and within it"—she paused briefly—"the Tear of Joy."

Amanda stifled a gasp. "In the skull?" she asked incredulously. "How did it get there?"

The rani shrugged. "Who knows? There it lay, undamaged after nearly a century. My husband gave it to me, before all the town. He was a pig, but politic. Before them, he gave it to me. In private, he took it back—for safekeeping, he said. He permitted me to keep a few baubles, and this figure, the only one which had not been destroyed in the temple's collapse. I was not pleased," she added with a faint smile.

There came a loud sniff from the doorway.

"What ails you, Padji?" the princess asked.

"Nothing, mistress."

"Then be silent." She turned back to Amanda. "Once and only once in my life have I loved," the rani said. "I speak not of ordinary love, which I have possessed in abundance. I speak of a great, all-consuming love, such as most persons merely read of or see performed in drama, but never experience in their lives. In your legends, it is the love of Tristan and Isolde. In mine, it is that of Krishna and Radha."

After a moment's consideration, Amanda said softly, "You mean sinful love, I think." She blushed as she spoke, not for any missish reason, but because to speak of sin to the rani was . . . oh, absurd, really. Her morality was not defined by the Church of England or English society.

"Yes," the Indian woman answered calmly. "Sinful love." She lazily drew upon the waterpipe.

While she awaited the rest of the story, Amanda gazed about her, trying to memorise her surroundings, for it would be the last time, perhaps. Thick with smoke and incense, these chambers would have frightened the ladylike Eustacia, and most gently bred British ladies. They would have perceived the place as a den of iniquity. Certainly it fit their image of the Rani Simhi as a dangerous woman whose history comprised one long career of sin.

Perhaps it *was* sin, Amanda reflected. Nonetheless, the princess's world was fascinating, and Amanda had been happier here than anywhere else she could remember. Whether legend or history, the universe her Indian friend revealed was a dream world, captivating as a fairy tale. It was also just as safe as one, for Amanda could never enter its pages.

A light breeze wafted from the garden, carrying the scent of flowers and the fresh fragrance of the carved vetiver entryway. Something else, Amanda thought, drawing an appreciative breath. Agarwood?

"My husband became one of the most powerful princes in India," the rani continued. "Thus the British soon arrived, to persuade him to accept their protection rather than that of the French. Among them was one, tall and fair. In his hair gleamed the golden light of the sun, and in his eyes the glistening sea. I saw him and love consumed me. This passion caused me to risk death, the punishment for adultresses. Richard Whitestone became my lover, and in time, I ran away with him."

Padji cried out, "Oh, mistress, would that I'd cut out the dog's heart!"

"Hold your tongue," said his mistress. "My friend does not wish to hear your ignorant babbling." She turned back to Amanda. "He is like a child sometimes. He thinks everything may be resolved by cutting out hearts. One cannot explain to him. He is not a woman."

Amanda's gaze slid from servant to mistress. She understood. "Your lover betrayed you."

The princess shrugged. "Men are easily confused. One night I awoke, and found my lover gone."

"He took everything," Padji growled. "The jewels—"

"He took from a thief," his mistress corrected. "Merely to abandon my husband was insufficient payment for his selfish cruelty. I stole from his treasures, took what he held

16

truly precious, gold and jewels. Yet this was not entirely revenge. My lover and I must live on something, and he was not a wealthy young man."

"Still, he took everything? Abandoned you and left you destitute? Whether you'd stolen the treasures or not, that was a despicable thing to do," Amanda said indignantly.

"There is more to be unfolded," the rani answered, "as it was unfolded to me. I later learned my husband had persuaded the Englishman to seduce and take me away."

Amanda's mouth fell open.

"My husband had grown to fear my influence. He was eager to be rid of me, but dared not kill me, for fear of an uprising. If I committed adultery, however, my own people would pursue me and put me to death, while he stood by, innocent, the injured spouse."

"Good heavens."

"As I told you, he was politic. Still, he also betrayed his English ally. He'd promised Richard Whitestone a considerable reward, which he failed to deliver. Thus my lover took his payment from me."

"That hardly excuses him," Amanda said, rubbing her forehead. "I know you believe each matter also contains its opposite, but all I see in this is villainy."

"So it is, memsahib," Padji solemnly agreed. "I might have caught and killed him, but my mistress would not permit it. Even then—"

"I was betrayed. What of it?" the princess interrupted. "Women are always betrayed. Yet I prospered. Did not this Englishman show me the Fire of Love, which so few experience? Did he not release me from my husband and carry me to safety? Within months my husband lay dead of fever—and I was spared the *sati*. Instead of burning on his pyre, I was free, many miles away. Did I not find another husband, worthy and loving, who gave me strong sons and showered me with wealth?"

All while she'd spoken, her voice calm and cool, the rani had continued stroking the statue.

After a moment's silence, she said, "Though he took all else, Richard Whitestone left me this figure. One night, as I lay weeping for him, Anumati came to me in a dream. In time, she said, I would discover the meaning of this suffering, and its end. The one object my lover had left me was her gift to me, which she would fill with all her blessings. This was her promise, and she kept it."

She must have observed dissatisfaction in Amanda's face then, because she laughed. "Ah, my young friend, the matter of love still troubles you."

"You speak as though you forgive him," Amanda said, "yet he behaved abominably in every way. He behaved like a—a prostitute. Then he stole all you had."

"Merely the acts of a desperate man. Yet I have no doubt he loved me. Such passion cannot be feigned. Perhaps that made him most desperate of all, for ours was the love that is madness and rapture at once."

"If it *is* a sort of madness," Amanda said reflectively, "then no wonder it is treacherous. As you said, most of us only read about it—yet the stories are always tragic, as yours seems."

"What tragedy?" was the cool response. "I found happiness after."

"But destructive, at least," Amanda argued, without quite knowing why she needed to argue. "I don't know about Krishna and Radha, but what about Tristan and Isolde? What about Romeo and Juliet?"

"Ah, yes," the princess said. "*Romeo and Juliet*. I have read this work of your great poet many times. A fine scene, that in the garden. She calls to her lover, as I called to mine in my sorrow and loneliness." In English, then, she quoted as she gazed towards her own garden, " 'O! for a falconer's voice, / To lure this tassel-gentle back again.' "

The Rani Simhi was still a beautiful woman. As she softly uttered the longing words, her face softened, too, and for an instant, Amanda saw in her profile the young girl who'd known rapturous passion. For that instant, Amanda almost envied her. Almost.

"Would you lure him back?" she whispered.

The princess's gaze, dark and liquid, came back to her. She smiled.

Padji shifted restlessly.

"We bore Padji beyond his little patience," his mistress said, her voice brisk again, "and I keep you overlong with my tales. Yet he understands," she added, throwing her servant a warning look, "that you must know the story, because now the statue belongs to you, my dear friend." So saying, she held the sandalwood figure out to Amanda.

Stunned, Amanda took it.

"Anumati's is a woman's gift, to be passed from mother to daughter. I have no daughters of my blood, but you have become the daughter of my heart. Thus I pass the Laughing Princess to you. May all her blessings enrich your life, as you have so enriched mine, child."

There was no holding back the tears then, a monsoon flood of them, so that Amanda scarcely saw the heap of gifts Padji began piling before her, barely comprehended the rani's affectionate words of farewell. Silks, kashmir shawls, perfumes, and incense—a rajah's treasure. In vain Amanda protested this largess. The princess waved away all objections.

"If you remained with me, my daughter, thus would I adorn you," she said. "Also, I would find you a fine husband, tall and strong and passionate. Unfortunately, I could find no one worthy in time."

Amanda gave a watery giggle. Indian women were often wed at puberty. At six and twenty, even by English standards she was at her last prayers.

"That is better," the rani said. "We part with smiles." She embraced Amanda, then added, "If I find you a husband, I shall dispatch him to England, never fear."

In the flurry of gift giving and leave taking, they did not hear the soft rustle in the dark garden beyond or the featherlight footsteps fading into the night.

=== 2 ===

AMANDA THOROUGHLY LOATHED the palanquin. She objected on principle to human beings used as beasts of burden. However, the rani always provided a palanquin to collect her English friend and bring her home again. Rather than professional bearers, who were notoriously untrustworthy, four of the rani's own sturdy, well-armed servants carried it.

They made their way speedily through the dark streets, Padji at their side to terrify any prospective evildoers with his muscular hulk and monstrous sword. Amanda doubted even Queen Charlotte's safety was so well provided for.

All the same, Amanda had never travelled with so much wealth, and the jewels in the lacquered box made her anxious. Still, who could know what she carried? Spies. Spies lurked everywhere. Not to mention that everyone by now had heard of the master thief, the Falcon. His vision, it was claimed, penetrated stone walls.

Roderick called the stories typical native nonsense. Certainly, he admitted, India abounded in cutthroats and thieves. Nonetheless, no man could turn himself into the night breeze and slip through keyholes. No man slithered into gardens in the guise of a snake, or flew through windows in the form of a dove. That, supposedly, was how the Falcon had made off with one woman's ruby necklace, and another's diamond bracelets. More likely, Roderick told his sister (when Eustacia was not nearby), the women had bestowed the jewels upon their lovers, and accounted for the missing gems as supernatural thefts. Lately, everything was blamed on the Falcon.

Yet Amanda had heard other tales—of documents, letters, political secrets bought or stolen, then sold. Always, one name was whispered: the Falcon. Only one name, but she little doubted it comprehended a vast network of spies and mercenaries, as likely controlled by the East India Company as by an Indian mastermind.

She sighed. She would miss India, but not its atmosphere of suspicion and treachery. She had grown accustomed to the stench, heat, and din of Calcutta, yet she would not miss those, certainly. Apart from the rani, her one friend, what would she miss, really?

A cry sheered the night, like a dying bird song, and the palanquin halted. Amanda heard Padji's voice in sharp Hindustani: "What message?"

"For the woman," an unfamiliar voice answered in the same language.

Amanda peered through the shutters.

In the darkness she made out Padji's immense form, then a flash of metal, whistling as it swooped to his neck, so swiftly she had no time to cry out a warning before the gleaming blade lay upon the servant's throat. Amanda blinked. That must be Padji's own sword, because his hand hung empty now. How had the man done it?

"Lay down your weapons," the strange voice commanded the bearers, "or he dies."

"Run, fools!" Padji cried. "Take her away. I die for—"

"No!" Amanda cried, before the bearers could move. "Do as the pig says."

"A wise woman," the voice said softly. "Down on your knees, my elephant," he told Padji.

"I kneel to no thieving pig. Cut my throat, then, fool, and the others will fall upon you."

"No!" Amanda screamed.

Too late. Silver gleamed as it swept through the air, and Padji crumpled to the ground. Instantly, the bearers set down their burden. To Amanda's amazement, the intrepid attacker fled, pursued by four shrieking avengers.

Amanda pushed open the palanquin shutters and scrambled out. She stared at the dark heap on the ground. "Oh, Padji," she whispered. Shaking in every limb, she crept towards him. Gingerly, she reached out to his shoulder, then jerked her hand back. What was she thinking of? The thief must have cut his throat. He'd be covered with blood . . . sticky . . . ghastly.

She scuttled back hastily, struggling to control the spasm of nausea. One . . . two . . . three deep breaths. Then she looked about her, while her heart seemed to pound in her ears. She was not far from home. Even if she could have endured touching the body, she certainly could not carry it with her. She returned to the palanquin and quickly collected her belongings.

The robber had chosen the site well. Large gardens sprawled on either side of the dark, narrow passageway's high walls. The houses' inhabitants were too far away to hear cries for help. Normally, the gates at both ends of the passage were kept locked. Tonight, though, with virtually all Calcutta's upper crust at the rani's celebration, it must have been more convenient to leave the way open. Or else the thief had broken in. Alone? Amanda glanced anxiously about her. A risky business for one man, wasn't it?

She held her breath, but the only sounds she made out came from a great distance: hoofbeats and voices. Nearby she heard only her own heart thundering.

Clutching her awkward bundles to her, she hiked up the skirts of her sari, ran blindly to the end of the passage, and turned the corner.

A dark form swept out of a gateway, a hand covered her mouth, another wrapped round her waist and dragged her backwards into the shadows.

"Drop it."

To her shock, it was the same voice she'd heard only minutes before.

She dropped the lacquered jewel box, then drove her elbow into her attacker's stomach and tore away from him. A foot shot out, tripping her. She stumbled, and the packet of silks slid out from under her arm. Still tightly clutching the Laughing Princess, Amanda regained her balance, only to be hauled up against the robber's body. The hand closed over her mouth again, choking her.

"Drop it, curse you!" he gasped.

Amanda squirmed, frantically trying to break free of the suffocating embrace. One strong hand pressed painfully over her mouth. The other crushed her rib cage. She stomped on his foot, pushed, kicked, and elbowed, all the while clutching the sandalwood figure as though it were her firstborn. That was all she wanted. Why wouldn't he take the rest and let her go? But he was pulling at her hands now.

Again she jammed madly with her elbow. This time he abruptly released her, and her own force unbalanced her. She fell against him, felt him dropping with her. They crashed to the ground . . . and she found herself pinned beneath him.

"Foolish woman," he said, panting. While the weight of his hard body held her down, he began prying her fingers loose from the figure.

"No!" she shrieked, as he wrenched the statue from her grasp. "You bastard! No!"

There was a heartbeat's pause, and Amanda realised she'd cried out in English.

"A thousand pardons, memsahib," he said.

Then he leapt to his feet . . . and vanished into the night with the Laughing Princess.

White hot, it churned round her, blinding her: Rage. Amanda dragged herself up onto her knees and screamed, "You filthy bastard! You bloody, thieving swine!" Silence answered. She pounded her fists into the dirt in impotent fury.

Something else pounded, somewhere beyond the vast,

23

surrounding wall of rage. Footsteps? She raised her head, just as a figure staggered into the narrow entryway.

"Oh, missy, what has that pig done to you? Fiend. A hell-fiend. We will find him. We will tear him in pieces and rip out his heart while it yet beats. We will—"

"Padji?" she croaked, disbelieving.

He fell to his knees beside her. "Aye, it is Padji, the worthless slave who has failed you." He took her hand and pressed it to his lips, repeatedly, while he muttered inarticulate lamentations.

Amanda pulled her hand away. "You're alive," she said. "I thought he'd murdered you."

"A blow only. Half a breath's less force and I should not have sunk under it. A moment less in blackness and I should have caught him and killed him, and thrown his polluted head at your feet. Ah, we have been tricked, and it is my folly. Aiyeeeeeee," he wailed. "I am a dead man."

"Do be quiet," Amanda snapped. "There's no point staying here moaning about it. We've got to get home."

The servants were all abed, and Roderick and Eustacia were still out when Amanda and Padji reached the house. This was exceedingly fortunate, for Roderick would have made an international incident out of the attack—after, that is, his wife had finished dropping in and out of fourteen fits of hysterics.

Mrs. Gales, Amanda's companion, possessed a less turbulent disposition. A tall, ample-figured woman in her mid-forties, the auburn-haired widow had small use for emotional displays. India was a treacherous, incomprehensible place, and the natives were, in general, demented. If one made a fuss about every objectionable episode that occurred, one would live in a constant state of fuss. This, to Mrs. Gales's mind, constituted a prodigious waste of time and energy.

Though distressed by her employer's shocking experience, the widow perceived no reason to compound the unpleasantness with swoons or hysteria. Instead, she calmly advised Amanda to wash and change. Mrs. Gales meanwhile saw to Padji's facial injuries in her usual efficient manner, ordered him to sit quietly in a corner, then set about making tea.

With the removal of grime and the resumption of proper English attire, Amanda discovered she didn't look nearly as ghastly as she felt. Her modest yellow muslin frock concealed her few outer bruises. Her mouth was sore, her jaw ached, and her ribs felt as though she'd been run through a gristmill. Nonetheless, her looking glass showed nothing obviously amiss.

As she entered the parlour, she found Padji in a considerably more colourful state. His face was bruised and cut where the paving stones had scraped it, and a large lump had sprung up on the back of his head. The villain had aimed beautifully, he grimly admitted. The man had struck with the sword hilt just below the cushioning turban.

"Indeed, the fellow sounds remarkable," said Mrs. Gales as she handed Padji a cup of tea. He shook his head and commenced to rocking to and fro in a melancholy manner. Mrs. Gales shrugged and placed the cup on the floor beside him.

"I can scarcely credit it," she said to Amanda. "That one man should attack so large and well-armed a party. How could he have robbed you while he was running away from four bearers? There must have been two robbers at least."

Amanda shook her head. "It was the same one. He must have tricked them somehow, then doubled back for me."

"So it was," Padji grumbled. "A master of deceit. How did he know my mistress's signal?"

Amanda put down her teacup and looked at him. "Is that what the strange bird sound was?" she asked. "Is that why you stopped?"

Padji covered his face with his hands. "I am a dead man. She will tear my tongue from my throat. She will flay my flesh and pour burning poison into the wounds. 'Protect my daughter,' she told me, and I failed. She will bury me alive and sing curses over my grave."

"She'll do no such thing," Amanda said briskly. "The man merely robbed me. I wasn't raped or murdered. Calcutta is filled with thieves. I shall send a note, explaining."

"No!" he shrieked, jumping up. "You must not tell her. She will know soon enough. My mistress learns everything. But there is time. I will go with you on the ship, and when she discovers, I will be far away."

"Go with us!" Mrs. Gales echoed. "Are you mad?"

"I must go. There is no place in all India I can hide. Her spies will find me out. They will put out my eyes with burning brands, because I was a blind man who did not see the Falcon as he swept down upon her beloved daughter. They will—"

"The Falcon?" Amanda cut in before he could commence another litany of horrors.

Padji covered his mouth with his hands.

Amanda rose from her chair and approached him. "That was the Falcon?"

"Forgive me, precious one. I am mad with grief. I know not what I say."

"Do you not?" Amanda responded. "Very well. I shall send to the rani for servants to guide you back, lest you lose your way in your confusion."

Padji fell to his knees before her. "No, missy, no, I pray you. She will make me die a thousand times."

"Then tell me what the Falcon wanted with me. He might have taken the jewels and silks easily enough. Why did he want only the Laughing Princess?"

"O beloved of my mistress, there are matters I do not understand. I have followed her since I was a child, slept in mud and eaten maggots when I must, yet even to me she does not reveal everything."

"If he wanted the statue, it must be of great value," Amanda said.

"Aye, so he must have believed." He raised his head to gaze at her. "You told me you dropped the box of jewels and the silks, but you fought him for the Laughing Princess. So what must he think, but that this statue is of the greatest value of all?"

"Damn," Amanda said softly. Padji was right, of course. A cleverer woman—the princess, for instance—would have instantly dropped the object she most valued and fought over trinkets. Amanda had lost her most treasured gift because she'd let emotion rule instead of reason. "It is not others who betray us," the rani had once told her, "but we who betray ourselves."

Amanda had lost only a wooden statue, perhaps a hundred years old, perhaps much less. As antiquities went—and India was thick with them—the Laughing Princess's monetary value was slight. To her, though, it was a piece of legend, a piece of India. More important, it was a gift of sentiment, the only treasure the rani's false lover had left her, the only physical reminder of one brief, intense passion . . . and betrayal. It was a gift to her "daughter," she had said. That word was perhaps dearest of all.

Amanda's own mother had existed briefly, a figure in a haze, a beautiful princess forever locked in the prison of her own fairy tale world. Smoke . . . and incense . . .

Amanda shook herself out of her reverie to find her two companions staring at her.

"What's done is done," she said. "Perhaps it will turn up. If the thief was the Falcon, and if he's as clever as reputed, he'll realise the figure's worthless and discard it. You may even find it on your way home," she told Padji. "If, that is, your knees haven't frozen into that position. *Will* you get up?"

"But I go with you," he said, gazing up at her with misty brown eyes.

Amanda stared back incredulously.

"You most certainly do not," Mrs. Gales said. Then, as though recollecting he was a native, and therefore congenitally irrational, she patiently explained, "We could never arrange your passage at this late date, even if Lord Cavencourt permitted it, which I strongly doubt. The end of our long war with Napoleon has left a great many former soldiers in need of employment. Lord Cavencourt cannot in good conscience pay a foreigner for what an English servant can do."

"Unless, of course, the foreigner is French," Amanda put in dryly, "and an excellent chef."

"My dear girl, you know I never meant—"

"I know, Leticia, but that argument won't wash."

"I can cook," Padji cried, still gazing soulfully up at Amanda, his hands now folded in supplication. "I am an excellent cook, even the English food." He launched into a staggering list of his gastronomic accomplishments, down to the art of soft-boiling eggs.

"I'm sorry," Amanda said gently. "Truly—because I'll miss you dreadfully. But even if we could arrange it—which I know we can't—to take you would be most unwise, and not fair to you at all. This is your country. You'd hate England. It's cold and damp, and many people will treat you unkindly because you're a foreigner and your skin is dark."

"I will be despised," he said. "I will live as an untouchable, a leper. But I will serve you faithfully. And my mistress will not fill my mouth with scorpions and—"

"Lud, but you have the most ghastly imagination, Padji. Oh, *will* you get up? What are you thinking of, to be grovelling in this way, a great strong man like you—and at your age."

Padji rose. "Then you will take me with you?"

Amanda sighed. "The ship sails tomorrow. To arrange passage at the last minute requires a great deal of money and influence. That means my brother must arrange it, and I assure you he won't."

"But if it can be arranged, you will let me serve you?"

"It can't be," she answered, her gaze flickering from the

huge Indian to Mrs. Gales. "Roderick would never permit it, let alone help."

"Never fear, mistress, O beautiful and compassionate one, whose eyes burn with golden flames and—"

"Padji, you must—"

"Tomorrow. I will arrange it all, and tomorrow I will commence a new life, as your adoring slave."

Oblivious to her half-hearted and Mrs. Gale's emphatic protests, Padji commenced a speech on the thousand ways he'd serve his new mistress. He'd just begun soaring to improbable heights of self-sacrifice—the eating of flies being deemed somehow necessary to satisfactory service — when the Cavencourt carriage was heard at the gate. Padji promptly crawled out a window and escaped through the garden.

══ 3 ══

RODERICK ACCOMPANIED HIS sister, her companion, and her maid on board ship, dutifully saw their belongings properly arranged, repeated for the hundredth time what Amanda must do upon reaching England, checked for the fiftieth time the papers entrusted to her, gave her a peck on the cheek, and departed.

Not ten minutes after he'd gone, one of the mates appeared, requesting Miss Cavencourt's appearance in the wardroom. The captain wished to speak with her.

"Miss Cavencourt has scarcely had time to catch her breath," Mrs. Gales said reprovingly, with a glance at the weary, unhappy Amanda. "Is the matter so urgent it cannot wait?"

The man apologised, but declared they could not weigh anchor until the problem was resolved.

Alarmed and puzzled, Amanda went with him, Mrs. Gales following with stiff disapproval.

As soon as Amanda entered the wardroom, her heart sank. Beside Captain Blayton, Padji stood at proud attention.

"We have a problem, Miss Cavencourt," said the captain after a brief, apologetic preamble. "In fact, we have had any number of problems in the last twelve hours," he added irritably.

30

"I do hope Padji has not created difficulties for you, sir," said Amanda.

Captain Blayton's stern countenance relaxed slightly. "Ah, so you *do* know him. When he claimed to be your cook, I must admit I was—well, that is neither here nor there. The case is this: my own cook failing to report for duty last night, I ordered a search. Just before dawn, this fellow—Padji, as you say—appeared, and led us to a certain tea shop, where we found Saunders in a state of delirium."

"Terrible fever," Padji said gravely. "I heard his cries. I have heard that terrible sound before."

Amanda threw Mrs. Gales a glance. The widow must have grasped the situation just as quickly, for she glared at Padji.

Sublimely oblivious to Mrs. Gales's sulphurous expression, Padji bent his own innocent gaze upon Amanda.

"I tell the great ship's master I have no more heart to cook for the family when my gracious mistress is gone," he said sadly. "My heart breaks because she leaves forever. In the night, I run away to see the ship that will bear her away across the world. I weep many tears into the waters, to send a part of me with her. It was Fate led me to the place, mistress, that I might find the poor man, my brother cook, in time to save his life. I carry him, gentle as one holds a baby, to the shop of a good friend. This friend recognises the man, Saunders. And so myself I seek out the wise captain, and myself do his bidding and find the doctor. With my own hands, I make a healing broth, which the doctor himself tastes."

"Yes, well, there's no question you were helpful," the captain interjected. "But we ought to get to the point, oughtn't we?" Turning to Amanda, he said, "The doctor has pronounced Saunders unfit to travel."

To move him from his bed would be death," Padji solemnly agreed. "I see at once the hand of Fate. The gods lead me to this man. Why? Inscrutable are the ways of the Eternal, yet this riddle is soon unlocked. The man is a cook. What is Padji? A cook. It is plain I am summoned in order to take his place, and continue near my beloved mistress."

"The point is," the captain said impatiently, "this fellow proposes to cook for us in exchange for passage to England. It is true I need a cook. On the other hand, I cannot possibly harbour runaway native servants. I considered speaking to Lord Cavencourt himself, but—well, I was reluctant to get your cook into difficulties, after he'd made himself so useful. He seemed exceedingly alarmed at the prospect of confronting your brother."

"Dear me," said Mrs. Gales sympathetically. "How awkward for you."

Amanda found her own sympathy inclining to Padji. He had done a terrible thing, but he was obviously desperate. She could not abandon him.

"How I wish I'd known sooner," she told Captain Blayton. "Had you spoken to Lord Cavencourt, you would have learned he'd have no objections. Padji has simply spared my brother the unhappy task of discharging him. You see," she quickly explained, before the captain could wonder what horrendous crime the Indian had committed, "the rest of us had grown accustomed to Padji's hearty style of cooking. Unfortunately, Lady Cavencourt found it too robust for her delicate palate."

An expression of relief washed over the captain's lined face and a greedy gleam appeared in his eyes. "Hearty?" he repeated eagerly. "Robust?"

"Oh, yes," Amanda said. "Padji's style, I'm afraid, is a deal better suited to keeping a fighting army—or navy—in trim. Plain English food, enlivened with a dash of Indian spice."

From that point on, the captain was hers. Amanda had only to assure him she'd take charge of Padji when they reached British soil, and the matter was settled. The captain agreed to allow Padji to cook his way to England.

Padji expressed his gratitude in his usual fashion. He

dropped to his knees and kissed the hem of Amanda's frock. "Oh, generous mistress. Oh, kind and wise—"

"Get up," Amanda snapped. "Don't grovel. You disgust the captain."

Padji scrambled to his feet.

"Furthermore," Amanda went on, "while we are on board this ship, I am not your mistress. Captain Blayton is your master, and you will obey him absolutely, or he will flog you. He has been exceedingly kind to take you on, considering the difficulty you've caused him. You will cause no further problems, do you understand?" She could only hope Padji understood that poisoning crew or passengers must be considered a problem.

Padji nodded, all humility, then turned to the captain. "Oh, wise and generous master," he said, "how may I serve you?"

Amanda stood at the railing, watching Bengal dissolve into the distance, and with it seven years of her life. So had she watched England recede on the grey, late spring day she and her parents had fled financial ruin and humiliation.

Not that they'd been entirely ruined. Roderick had managed to salvage the manor house in Yorkshire at least, and it would be awaiting her. Humiliation, too, was perhaps an exaggeration. Mama was oblivious, as she was to virtually everything. Papa, who'd spent most of his life pretending all was well—regardless what facts loudly contradicted—had evidently come to believe it. At the time, Amanda had felt she alone was aware that her mother was hopelessly ill, her father had just lost a fortune, and she had lost her betrothed in consequence.

Though nothing at all was wrong, in Papa's view, India and Roderick were expected to set it all right. Papa had made his fortune there, and met his wife. He must have believed he could return to a happier past. He returned, and India killed first his wife, then him, in less than a year. Though Amanda had mourned them, she could not say she missed them. All the life before their passing seemed too much like a troubled dream. She had simply looked on, always outside, always helpless. When they'd gone at last, the sad dream had ended.

Amanda would miss the rani though, for she was solid and real, the product of a harsh Oriental reality. She'd embraced and welcomed Amanda into her world, where Amanda had found a friend, a sister, even a mother. Padji formed part of that welcoming world. No wonder that, after the first moment's stunned dismay, Amanda's heart had soared with relief. In a moment, the huge Indian had become her bulwark, and she no longer felt so alone and vulnerable.

Oh, certainly she had her companion and her maid, Bella. Both were fond of her, but they could never understand how afraid she was of England. She'd needed Padji, and he, needing her, had come. Perhaps it was Fate, as he claimed.

One could only hope the princess would forgive both her friend and her servant. Yet she must. She knew how difficult it was for mere mortals to manage Padji. The princess herself had said that once he got an idea into his head, no power on earth could get it out again.

He'd seemed uncharacteristically restless the whole time his mistress had related last night's story, and very unhappy when she'd given Amanda the Laughing Princess. Or had Amanda only imagined that? She was no longer certain what she imagined, what was part of the story and what was not. The goddess Anumati, the marauders, the vindictive husband, the false lover—layer upon layer the tale had unfolded, like the petals of a lotus. Even at the end, Amanda had felt there must be more.

The robbery brought more. It had seemed another piece, another unfolding petal, opening and drawing Amanda towards the dark centre of its heart . . . dark, like the passage last night, and dangerous.

She winced, recollecting the strong fingers relentlessly prying hers loose from the figure. Of course the thief must be strong. The masculine form she'd watched through the palanquin shutters had seemed so slender next to Padji's bulk, yet the robber had felled the muscular servant with a single, well-aimed blow. When he'd fled before the pursuing bearers, the thief had moved with cat grace, leaping lightly into the shadows. Then, out of the shadows he'd leapt upon her, and she had felt his taut, merciless strength.

Why had he not knocked her unconscious as well? Surely that would have been simpler than wrestling with her for a piece of wood. Moreover, he would have ensured her silence . . . and oblivion.

Smoke and the scent of agarwood . . . rough muslin and the crushing trap of hard muscle . . . a long body pressed to her back . . . and the confusion, black and hot. Amanda shuddered at the recollection. Turning from the hypnotic sea, she found an intent, blue-eyed gaze upon her.

The man looked away to the ocean.

In his hair gleamed the golden light of the sun and in his eyes the glistening sea. Amanda smiled. The rani's description of her English lover would aptly describe a considerable portion of the British male population. In any case, this man's eyes were not the shifting, unreliable colour of the sea, but deep, deep blue. Even at a distance of several yards, Amanda had not mistaken that. He wore no hat, and the ocean breeze tumbled and tossed his thick, dark gold hair.

His profile ought to have been sculpted, she thought with critical appraisal: the high forehead and clear ridge of brow, the aquiline nose, the firm, well-shaped jaw. She sensed a slight movement then, and hastily withdrew her gaze.

He was undoubtedly handsome, but that was no excuse for staring at him as though she were a cobra intent upon her next meal. Furthermore, any man so splendidly attractive must surely be vain, accepting as his due the admiring gazes of scores of stunning women, which Amanda most assuredly was not. Not to mention it was silly at her age . . . Lud, she must be overtired.

Without sparing him another glance, Amanda made her way back to her cabin.

Bloody hell. Over a million square miles of subcontinent, vessels swarming up and down the coasts, and the curst Indian was aboard *this ship*.

Not until early afternoon, when the *Evelina* had sailed out into the Bay of Bengal, had word trickled down from crew to passengers about the cook's replacement. Not until very late in the day had Philip discovered who the new cook was.

Philip had, wisely, he'd thought, kept within the cabin until they'd sailed well beyond reach of Calcutta. He knew the rani's spies must be mingling among the crowds at the docks. He knew better than to let them catch a glimpse of him in daylight.

Escaping the cramped cabin at last, he'd come above for a preliminary scout of the deck. He'd scarcely taken in his surroundings when his gaze lit upon a turbaned giant, standing by the ship's bell. The massive brown being gravely listened to a mate, who explained the six four-hour watches and pointed out the inadvisability of tardiness in producing the daily ration of grog. The few words the giant spoke merely confirmed his identity. Philip never mistook a voice.

Luckily, he'd been staring at the Indian's broad back, and Padji hadn't seen him. Philip had slipped away to the stern to weigh his options. He considered stealing a lifeboat, but instantly discarded that notion. He couldn't leave Jessup behind, and he certainly couldn't take him along. They were trapped.

Philip glanced about him. The woman had left. She must be Miss Cavencourt. The Bullerhams and their staff had boarded shortly after he had, and he'd helped their servants with the trunks. That left three female passengers, and the one standing by the rail seemed far too young to be the widowed companion Randall had described. She was also, obviously, not a servant. Her dress would have told him so, even if Philip hadn't noted unmistakable signs of breeding in her profile and carriage.

He'd sensed something else, though, and he'd stared at her overlong, trying to determine what it was. Some nagging recollection. He swore again. If it nagged, it must be attended to, whatever it was. As if he hadn't enough to cope with already.

"My dear," said Mrs. Gales, "Bella is perfectly capable of seeing to your frocks. You'd do better to nap. This morning you looked as though you hadn't slept a wink, and our interview with the captain cannot have been restful. Padji was most thoughtless to oblige us to tell falsehoods. My conscience is most troubled." Troubled or no, Mrs. Gales continued steadily with her needlework.

Amanda was bent over her trunk. She'd been examining her frocks, trying to decide what she'd wear for her first dinner at the captain's table. The blue was more fashionable, but the rose was more becoming . . . She flushed and pulled herself out of her fantasies. "You weren't the one told all the fibs, Leticia."

"I didn't contradict you, though, did I? And poor Captain Blayton. Such a dreadful morning he must have had." She sighed.

Amanda looked up. "He seemed happy enough about replacing his cook so speedily. Nor did he seem remotely displeased to be talking with you near a whole hour after," she added slyly.

"My dear, I do not find endless miles of ocean nearly so fascinating as you do. We shall see enough of it, I daresay, and there is no harm in allowing a harassed gentleman to unburden himself."

Older gentlemen did tend to confide in Mrs. Gales. She was well-rounded and comfortable in form, and equally comfortable in personality. Having no pretensions to beauty, the widow was neither vain nor flirtatious, but a sensible, well-bred, and tolerant female. Perhaps that was why so many mature men were drawn to her. One could not be amazed to learn the captain had, so soon after meeting her, commenced confiding his woes.

Amanda frowned at a crease in the bodice of the blue muslin. "I take it more than Padji harassed him, then?"

"I'm afraid so. Captain Blayton has apparently fallen victim of the whims of the aristocracy. He was obliged to leave Mr. Larchmere behind in order to take on an invalid solicitor and his valet. The Marquess of Hedgrave's solicitor," Mrs. Gales added significantly. "Naturally, a mere 'Honourable' must give way."

"How sick is this man?" Amanda asked. "He can't be seriously unwell if he undertakes a long sea voyage."

"But that is just the point, my dear, and no wonder the captain is so provoked. Mr. Wringle was carried on board and, according to Captain Blayton, looked even worse than the cook he hadn't dared move from Calcutta! Did you ever hear the like?"

The blue-eyed man was the valet, then. Miss Cavencourt's colour rose once more. She let the lid of the trunk fall shut. "It seems most inconsiderate to me," she said, ruthlessly squelching a flutter of disappointment. "This is hardly a hospital ship, and I daresay we'll all be tried enough with Mrs. Bullerham's digestion."

"Mrs. Bullerham's only problem is a revolting tendency to overeat," said Mrs. Gales with a sniff. "I expect she'll be running Padji ragged demanding special teas and broths, and complaining the whole time. When I heard the news, I was nearly as irritated as the captain. Though Mr. Larchmere is rather full of himself, he does relate the most charming anecdotes, and I had counted on him to relieve the tedium of our mealtimes at least. Not that the captain is tedious," she added, "but he is responsible for everything. One cannot expect him to carry the entire burden of entertainment. I do not blame him a whit for feeling as he does. I should feel put upon myself. Yet, as I told him, the Whitestones have always been high-handed. One might as well complain of the ocean being damp, you know."

Amanda sat back on her heels. "I beg your pardon," she said. "Did you say Whitestone? Whom do you mean?"

"Richard Whitestone, Marquess of Hedgrave, my dear," Mrs. Gales said patiently. "Very high-handed they all are. Or were, since he's the last of his branch of the family. His heir presumptive is a distant cousin, I believe. There is the marquess, half a world away, yet the commander of an East Indiaman must do his bidding, regardless who is inconvenienced. Not that one is surprised, when most of the East India Company dances to Lord Hedgrave's tune." She shook her head. "Really, Amanda, I must insist you lie down and rest. You are as white as a sheet."

"He's far too sick to undertake a voyage of any sort," the ship's surgeon said brusquely as he followed Philip out of the cabin. "Just as I told Mr. Groves last night. If it's fever, it's not like any I've ever seen." He paused. "Well, not since this morning, actually. Our cook showed similar symptoms."

For a moment, Philip felt ill himself. So that was how the murderous Indian had gotten on board the ship. But Jessup would not die, Philip told himself. He would *not*.

"The physician in Calcutta seemed to think my master risked greater danger in remaining," he said, in as placating tones as he could manage. "The climate had already weakened his constitution, and the doctor believed he'd not survive the monsoon season. Surely his case isn't hopeless, Mr. Lambeth. I was given to understand the present ailment resulted from ingesting tainted food."

The surgeon continued on towards the upper deck. "No surprise, that. Confounded Indian food," he muttered. "Spiced so hot you never know what you're eating." He scowled. "Blayton's a damned fool, hiring that Indian. Miss Cavencourt herself admitted her sister-in-law couldn't stomach the man's cooking."

The queasy feeling washed through Philip again. He blamed the rolling vessel.

"The Indian was employed by Miss Cavencourt's family?" he asked with no more than ordinary polite curiosity. "I wasn't aware of that."

"*Was.* Unreliable, like all of 'em. Not a native you could trust as far as you could throw him. A sneaking runaway, that one. Admitted it himself—boasted, even. Should have been flogged, to my way of thinking. But the lady stood up for him, and who's going to contradict Lord Cavencourt's sister?" Mr. Lambeth hesitated a moment, then added reluctantly, "Still and all, she don't seem a fool, and the Indian seems to worship the ground she walks on. Whatever he gave Saunders seemed to do the man some good. Maybe you can get him to mix up one of them messes for your master. Worst it can do is kill him, and he's not likely to last more than a week anyhow."

On this uplifting note, the surgeon took his leave.

Cold-hearted swine.

Philip returned to the cabin. Jessup lay upon his stomach, moaning faintly.

"Is it very bad, old man?" Philip asked softly.

"Unh."

"Are you thirsty? Can I give you some water?"

"Nunh."

"You have to take something. You've got to keep up your strength, soldier," Philip said with an attempt at heartiness.

Under the rusty brown stubble, Jessup's normally ruddy flesh lay flaccid and damp, a jaundiced green. The whites of the eyes he painfully opened had turned pale yellow, webbed with spidery red lines, and the brown irises were cloudy, unseeing. He mumbled something. Philip bent closer.

"Throw . . . me . . . over," came the gasping words.

Philip swallowed. "Can't," he said. "They'll keelhaul me. Just isn't done. You're going to have to hang on. But of course you will," he added encouragingly. "Fifty thousand pounds, and half that's yours, my lad. There it waits, safe and snug in the bottom of the trunk. You're not going to pass up twenty-five thousand quid, are you? We'll get you a pair of roly-poly tarts, one for each arm. And we'll dress you like a lord—shining boots from Hoby, one of Locke's hats, and Weston's best cut of suit. It's Weston now, you know, for the Beau's brought him into fashion . . ."

On through the long afternoon and into the twilight, Philip sat by his servant and talked until he was hoarse, because words were all he could offer. He must give the man reason to live, to hold on. If Jessup held on this night, if he managed to sleep a bit, perhaps he'd wake stronger tomorrow. Perhaps he'd swallow a bite then, and grow stronger yet.

If and if, perhaps and maybe. Philip Astonley had never felt so helpless since the day, fifteen years ago, he'd made his decision. Was this the end of it, of the dream that never quite came true, but never quite proved false, either? Trapped on a ship bound for England, his one friend in the world about to die, his worst enemy about to kill him? The Falcon had always known he'd be murdered one day. He was not afraid to die. He was simply curious: Would Padji snuff him out quickly, or would the giant take his time, to draw the thing out with supreme, unruffled Indian patience?

However the end came, it would be his own damned fault, Philip reflected disgustedly. Rage edged to the surface again. The rani . . . imbecilic Randall . . . the woman . . .

Jessup groaned. Banishing his growing fury, the Falcon focused mind and energy on keeping his servant alive.

4

MORNING CAME AT LAST, and Jessup finally fell into exhausted sleep. He was sinking, though. His colour had deteriorated to grey.

Philip recalled the surgeon's words: "Maybe you can get him to mix up one of those messes for your master." He'd have to hazard it. There was a chance the Indian would recognise him. On the other hand, Jessup at present had no chance at all.

After all, Philip—in the disguise of a plump, prosperous hookah merchant, complete with beard and thick padding—had merely passed Padji briefly in the hallway of the rani's palace. For the robbery, he'd shaved and foregone the padding. Thus Padji was unlikely to equate the merchant with the robber. Would he note a resemblance between Mr. Brentick, valet, and the thief, though? Perhaps not. Philip had, as usual, disguised his voice that night. The Falcon could mimic virtually any masculine voice he heard, and more than a few feminine ones. What Padji had heard was an excellent imitation of the Bhonsla Raja.

His decision made, Philip dressed quickly but carefully, discarding any garments that still bore traces of agarwood. The expensive incense was too distinctive. He would have to adjust his posture and stride. He'd imitate Monty Larchmere's stiff and graceless valet.

That left one's countenance, but it was too late for cosmetic adjustments. Virtually everyone on board had already seen him. In any case, Padji could not have seen the robber's face in the unlit passage. Even the rani— who was aware the merchant was the Falcon or the Falcon's accomplice— would recognise the eyes only. Padji hadn't her opportunity to study the ersatz merchant at close hand. Had they ever seen Jessup, though? Philip swore under his breath. Never mind. The Indian might make the connexion. He might not. Half a chance, then.

Philip headed for the upper deck and turned towards the forecastle, hoping to find the cook there. A confrontation in plain view of others was vastly preferable to a private one in the galley's hot confines.

Philip had scarcely taken five steps before something struck the back of his head. Instinctively, the Falcon's hand went for the knife under his coat, and he whirled round. His glance darted about, seeking his attacker . . . and lit on a woman. Miss Cavencourt. He drew his hand, empty, from the coat. She hurried towards him, her face flushed, and her coffee-coloured hair whipping in the stiff sea breeze.

Something tapped at his leg. He glanced down and saw a bonnet, which the wind knocked against his leg. He'd stepped on one of the ribbons. He snatched up the hat and held it out to her.

"I take it the missile is yours, miss?" he said, then cursed himself. Servants didn't make facetious remarks to their betters.

The colour rose higher in her cheeks. Dusky rose on mellow ivory.

"Yes. Thank you." Gingerly she took it.

"I'm afraid I accidentally trod on the ribbon," Philip said with great deference while his brain clawed and scratched, trying to place her voice. It wasn't enough. He needed another few words, and he'd already said more than he ought. Ladies didn't speak to strange gentlemen, and he wasn't even supposed to be a gentleman. Drat that idiot, Randall.

She'd turned away slightly to examine the bonnet. Now her gaze slid slowly up to meet his. Her eyes were very unusual, large and amber-coloured.

"Oh, it doesn't matter," she said. "I'm—I'm sorry it hit you. I'd taken it off, you see, because the wind was knocking it about, and then I forgot I had it . . . Oh, well. At least it didn't fly into the sea." She flashed a nervous smile. "Thank you." She turned and made quickly for the forecastle.

No.

Not possible.

Not the same woman.

But he was already following, calling out, "Miss? I say, Miss Cavencourt!"

She halted and turned around.

"I beg your pardon, miss, but you can't go there," Philip said, his brain working rapidly while he schooled his features to a proper servantlike blank.

Her surprise stiffened into chilly hauteur. "Indeed," she said coldly. "Are you a sentry?"

"No, miss, certainly not," he answered, his tones humbler still. "I only guessed you might not be aware the forecastle is no place for ladies."

Though her expression remained chilly, he discerned a shade of indecision in the glance she threw behind her.

"That's where the off-duty crew customarily take their leisure," Philip explained. "They may be about soon, and you'll find the company a bit rough, miss, especially without an escort. I rather think the commander would prefer you kept away, escort or no."

She stared at him as though he were foaming at the mouth.

"That is quite absurd," she said. "That is, I realise it was kindly meant, but I assure you I have nothing to fear."

Definitely the same woman. The same height, the same form, the same voice, with its husky overtones.

At that moment, Padji emerged from the galley. His gaze swept the deck and flitted past Philip without a glimmer of interest before lighting upon Miss Cavencourt.

She turned to Philip. "That man is my servant. As you see, I can have nothing to fear, on the forecastle, or anywhere upon this vessel." Again she began to walk away.

Crushing the wild urge to heave her arrogant person over the rail, he followed. Jessup first, he reminded himself. The woman could provide a less risky way to get what Jessup needed, if Philip could but control his temper.

"I beg your pardon, miss," he managed to choke out. "I meant no offence."

"None taken," she said dismissively, still walking.

"I didn't realise the cook was your servant," he said hurriedly, as the immense form loomed nearer. Philip kept his eyes downcast. "I was about to speak with him myself. You see, I need his help."

Miss Cavencourt paused.

Philip didn't grovel, precisely, but near enough, while he explained "Mr. Wringle's" condition and the surgeon's estimation of the invalid's prospects.

"Mr. Lambeth sounds monstrous disobliging," she said when he was done. "He should have spoken to Padji directly."

"I am in no position to make demands of anybody, miss. I regret to say we caused considerable inconvenience to several people, and I understand Mr. Groves handled the emergency less diplomatically than one could wish."

Imbecilely was more like it. Had Groves allotted Philip the role of master, he'd not be in this humiliating position. He'd have had them all running briskly at his beck and call. He'd learned that, if nothing else, from his overbearing sire. Small good it did him now. Leave it to Randall to behave like a blithering idiot at the first hint of difficulty.

Aye, but you left it to Randall, didn't you? nagged a sardonic voice in his head. *Had to dash off like an adolescent hothead, didn't you, wild for revenge?*

Miss Cavencourt's low, crisp tones broke through the red fury in his brain.

"I shall speak to Padji, of course," she said, "but it would be best if he examined your master himself."

"There's no need to put him to the trouble," Philip said smoothly, "though you're most kind to offer. I've told you exactly what the surgeon told me. I listened very carefully, you may be sure. My master does need to eat something and—and I can scarcely get him to swallow water."

He felt her studying gaze upon him then, even as he watched the Indian out of the corner of his eye.

"I see," she said, her tones less frosty. "You are very anxious, Mr.—Brentick, isn't it?"

"Yes, miss."

"I shall ask Padji to prepare something as quickly as possible, and he'll send for you when it's ready."

Except for the sentry, the forecastle was deserted. Nonetheless, Amanda took no chances. In Hindustani she repeated Mrs. Gales's revelations and voiced her own suspicions.

Padji shrugged. "What did the servant want of you?" he asked.

"Haven't you heard a word I've said? Mr. Wringle, who was hurried on board in the dead of night—the night I was robbed—works for the Marquess of Hedgrave, who happens to be *Richard Whitestone*."

"What did the servant want of you?"

"Gruel—broth—I don't know. Something for that wretched, thieving master of his. Did you poison him, too?"

"A healing broth. I see. I shall make it now." Oblivious to Amanda's look of outrage, Padji turned and descended into the galley. She followed.

The brick-lined space was as hot as Hades. Padji promptly began crushing herbs. Amanda perched on a cask and glared at him.

"You can't poison him, you know," she said. "I'm not saying I'd object if you did, but you can't. You'd be the first suspect, and you've nowhere to hide."

"Why should I poison this man? He has done me no ill."

"It's obvious what happened. The Falcon turned the statue over to Mr. Wringle, who hastened aboard the first ship bound for England."

Padji shrugged.

"There's no need to get inscrutable with me," Amanda said irritably. "You said yourself the Falcon stole my statue, and the more I've considered your explanation, the less sense it makes. He always steals for *someone else.*"

"May you cut out my tongue for contradicting, mistress, but I know nothing of that. He's a thief."

"He's a professional—or one of a group of professionals—and you know as well as I that the services are hired out."

"I am but an ignorant servant, O adored one. I know nothing," Padji said imperturbably as he mixed the herbs into hot liquid.

This approach, obviously, would lead nowhere. Amanda considered. "I see," she said after a moment. "You know nothing, ask no questions, merely follow orders. Is that correct?"

"Such is my lowly ability, O daughter of the moon."

"Then who ordered you to poison the cook, you deceitful creature? I know you poisoned him, so you needn't waste breath denying it. I know, in fact, precisely the mixture you used. Did your mistress not tell me of her old family recipe? A fungus, is it not, which grows on—"

"It is unseemly for the mistress to speak of these matters," Padji cut in reprovingly. "They are the concern of the lowly slave."

"Is it seemly to tease and mock your mistress?" Amanda retorted. "Is it honourable to keep secrets from me, when I risked my honour, and that of my family, to save you? Did I not tell monstrous falsehoods on your behalf?" She drew out her handkerchief and wiped her perspiring forehead. Then, recollecting her irritating sister-in-law's methods, she dabbed at her eyes. "This is my thanks for taking pity on you," she said in a choked voice.

"Aiyeeee," Padji wailed softly, pushing the bowl aside and gazing at her in anguish. "She is the true daughter of my mistress. With a word she stabs at my heart."

"Your own mistress would have cut out your heart by now, if you so vexed her," Amanda answered. "But you know I am soft-hearted and sentimental, and so you take advantage of my weakness and mock me."

Instantly, Padji dropped to his knees. "No, beloved, no mockery. It is not so. Ah, I am a man torn between two lionesses. 'Protect her from all danger,' my princess orders me, and so I do my lowly best. Yet her too-wise daughter sniffs trouble and wishes to throw herself into it. What is to be done with such women?"

Amanda withdrew the handkerchief from her eyes. Trouble, he'd said. Then she was right.

"For a start," she said briskly, "you might tell me the truth. The rani left something out of her story, did she not? The value of the statue, for instance. Why should the Falcon steal a piece of carved sandalwood? And *will* you get up?"

Heaving a great sigh, Padji rose. He would tell her, he said, and she would not believe him, but he was a man beset on all sides.

Miss Cavencourt expressing impatience with a brisk tapping of fingers upon the cask, Padji hurried on to offer what he called his humble theory. He was unaware of any great monetary value to the statue. Still, he knew someone wanted it. Offers had been made, thefts had been attempted. These were all quashed, of course, for Anumati's wishes must be consulted, and the goddess had not at that point named the heir.

"Never mind that," Amanda said, disregarding dreams and visions and settling to facts. "Who wanted it?"

"What other but the man she told you of?" Padji asked sadly. He shook his head. "Why will they not leave each other in peace? He abandoned her. I might have killed him and put an end to it, but she will not have an end to it. She puts a curse upon him and writes the curse down in a letter, that he will know who has done it. He took her heart, she writes in this letter, and so she takes in return the new life from his loins. He shall sire no sons, and his name will be forgotten, as he's forgotten her."

While this threw an interesting light on the rani's response to seduction and abandonment, it hardly answered the question.

"That was a suitable curse, I admit," Amanda said, "but what has it to do with the statue?"

"He has no sons, and his wife has been dead five years now. Perhaps he wishes to wed again," Padji answered.

Amanda stared at him. "Are you trying to tell me he wants the statue back because he thinks it will undo the princess's curse?"

Padji nodded. "Did she not tell him in her letter that he had left the thing of most value behind? Did she not say he would know nothing of true happiness until—" He stopped short, his brown eyes wary, his stance alert. "No more," he whispered. "These matters are not for others' ears."

His hearing must be prodigious acute. Hard as she listened, a long, tense moment passed before Amanda could hear the approaching footsteps over the noise of the crackling stove and the endlessly creaking timbers. A moment later, the ship's surgeon descended the steps into view.

As soon as he spied her, Mr. Lambeth's heavy features knit into a frown. "Galley's no place for ladies, Miss Cavencourt," he growled.

With slow dignity, she rose from the cask. "On errands of mercy," she answered coolly, "one regards the errand first, and the surroundings not at all." In a few crisp words, she informed him that she'd come to compensate for his neglect of the ailing solicitor. While she lectured, Amanda covered the bowl of broth and set it on a platter.

The surgeon's countenance darkened. "The man's done for," he answered defensively. "My time's better spent with those I can help."

"Indeed. Attending to Mrs. Bullerham's indigestion— a

permanent condition, as all of us who know her will attest—
is of far greater importance than attempting to make a dying
man's last hours endurable."

On this self-righteous note, Amanda took up bowl and
platter and stalked out.

Not until she'd marched halfway across the deck did she
recollect she was to have sent for the valet. Just as well, she
told herself. She wanted a look at his master, didn't she?

The door opened immediately in response to her reso-
lute knock, and the tall form of Mr. Brentick promptly
blocked it.

"Miss Cavencourt," he gasped.

A mere fraction of a moment passed before he schooled
his features to polite blankness, yet that was time enough.
She spied the sorrow and anxiety in his countenance, and
simultaneously recalled the edge of bleakness in his voice
earlier, when he'd asked for help. He was genuinely distressed about his conniving employer. Amanda experienced
an irrational twinge of guilt. She promptly smothered it.

"Padji had the broth ready while I was there," she said.
"It seemed foolish to let it cool while someone came to
fetch you, especially when I was returning this way. Or
nearly this way," she amended with strict regard for accuracy.
Her cabin was at the stern, well-lit, large, and luxurious.
This, she saw as she peered past the tall, dark-coated figure,
was a tiny, dark cell.

"That was very kind of you, miss." Mr. Brentick tried to
take the broth from her, but she held fast and raised one
autocratic eyebrow in perfect imitation of her brother. The
valet retreated to let her pass.

"Oh, dear, the poor man," she said softly, involuntarily,
as she approached the invalid. He looked ghastly. "No
wonder you are so alarmed." She looked up to meet a stony
blue gaze.

Amanda decided to disregard Mr. Brentick's facial ex-
pressions. "Can you prop him up a bit?" she asked. "If you
will hold him, I can feed him."

The valet hesitated, his face stonier yet.

"It wants two people, Mr. Brentick," she said impatiently. "While you dawdle, the broth grows cold."

Under the stiff mask, he seemed to struggle with something, but it was a brief combat. Then, his piercing blue gaze fixed on her as though in challenge, he moved to the cot to do as she asked.

Before she'd left the cabin, Amanda had promised to send Bella on the same errand in two hours. Mr. Brentick had protested, citing the needless trouble to herself and her servant, and he had got an unpleasant glint in his eyes. Amanda had firmly ignored both words and look, and in the end, she'd won the skirmish.

She waited until Bella was gone before taking Mrs. Gales into her confidence. Then Amanda quickly outlined the rani's tale, her own suspicions, and the information Padji had so reluctantly offered.

Mrs. Gales listened composedly throughout, occasionally interjecting a calm question. When Amanda was done, the older woman shook her head.

"Five years in India may have disordered my reason," she said. "On the other hand, it has taught me to accept the possibility of such mad goings-on. Once one has seen a man—of his own free will—swinging from a hook, which has been inserted into the flesh of his back, one is prepared to see or hear *anything*."

"Then you do believe it's possible Lord Hedgrave hired the Falcon to steal my statue?" Amanda said with some relief. She had feared Mrs. Gales would think she'd taken leave of her senses.

"It's possible." Mrs. Gales took up her needlework once more. "I will not pretend to understand the Rani Simhi," she went on. "She is an Indian, and therefore incomprehensible. She most certainly ought not have told so lurid a tale to an unmarried young lady. On the other hand, at least she did not pretend to virtue, and one must respect her honesty. As to Lord Hedgrave, I'm obliged to admit I would not put it past him. My late husband had dealings with him, as did many of his colleagues. When the marquess wants something, he goes after it with all the inexorable force and disregard of obstacles of the Juggernaut. Whatever or whoever lies in his path is simply mowed down."

"Would he go to such lengths for a wooden statue?" Amanda asked. "That's what bothers me most of all. It hardly makes sense, does it?"

Mrs. Gales hesitated, her usually smooth brow knit. After a moment, she said, "In England, more than one gentleman has paid a large sum for the privilege of lying in Dr. John Graham's Celestial Bed. If they believe a bed will instantly correct their inability to beget offspring, why should not Lord Hedgrave believe in the efficacy of a wooden statue? I suppose a marquess might be as superstitious as the next man. When it comes to these matters, my dear, otherwise sane and sensible men can prove amazingly irrational." She smiled faintly. "What an extraordinary woman the rani is. Her letter must have acted on him over the years like slow poison. One ought not admire her, to be sure, yet it is so seldom a woman can achieve so effective a revenge for ruination. With words only. How very clever of her! Wicked, of course, but clever."

"I should say lucky, rather," said Amanda. "If he had produced an heir, her curse would have been a joke."

"I daresay she'd have found some other means of torturing him," Mrs. Gales answered dryly. "In any case, they are both quite wicked creatures, which makes it difficult to choose between them. Still, my sympathies naturally incline to my own sex, and it *is* your statue. I do not see why Lord Hedgrave should have it. The idea! To set a murderous Indian thief after a British subject—an innocent young lady, no less."

"If the theft *is* Lord Hedgrave's doing," Amanda reminded her. "We don't know that for certain, any more than we know Mr. Wringle's got my statue. But I mean to find out. I'll speak to Padji again, tomorrow." Her colour rose slightly and her folded hands tightened in her lap. "I expect we shall have to be underhand, but I see no alternative. Mr. Wringle comes with a deal of influence. Randall Groves himself, no less, escorted him on board, and all the Marquess of Hedgrave's power looms behind him."

Mrs. Gales looked up from her needlework. "You are quite determined to have it back, my dear? Are you sure?"

"Yes." Amanda met her gaze squarely. "I cannot explain, but the statue means a great deal to me."

"You needn't explain. As I said, I do not see why that arrogant man should have it, especially via such abhorrent methods. You ought be able to simply demand what is rightfully yours from this Mr. Wringle."

"He has only to deny it," Amanda said, "and if I demand a search—"

"Yes, my dear, we both know how the world works. Unfortunately, I also know how Lord Hedgrave works." Mrs. Gales paused, a shadow of concern crossing her countenance. "He can destroy you, Amanda. He can ruin Roderick. Even for a wooden statue."

"I know," Amanda answered quietly. "I intend to be careful."

5

THE PLUMP, DARK-EYED maid appeared five times a day with the odd-smelling broth. Five times a day, Philip propped Jessup up, while Miss Jones patiently spooned the liquid into him. By the end of a week, Jessup seemed marginally better. By the end of the second week, he'd definitely improved. During this time, Miss Cavencourt also supplied plump pillows and fresh linens from her own stores.

Philip was none too happy to find himself under so great an obligation to her. Still, he reminded himself, she had saved Jessup's life.

Accordingly, Philip sought her out that afternoon to thank her. He found her, as he'd expected, above, standing at the rail and gazing out at the sea. She spent most of the day at the rail, it seemed, sometimes with Mrs. Gales or Bella, but most often alone. Time and again he'd come up for a five-minute breath of air, and find Miss Cavencourt standing so. An hour later, he'd be back for another hasty gulp, and behold her there yet, apparently lost to all the world, her gaze fixed upon the water.

At his polite greeting now, she started, and, as though she had been someplace very far away, a long moment passed before her golden eyes brightened with recognition.

Halfway through the proper little speech he'd prepared, Philip became aware of a new scent mingling with the salt air. Patchouli. But light, only a hint. It must be in the shawl. Kashmir was often stored in patchouli, to ward off insects. Nothing ominous about that, he thought, as he continued somewhat distractedly to describe Jessup's improved condition and express his gratitude.

"It's very pleasant to be applauded," she said when Philip finally ground to a halt, "but most of the credit goes to Padji. It's his secret receipt, you know."

"Indeed. We are most fortunate you brought him with you," Philip replied stiffly.

"You seem devoted to Mr. Wringle," she said, her gaze upon his left lapel. "Have you been long in his employ?"

Now it begins, he thought cynically. Still, expecting an examination sooner or later, he'd prepared his answers. As usual, he'd offer no more truth or falsehood than absolutely necessary.

"I have been acquainted with Mr. Wringle some time," he said, "but came into his employ only very recently, thanks to Mr. Groves." Mr. Groves the incompetent. Jessup a solicitor and Philip the valet, when it was supposed to be the other way about! But that wasn't all Randall's fault, was it? With Philip unavailable at the time, Jessup had to play the master. They'd hardly chuck Monty Larchmere out on account of a mere servant, regardless how desperate the case.

"Then your loyalty is all the more admirable." Her gaze swept upward, and he found himself gazing into golden light, where shadows flickered. "You've scarce left his bedside this fortnight."

"Naturally, one would wish to be at hand if the master needed anything."

"All the same, you will not wish to wear yourself out. You'll be no use to him if you sicken as well, and your pallor tells me you haven't enjoyed a decent night's sleep—or a proper meal—the whole time."

Until that moment, Philip had not felt the least unwell. Abruptly he became aware of his aching muscles, and with that awareness, weariness began to steal through him. It was as though he'd been an automaton these last two weeks.

Now she'd said the words, the mechanism proceeded to disintegrate.

"It can't be healthy for you to remain so long in that close space," she went on, ignoring the denial he murmured. "At least when Bella is there, you might leave with clear conscience, and take a stroll in the fresh air."

Fresh air. Damn her. But she couldn't know about *that*. She only wanted him out of the way.

"I appreciate your concern, miss, but I'm afraid the nursing still wants two people."

"Oh . . . yes . . . naturally. In any event, you are here now, aren't you? How silly to tell you to do what you're already doing. Sillier still to make you stand and endure a lecture, when I have just recommended exercise. Pray don't let me keep you." She turned back to the sea.

Philip hurried back to the cabin, certain one of Miss Cavencourt's minions was nosing about. That he found no minion, nor a single article disturbed, did not appease him. He crawled into his uncomfortable hammock and tried to nap. Too late. She'd killed sleep, hadn't she?

For Jessup's sake, Philip had clamped down his own feelings, locked and sealed them away. He hated the cabin. Monty Larchmere was as hard up as everyone suspected, or he'd never have settled for this miserable hole. The place was narrow and dark, and the air was stale at best, but mostly foul. Philip would have slept above on deck, if he dared. He didn't. He couldn't leave the cabin unguarded at night, even locked. What was a lock to the sly Indian, curse him. Curse her as well—Pandora, with those deceitful golden eyes. She'd uttered the words and the demon he'd locked away had sprung out to smother him.

It was early afternoon, but light scarcely reached this place. It was dark, rank, suffocating. Too familiar.

That was all a lifetime ago, he told himself as he forced his eyes closed. Another life, a child's, and he was a man. How many times in the last fifteen years had he hastened fearlessly towards certain death? He was no longer a weak, helpless little boy. He was not afraid . . . of anything.

All the same, he felt it steal over him in a slow, icy stream: Dread. Groundless, irrational, his adult mind insisted, even as it sank under the cold horror.

In minutes, Philip was out of the cabin, hurrying blindly through the passage. Then he was into the light at last, into the air, gulping it greedily until his mind rose out of the icy trap and his heart returned to its normal, steady beat. Damn her to hell.

Jessup's recovery continued at the same faltering pace, and the ensuing week was slow torture. Of course one must eat and rest and exercise. Philip was not a fool. Yet his appetite dwindled, suffocated, as his reason was, by the endless watching in the hot, tiny cell. The sight of food sickened him, and he grew bone-achingly weary, so that climbing to the upper deck this day was like scaling a thousand-foot cliff.

Catching sight of him, Miss Cavencourt marched across the deck and commenced another lecture. Philip stared at her, utterly unable to comprehend a syllable. Then something began to buzz very loudly in his ears, his muscles jerked crazily, and Miss Cavencourt and all the world were submerged in a heavy black blanket.

A child was screaming, sobbing, somewhere. A door, thick and heavy . . . and oppressive, stifling darkness. He couldn't breathe. His little hands burned, raw with pounding on the immovable barrier. "Please, I won't do it again, Papa. Please, Papa. I'm sorry."

Something cool and wet touched him then, and a gentle hand brushed his forehead. Philip's eyes opened to golden light shimmering amid the shadows. Autumn at Felkonwood, safe in the forest. The light fell warm, and the breeze blew sweet with . . . patchouli?

His mind shot back to the world and discovered a woman

bent over him. He tried to pull himself up.

"No, Mr. Brentick, not so quickly," Miss Cavencourt said softly. "You'll make yourself sick."

Nausea rose in a dizzying wave. He lay back again and took a long, steadying breath. "What happened?" he asked. His voice seemed to come from miles away.

"You collapsed," she said, "under the weight of my disapproval."

A disconcerting warmth overspread his face. Devil take it! He'd swooned at her feet—he, the Falcon—and now he must be blushing like a schoolboy.

A faint smile curved her full mouth, but her gaze softened to smoky amber. "You should have listened to me, Mr. Brentick. But that will be my only 'I told you so,' " she added, the smile fading, "so long as you follow my directions henceforth. Fortunately, there is no fever. You are simply overtired and weak from hunger. I want you to try to sleep. When Bella comes by later to feed your master, she'll bring you some broth as well. You must try to finish it. Even if you feel a bit queasy at first, it will do you a deal of good, I promise."

She rose, and only then did he realise he lay, not in the hammock above Jessup's cot, but on a narrow mattress on the floor. How the devil had she managed that? As she moved away, Philip glimpsed a large brown shoulder at the corner of the open doorway. Padji. So that was how.

Gad, how long had he lain unconscious? They might have ransacked the entire cabin by now.

Philip waited patiently until the pair had departed and their footsteps faded away. Then he sat up slowly, fighting the urge to vomit, and crawled onto his hands and knees. The trunk was still wedged against the wall, and his mattress had been pushed against it. He fumbled in his coat, found the key, and unlocked the trunk. His arms seemed to be made of blancmange. He needed three attempts to get the lid up.

A few endless, stomach-churning minutes later, he sank

back onto the mattress. They'd touched nothing. The tiny telltale feather lay exactly as he'd placed it, upon the small rug in which the Laughing Princess still nestled. He'd made certain all was as it should be before replacing all as it had been.

What the devil was she about? A golden opportunity, and she and the Indian had ignored it. Why did she bother with him, with Jessup? Why hadn't she let Jessup die? That would be one obstacle out of the way. And today—an ideal opportunity for Padji to eliminate Philip himself. Easy enough to render a swoon fatal, with the mistress by to create any needed distraction. Why had nothing happened? Was it possible she didn't know, after all? Or was she more cunning than he imagined?

He couldn't think any more. Not now. Later. His head fell back upon the pillow, and in minutes he was asleep.

"It's in the trunk," Amanda said. With trembling hands she brought the tumbler of wine to her lips and sipped. She and Mrs. Gales sat on the cushioned banquette under the row of windows.

Mrs. Gales's needle was not so steady as usual. "You promised to be careful," she said. "That was foolhardy, Amanda. Suppose he or Mr. Wringle had wakened?"

"Padji saw to that. I don't know what he used. At any rate, I had the cloth over Mr. Brentick's eyes, and Padji was very quick. He'd got the keys when he was carrying Mr. Brentick to the cabin. Then we had all the bustle of carrying in the mattress. I made sure to ask whether there were clean linens. If either had awakened, that would have been our excuse for rummaging." Amanda swallowed a bit more wine before adding, "Padji was in and out of the trunk in about a minute. I'd hardly turned my head before he was done."

"Indeed. Practice makes perfect, I suppose," Mrs. Gales said dryly. "Still, *your* aptitude in the matter is a surprise. Your presence of mind seems nothing short of miraculous."

"Hardly. If Padji hadn't been nearby, it would never have occurred to me to take advantage of the situation. When Mr. Brentick fainted, I nearly did, too, I was so . . . taken aback."

Frightened, half to death. Every day she'd watched his brief ventures above, and her heart had gone out to him, so sick and miserable he seemed.

At first she'd told herself this was just as he deserved for associating with a low criminal like Mr. Wringle. But Reason had promptly pointed out it was fully possible the valet had no idea what his employer had been up to. Why should Wringle tell his servant? If he had, why should the valet risk his own health to care for such a man? Just suppose Mr. Brentick were of the same dishonest ilk. Wouldn't he do far better to let his master die, and collect the reward himself? There must be a reward—a considerable one—to drive Wringle from Calcutta in his condition.

The more she'd reflected, the more evidence Amanda found to make the valet an innocent bystander. And today . . .

How she wished she'd not remained in the cabin to nurse him. She should have summoned Bella. As yet, the maid knew nothing about the statue, except that it had been stolen in Calcutta. *Her* conscience would not have shrieked while she listened to Mr. Brentick's delirious mutterings. The poor man had cried out to his papa.

Some childhood terror must have seized him. Amanda could understand that. She had her own nightmares. Everyone did. Yet her heart had ached at the pitiful pleas, and again later, when his eyes had opened. Horror lingered in those deep blue depths, and in the fleeting moment before he came fully awake, they'd seemed the innocent, terrified eyes of a little boy. She had wanted . . . really, how stupid. He was a grown man, and ill. He'd simply had a nightmare, or a hallucination brought on by exhaustion—or by whatever Padji had used on him.

Mrs. Gales was saying something, and looking at her rather strangely.

"I beg your pardon," Amanda said. "I fear my mind wandered."

"I asked why you didn't take the statue when you had the opportunity."

Amanda thrust the valet's image aside. "Far too risky," she answered. "Padji, Bella, and I are the only outsiders who've entered that cabin, which would make us prime suspects. The instant the theft was discovered, the commander would have to comb every square inch of the vessel. Eventually they'd find the statue, and then it would be only my word against Mr. Wringle's that the Laughing Princess is rightfully mine."

The widow sighed. "I see. The captain would probably leave the matter to be settled in England, and—"

"And the Juggernaut—Hedgrave—would crush me." Amanda swallowed the last of her wine. "The task, you see, wants subtlety, cunning, and patience, at the very least. It wants the Falcon, actually, but as we haven't got *him*, we shall have to make do with Padji."

"Beg pardon for mentionin' it, guv, but a body'd think you was turnin' into a fusspot is what," said Jessup as he hauled himself up to a sitting position. "Ain't the damned thing hid good enough? Don't I have this here pistol under the pillow? Don't I keep a sharp lookout the whole time the gal's here? Not to mention which, they do say two's company, if you take my meaning."

"You're in no condition to dally with ladies' maids," Philip said. "And do I have to remind you the abigail belongs to the woman I robbed?"

He'd already had an unsatisfactory discussion the day before with Bella, who'd taken umbrage at his offer to relieve her. Two months they'd been at sea, and Jessup, though still weak, was sufficiently alert to take note of his surroundings. That was the trouble. He'd taken note of the plump Bella—and she of him, evidently, for the two were at present behaving like a pair of moonstruck adolescents.

All by himself, Jessup had contrived an explanation for his lowly speech and coarse manner, because, he said, he was tired of giving one-word answers. He had only to "confess" that Mr. Groves had exaggerated his position—he was merely a solicitor's clerk. Bella would pass along the revelation. Thus, when Jessup at last became well enough to venture among the others, no one would expect anything but the common sort of fellow he was. Meanwhile, he wanted more privacy.

"I ain't like to forget when you call it to my attention every other word," Jessup answered grumpily. "Like I ain't been through half a hundred battles with you, not to mention we been through a deal worse since we left off soldierin' for thievin'. Leastways in a battle, a fellow gets his leg shot off or his arm, or something clean-like. He don't get poisoned and drove all the way to Bedlam and back with no hope of dyin' and bein' done with it."

When all else failed, Jessup was not above applying guilt. He was entitled, considering his master was to blame for his condition. The poison had so weakened Jessup's constitution that many months would pass before he was his sturdy old self again. Now his employer wished to deny him the comfort of a woman: a plump, amiable maid with gentle hands and a soft, soothing voice.

In Jessup's place, Philip would have wanted the same. Besides, this was a man of five and thirty summers, not a callow youth. While perhaps unequal to the rani's fiendish tricks, Jessup was nonetheless up to every other sort of rig. He knew the wooden statue's value. He'd not risk his share of the reward for a tumble with any female.

"I suppose I am behaving like a fussy nursemaid," said Philip ruefully, as he commenced pacing the tiny cabin space.

"Worse," his servant answered tactlessly. "I never seen such a case of fidgets in my life. Whyn't you go run about the deck and leave me in peace?"

"I do not fidget," Philip snapped. "And I have been 'running about the deck' as you say, the whole curst afternoon. There is not one thing for me to do, and not one person to talk to except sailors, and they'd prefer spending their leisure jabbering at each other in their incomprehensible argot. Why can't they say 'right' and 'left' like normal people? What's wrong with front and back, forwards and rear? Do you know how many sails are on this ship? A least a thousand, and each with a different name, I expect," he concluded in exasperation.

"Is she pretty?" Jessup asked.

"What?" Philip whipped round so quickly that the top of his head grazed a beam. "What the devil are you talking about?"

"Miss Cavencourt. Is she pretty?"

"Are your wits wandering again? What has that to say to anything?"

"Just askin', guv. No need to get your innards in an uproar. I was too sick to notice when she was here, and I ain't seen her since I been better. Just wonderin' if she's plump like her maid."

"She is not plump at all, so you needn't drool over both of them."

"Aye, one of them scrawny ones, I expect. A spinster, I think you said she was?"

"I did not at any time say she was a skinny old maid. Not that it's any of your concern."

"We got her statue, so she's some worry, ain't she?"

"It was hers for less than an hour. It was Her Royal Hellcat's for a curst eternity. Or, to be more accurate, it was in her possession. We both know Madam Fiend stole it from Hedgrave."

"That's so, but Miss Cavencourt don't seem the same kind, do she? From what I hear, she was worritin' over you like a mother hen."

"Certainly. The lady of the manor always looks after the ailing peasants," Philip answered irritably.

The servant rubbed his eyes. "Well, I don't blame you

for feelin' the way you do. Bound to stick in your craw, it is, havin' to bow and scrape and be ordered this way 'n' that. Still, it's in the way of business, and you won't hurry this ship any faster, for all your fussin' and fidgetin'." Jessup sank back into the pillows. "I never seen you so jumpy, like a cat in a tub o' water. Wears me out, just watchin' you."

"What sticks in my craw," Philip gritted out, "is being trapped on a ship with a carved figure worth fifty thousand pounds, an Indian as like to murder us in our sleep as not, and the woman, supposedly his employer, I robbed. Think, man. She's breached the security of this cabin. You're infatuated with her fat maid. Do you wonder that I'm *jumpy?*"

"No, I don't wonder, guv," was the weary reply. "I just wish you'd go be jumpy somewheres else."

= 6 =

HE WAS NOT avoiding her, Amanda told herself as she dragged her gaze from the tall, golden-haired figure prowling the deck. Mr. Brentick was a servant, and he knew his place. Her only excuse for talking with him was to enquire after his master, which added up to no excuse, since he must know Bella would report to her.

Certainly Amanda had no need to lure the valet from his cabin and occupy him in conversation while Bella did her own part. The abigail had at last been taken into confidence. Once she understood what Amanda required of her, Bella had made short work of the valet.

All the same, one could not help feeling uneasy about him, or sorry for him, perhaps. So restless he was, roaming the vessel like a caged cat in the Royal Menagerie. He did remind her of a cat. At first he'd seemed so stiff and formal, even awkward. But that was only on the rare occasions they spoke.

When he wandered, as he did now, it was with the lithe grace of a tiger. He even seemed to exude the same aura of power . . . or danger. Amanda was not sure what it was, exactly, only that now and again it seemed to lurk in his eyes as well, and it fascinated her, even as she instinctively shrank from it. Well, really, what had that to do with feeling sorry for him?

Amanda fixed her gaze firmly on the choppy sea. More than three months had passed since they'd left Calcutta. If the weather held, they'd reach Capetown in another week or so, according to the commander. Then, in as little as a month—though more likely longer—they'd reach England. East Indiamen had been known to sail all the way from China to the Thames in a bit over three months, but that was rare. One storm could drive a vessel far off course, or damage it severely enough to require months of repairs at the nearest port. Furthermore, the *Evelina* had been becalmed twice and could be again. She must not think about time, Amanda chided herself.

The wind seemed to grow stronger as morning gave way to grey afternoon. Certainly Mrs. Bullerham's usual complaints had increased significantly in volume. Two servants had hauled the obese harridan up, as they did nearly every day. She had, as usual, found fault with them throughout the process. Now, outraged with the ship's rocking, she was venting her displeasure upon her spineless spouse.

Amanda moved some distance aft, where she wouldn't be able to hear them—or at least not so clearly. The clouds thickened and the vessel rose and fell on the choppy sea. Ten minutes later, Mrs. Bullerham's booming tones rose suddenly, audible even over the wind and the moan of the timbers. Blast the woman! Why the devil didn't she go below if a hint of rough weather so overset her?

Amanda glanced back and drew a sigh of relief. The Bullerhams were preparing to descend. Amanda strolled back to her preferred spot and, gazing idly about, saw Mr. Brentick scowling after the clumsy parade. Abruptly, he looked towards Amanda, meeting her curious gaze before she thought to withdraw it. He bowed—no, it was more like a nod—and equally unthinkingly, she smiled. He hesitated a moment, then, to her surprise, crossed the deck to her.

"Does the smoke sicken *you*, Miss Cavencourt?" he asked.

"The smoke?"

"From the galley. The cooking odour and smoke, Mrs. Bullerham declares, is intolerable."

"Mrs. Bullerham's toleration is of exceedingly limited quantity," Amanda said.

"I wish I'd been warned. I had the temerity to suggest she move farther aft, away from the smoke."

"Did you? I hope you didn't suggest how far aft. In the vessel's wake, for instance."

"Swimming is reputed a healthful exercise," he said blandly.

"Indeed. I wonder no one's recommended it to her ere now."

"Evidently, no one recommends anything to Mrs. Bullerham, as my still-tingling ears will attest."

Amanda glanced up. His face was devoid of expression, except for those unreasonably blue eyes. The glint she discerned there was not entirely humour. Mrs. Bullerham must have been exceptionally vindictive today.

"Oh, dear," she said. "She gave you a nasty dressing down, didn't she? I hope you will not regard her. Discontent has poisoned her mind long since, and the boredom of the voyage makes her even more beastly, though it hardly seems possible."

"I fear there was too much truth in what she said to be disregarded. She wondered I had nothing better to do than idle about the livelong day, and no better sense of propriety than to accost my superiors with my unsolicited opinions." He paused, his face stiffening. "As I seem to have accosted you, Miss Cavencourt. I do beg your pardon."

"You needn't," she answered, instantly wishing Mrs. Bullerham at the bottom of the sea. "Whenever she provokes me, I stomp off to vent my feelings to Mrs. Gales or Bella. Otherwise, I should probably throttle her. Rage all you like, Mr. Brentick. You'll feel better after."

His blue gaze swept her countenance in a swift, cool assessment that left her unaccountably flustered.

"Thank you, miss," he answered quietly. "Your indignation on my account is sufficient. Mrs. Bullerham would say 'excessive,' in that it has led you to tolerate an impropriety."

Amanda flushed. She'd considered only his injured feelings, not their relative stations. Now she wished she'd left him to stew.

"Mrs. Bullerham would likely add that my grasp of etiquette leaves a great deal to be desired, and I wouldn't know an impropriety if it bit me on the nose," she answered tartly. "Though I don't see why it is ill-bred to commiserate with another human being. I wasn't inviting you to—to flirt with me, Mr. Brentick, merely to relieve yourself of the string of oaths burning your tongue." She could have bit off her own tongue then, but it was too late to recall the infelicitous words. Mortified, she turned back to the sea.

"I beg your pardon, miss," he said after a long, tense moment. "Naturally, the thought of flirting never crossed my mind."

She understood the words well enough. It was his tone that puzzled her. Was he laughing at her, a plain, aging spinster who talked of flirting?

"Actually, I wish you hadn't mentioned it," he went on. "It's rather like opening Pandora's box, isn't it?"

She threw him a scathing glance. "I was not trying to put ideas into your head. My temper got the better of my reason, perhaps, or I should have chosen less absurd phrasing."

"It's too late," he answered hollowly. "The damage is done. I can't think of a single remark that would not be construed as flirtatious."

Incredulous, she turned around full to stare at him. She'd always found him painfully handsome, but now, with that amused gleam in his eyes, he was . . . devastating. Gad, what had she done? Was it the ship rocking so hard, or her heart? She drew a steadying breath.

"Well. Then. At least I have taken your mind off Mrs. Bullerham," she said.

"Entirely."

"She's bored, you know, and when some people are bored, they become ill-tempered—in her case, more ill-tempered than usual. Bella, on the other hand, becomes a fiend for work," she went on, nervous under his unwinking cobalt stare. "She will clean the cabin a dozen times a day. Mrs. Gales merely switches from knitting to crochet or embroidery."

"And you, miss? What do you do when you're bored?"

She dropped her gaze to his lapel. "I'm never bored," she said.

"I envy you. I am—*was* bored out of my wits. Apparently, it makes me . . . impertinent. I have nothing to clean, because Miss Jones won't let me. She cleans our cabin as well. I have never learned needlework of any kind and—*ahem!*"

Her head shot up. "I beg your pardon?"

His countenance remained blank. "The rest was flirtatious, Miss Cavencourt. I suppressed it."

"Oh. Are you an accomplished flirt?" she icily enquired.

"Yes, I regret to say."

"I wonder you regret acquiring such a skill. To me it has always seemed a most difficult art to master."

"In that case, I applaud your *instincts*."

Heat washed over her face once more.

"That blush, for instance," he remarked soberly, "could be fatal to a faint-hearted man."

She quickly recovered. "Pray do not put fainting into your head, Mr. Brentick. You seem overly susceptible to every stray remark, and I know you are inclined to swoon on occasion."

"Touché, miss. Very well aimed, that one."

"I was not *practising*," she said, exasperated. "You needn't congratulate me, as though I were an apt pupil. Don't you know a setdown when you hear one?"

"Yes," he said. "Fortunately, I am a stoic."

Not a wisp of a smile, only that provoking glint in his blue eyes. She ought to box his ears. She ought to, at the very least, put him firmly in his place. Yet she felt he was daring her, goading her to do so, and she refused to be manipulated. Her own eyes opened wide and innocent. "Are you indeed, Mr. Brentick? I wish you had mentioned that earlier. I might have spared my sympathy for a more needy object."

For more than a week after that exchange, Philip kept a decorous distance from Miss Cavencourt. He felt certain he hadn't misjudged. The beckoning smile he'd responded to was of a kind familiar to him. He knew what she wanted: to win him over, allay his suspicions, distract him with a bit of flirtation. He was quite willing to play. He'd played the game too often to fear distraction. His senses might respond to an alluring countenance and a slim, shapely figure. Why not, after so many months without feminine companionship? Nevertheless, his mind would remain alert, as always.

No, he'd not misjudged, precisely, merely overstepped a shade too far, moved a bit too quickly for her. Very well. He could wait. Plenty of time.

So he reminded himself as he stood at the rail, his gaze fixed on Capetown. They'd drop anchor soon, and all the port's diversions would offer themselves to his needy senses: fresh meat, vegetables and fruit, drinkable wine, and women—scores of lively, accommodating tarts.

About damned time, too. These last few days had passed with intolerable slowness, each more provokingly tedious than the one preceding. Hardly surprising, in the circumstances. Now he'd no need to worry about Jessup, Philip's restless mind found no other important matter to occupy it. Thus that mind had taken hold of minor matters. Such as how long he'd been without a woman.

Capetown neared, and the deck swarmed with fleet-footed seamen, while the air rang with a babel of commands. Philip smiled. These hardened sailors were as impatient as he for dry land and all its pleasures.

In a tremendous hurry to get his enormous cargo home, Captain Blayton had refused to linger long at any port. Here, however, he'd remain two days at least, replenishing supplies while his passengers tasted the delights of Capetown's brand of civilisation.

Delight, indeed, Philip thought happily. A proper bath and proper food . . . and improper women . . . at last. As he surveyed the deck's activity, his glance fell upon the forecastle. There Padji stood, gazing about as well, his round, brown countenance sublimely indifferent.

At that moment, the door to pleasure and freedom swung shut with a deafening clang. Philip closed his eyes and uttered a low stream of oaths. How could he have been so stupid?

How the deuce could he think of leaving the *Evelina*? What better opportunity for the Indian but then? Padji might make off with the statue and easily lose himself in the crowds. The Indian might find it difficult, but certainly not impossible, to make his way back to Calcutta, devil take him.

Seething, Philip watched the passengers and most of the crew disembark, then stomped back to his cabin.

"You ain't goin' ashore?" Jessup asked, astonished.

In a few curt sentences, Philip outlined his concerns.

Jessup was affronted. "*I'm* here, ain't I?" he demanded. "You think I'd let that scurvy Indian get anywheres near it?"

"I think," Philip said tightly, "that scurvy Indian would have the pillow over your face and the breath crushed out of you before you could lay one finger on your pistol. We don't have a prayer unless we're both here—you exactly where you are, and my humble self at the door."

Thus they spent three interminable days and nights while their fellow passengers ate, drank, shopped, and toured by day, and ate, drank, and danced by night. That Padji never came within a mile of their cabin the whole time was a circumstance nicely calculated to drive Philip into a murderous rage.

On the fourth day, the vessel once again set sail.

"Should've gone ashore like I told you, guv, and got a

woman," Jessup said, shaking his head. "Won't be no livin' with you now."

"Go to blazes," Philip snarled. He stalked out, slamming the cabin door behind him.

As he emerged into the sun, the first person his eyes lit upon was Miss Cavencourt. She stood at her usual place at the rail, leaning on her elbows and gazing at the sea. She'd given up her bonnets weeks ago, and the wind tossed and tangled her coffee-coloured hair and whipped it against her cheeks. Philip glared at her.

The temptation to heave her over the rail was well-nigh irresistible. Unfortunately, at the same instant this prospect beckoned, the mischievous wind began gusting about her, driving her skirts up to reveal, for one devastating moment, a pair of elegantly turned ankles and slim, shapely calves. Philip's gaze slid up to her narrow waist and on to the agreeably proportioned curves above. At that moment, the urge to mayhem gave way to one equally primitive, though less homicidal.

His glance swiftly took in his surroundings. He spied Mrs. Gales at the stern, talking with the captain. Philip's face smoothed, his narrowed eyes gentled, and his muscles relaxed. With the unconscious grace of a stalking cat, he closed in upon his prey.

Miss Cavencourt may have sensed his approach, for she turned while he was yet some distance away. She didn't smile this time. When he neared, she responded warily to his greeting.

"I hope you enjoyed your visit ashore, miss," he said obsequiously.

"It was interesting," she said. "Yet I rather wish I hadn't gone. I scarcely got used to walking on solid land before I was back on the ship. Now I must grow used to that again."

"By tomorrow you'll have forgotten what solid land is like. It's amazing how swiftly the human bod—being adapts." *Oh, nice slip there. Try thinking with your brain, Astonley.*

"I collect you decided to spare yourself that exercise,

Mr. Brentick. Bella tells me you elected to remain with your master. Your devotion is commendable."

"I perceived no alternative at the time," he answered. "In any case, we got along well enough by day. At night, though, when he was asleep and I came above, I felt as though I walked a ghost ship. It was so quiet—a mere handful of seamen aboard. Just the creaking timbers and the waves plashing against the hull."

"How peaceful it sounds," she said softly. Her eyes, focused somewhere past him, softened, too, from sunlit gold to smoky amber. "I rather envy you."

"I thought you enjoyed Capetown, miss."

"I found it interesting. I'm not partial to—to crowds and social gaieties. I am rather a recluse, I'm afraid."

The teasing breeze lifted her scent to his nostrils, only to sweep it away again in the next instant.

Instinctively, he moved a step closer. "Then had you been in my place, you'd not have wished for company, as I did."

The shadowy amber glance flickered to his face. "Solitude and loneliness are not the same thing," she said.

"Perhaps not. Perhaps I was just bored. I think there was one mad moment when I actually yearned for a dressing down from Mrs. Bullerham," he said ruefully.

She smiled then, disarmed. Finally. "You make yourself sound desperate, Mr. Brentick, yet I cannot believe you could sink to so pathetic a state."

"No. What I actually wished was far more audacious. I wished I had not trespassed on your kind nature." He dropped his voice. "Among other regrets."

She turned away and fixed her gaze on the sea. "Is that an apology?"

"Yes."

"Oh."

He saw her hand tighten on the rail. Small and slim it was, its mellow ivory deepened to burnished gold by weeks in the sun. He wanted to touch its softness. His own fingers curled frustratedly into his palm. What the devil did he think he could accomplish in a few minutes? He had a rift to mend, and that wanted a clear head. Very well. He'd already made better progress than expected. After all, she could have chosen not to understand.

"Am I pardoned?" he asked.

"That depends on what you're apologising for."

"For having the effrontery to flirt with you, Miss Cavencourt, and insult your intelligence by pretending I wasn't," he answered boldly.

To his surprise, she didn't colour up.

"Gad, so that's what it was," she said wonderingly. "Mrs. Bullerham overset you more than I thought that day—or you are, truly, bored out of your wits." She turned an amused countenance to him. "They say the insane have flights of genius, though, and I must say your performance—well, you are very subtle, or I am very thickheaded. But you must not do it again."

"Oh, I know I mustn't," he said.

"Of course not. You would be casting your pearls before swine."

"Miss Cavencourt, I must beg leave to protest that choice of phrase, figure of speech or no."

"Mr. Brentick, you are all that is gallant, but if you do not dismiss yourself on the instant, I shall choke myself laughing." She bit her twitching lip and turned away again. What, he asked himself crossly, was so hilarious

"But, my dear, he admitted he tried to flirt with you," Mrs. Gales said as she knotted a silk thread. "You cannot wish to encourage him."

"I'm certain I discouraged *that*," Amanda said, smiling at the memory of his bemused face. "My experience of men is limited, I admit, but I'm sure they don't care to be laughed at. Yet it seemed so funny, or perhaps I was relieved. I'd thought he'd been mocking me that day. Now I realise he was—or is—quite desperate. His days must seem to him like solitary confinement. His sole company is a cross, recuperating invalid—whom Bella has monopolised."

"You feel *sorry* for the valet?"

Amanda recalled the terrified muttering she'd heard one day, and the nightmare lingering in deep blue eyes. Yes, that made her feel sorry for him, but it was the restlessness, too. His inability to be at peace with himself made solitude—which she welcomed—lonely and dreary for him. She pitied as well his intolerable boredom, which drove him to flirt with an ape leader like Amanda Cavencourt.

There was more, and that she could voice. "I think he's overbred and overeducated for his station in life," she said slowly.

"I think he is far too handsome." Mrs. Gales deftly guided her needle through the linen. "I expect he wreaks havoc with the maids, wherever he goes."

Amanda grinned. "More than the maids, I'll wager. I guessed today he's a rake of sorts. That seemed funny, too—a rakish valet, a self-proclaimed accomplished flirt, in such desperate case as to practise his skills on *me*. I shouldn't be surprised to learn he'd thrown one of those luring looks at Mrs. Bullerham, and that was what hurtled her up into the boughs."

Mrs. Gales's steady hand arrested midstitch. "What sort of look was that, my dear?" she asked mildly.

Amanda was staring into some distance beyond the cabin walls. "I once saw a painting of Krishna as a young man. He stood, surrounded by women, in a stream. He had his arms about two of them, and gazed at one in just that way. Intently." She shrugged, and her tones lightened again. "In any case, Krishna was quite the rake, was he not? The look must be commonplace enough, if the painter knew precisely how to convey it."

"A great deal too common, if you ask my opinion. If you catch the fellow gazing at you in such a way again, Amanda, you are well advised to box his ears."

"For a *look*?" Amanda laughed. "I daresay the poor man

can't help it. For a flirt, it must be an uncontrollable habit, rather like a nervous tic."

"Amanda," said Mrs. Gales, "overeducated, overbred, he remains a servant. Pray recollect as well, he is also a *man*. I shall say no more."

=== 7 ===

THOUGH SHE UNDERSTOOD well enough what the widow left unsaid, Amanda's common sense told her the warning was ludicrous. Long ago she'd learned she was not the sort of woman men wanted. All her one beau had desired was Papa's wealth. Thus, the following day, when the valet paused in his perambulations to greet her, Amanda saw no harm in leading him into conversation.

She soon learned he'd been a soldier, and had spent most of his service in Central India. He treated her to a few military anecdotes, and she found him both witty and surprisingly knowledgeable regarding Indian ways.

When he joined her at the rail the day after, the discussion continued where it had left off. Every day thereafter they met at the same place, at the same time, and talked. By the end of a week, their half-hour conversations had stretched into an hour, and even that time began to seem far too short.

Mr. Brentick was clever and very amusing, yet she'd met scores of clever, amusing men. The difference was that he appeared to find her so, too. When she lapsed into Hindu philosophy, one of her pet topics, he seemed fascinated. He asked intelligent, perceptive questions, and never hesitated to debate if he questioned her opinion. Amanda was accustomed to blank stares or, worse, condescending indulgence of her unwomanly and most un-British interests.

She found Mr. Brentick not simply superior to the common run of manservant, but a superior, rare species of man. Most important, she felt she'd found a friend. At the end of a fortnight, she felt as though they'd been friends all their lives

Amanda was on her way to the upper deck when the door to the Bullerhams' cabin opened, and Mrs. Bullerham, leaning heavily upon her cane, lumbered through. Her mind elsewhere, Amanda didn't notice the massive figure emerging until she was upon her. Then she stopped short, missing a collision by mere inches.

"This isn't a race course," Mrs. Bullerham announced in booming tones, "though one should not be required to remind you that ladies do not run. Did your mama not tell you it was unseemly?" Moving farther into the passage and thus blocking it, she boomed on, "But I forget. Your mama was ill-equipped to oversee your education."

Amanda's face set and her heart began to pump with hurt and rage, but she said not a word, only waited for the detestable woman to move out of the way.

"I am, of course, aware of your awkward situation," the heavy voice went on. "You are not entirely to blame for your ignorance. I'd hoped Mrs. Gales would drop a word in your ear, but she, evidently, is preoccupied with the captain. I have held my own tongue out of pity. But it will *not* do."

"I have often found that holding one's tongue does well enough," Amanda answered tightly.

"You are pert, miss, as I have remarked before."

"Then I wonder you wish to speak with me at all."

"Duty calls louder than personal feelings. As it should in your case," Mrs. Bullerham rumbled. "Your brother is a peer as well as a justice. Whatever your mother was, noble blood runs in your veins. Even if you are without self-respect, you ought consider your family."

"I would appreciate it, ma'am," said Amanda, "if you would step aside and permit me to proceed."

"So that you may hasten to your rendezvous? Are you

78

afraid the cit's valet will make off with your maid if you dally?" came the taunting reply. "Have you no pride?"

"Too much, ma'am, to respond to ignorance." Amanda turned away.

A fat hand clamped upon her arm. "Don't be a fool, girl. You're no beauty, but you can't be so desperate. Certainly you don't wish others to speculate that you are so starved for masculine attentions you must stoop to dallying with servants. You will become a laughingstock."

Amanda reached up and pried the fat fingers loose, then jerked her arm away. "I trust you are finished."

"I'm not, Miss Impertinence—not by—"

"Ah, Mrs. Bullerham," a cool, deferential voice interposed. "Did you wish assistance ascending the steps?"

Amanda's head whipped round, and her face flamed as she saw Mr. Brentick striding towards them. The blaze in his blue eyes seemed to crackle through the dim passage.

"Or had you rather," he went on in more ominous tones as he neared, "return to your cabin to *rest*?"

Mrs. Bullerham opened her mouth. Mr. Brentick took one step closer. Mrs. Bullerham shut her mouth, turned, and scuttled back into her cabin.

The blazing blue gaze fell upon Amanda then, and her heart seemed to clench into a hard little fist. She couldn't breathe.

"Miss Cavencourt, may I invite you above, to relieve yourself of the string of oaths burning your tongue?"

He'd heard. What burned then was her face.

"It seems the Devil also makes work for idle tongues," Mr. Brentick said as they reached the rail. "Mrs. Bullerham has the true instinct of a killer."

"It would be more gallant to pretend you'd heard nothing," Amanda said, forcing a smile.

"I thought that would be cowardly. I'm already disgusted with myself for not intruding sooner, but I was caught between Scylla and Charybdis, you see."

She was far too hurt, bewildered, and mortified to see anything at the moment, and her smile felt like a hideous facial contortion. Looking away, she inhaled deeply of the brisk salt air.

"I thought at first that if I dashed to your rescue, it would make matters worse," he continued. "I didn't realise my presence was unnecessary to accomplish that."

"If you will not be gallant," she said, "then please don't be kind, either." She swallowed, and made herself meet his sympathetic gaze. "Is it true? Is that what others think?"

"As you told me a while ago, Miss Cavencourt, her mind is poisoned. It was all venom."

She shook her head. "No, and that's the worst of her. However venomous, there's always truth in what she says. What enrages everyone is that she's insensitive enough to say it. It *is* what others think, isn't it? That I'm so desperate—"

"Why would anyone but a miserable, dyspeptic old cow think anything like that? Her mind is as sick as her infernal liver," he answered angrily.

"Do *you* think it?" she asked.

He stared at her a moment incredulously, then, to her confusion, he smiled. "If you'll pardon the impertinence, miss—are you mad?"

"What do you mean?"

"She said you were at your last prayers," he answered with the excessive patience usually offered the mentally enfeebled. "Whatever other twisted 'truths' she may have uttered, you cannot be so overset as to credit *that*."

Amanda stared at him blankly.

He returned the stare. "You aren't," he said. "It's quite impossible. Do strive to collect your wits."

"I wish you'd collect yours, Mr. Brentick. I most certainly am at my last prayers. I am *six and twenty*."

"And?"

She coloured. "And—and I have a looking glass."

"If you can't gaze into it in a rational manner, I can't imagine what possible good it does you."

Her eyes narrowed. "I hope you are not trying to persuade me I am some sort of *femme fatale.*"

"I should not presume, miss."

"If that is your notion how to appease my wounded dignity, I must point out you are altogether off the mark." As she met his expressionless gaze, another suspicion arose. "You aren't—you aren't flirting with me again, and pretending you're not, are you?"

His eyes opened very wide. "I wouldn't dream of it, miss."

"I should hope not. You did promise you wouldn't."

"If memory serves, I said I *mustn't.*"

"And so you mustn't," she said, growing flustered in quite a different way. "It makes me most—most uncomfortable."

"I'm painfully aware of that, miss. It is most provoking." His tones were aggrieved, but a devil danced in his blue eyes.

She answered the devil. "Oh, I nearly forgot. No doubt you fear your skills will grow rusty from disuse."

"That is not what concerns me," he said. He paused a moment. "I perceive a refreshingly independent spirit abruptly cowed by the perverted utterances of a foul-minded rhinoceros. I do all in my humble powers to distract you, and you do not attend. Instead, your beautiful eyes dart about, as though you were a hunted creature. It *is* provoking."

She caught her breath. "My what?"

"Of course there's no point reminding you your eyes are beautiful, because you're irrational. Your abigail has probably told you a hundred times, not to mention your beaux, but all those sensible voices are drowned out by the noise of that squealing sow."

No. He didn't really think she was . . . no, certainly not. He spoke so out of kindness, because he pitied her or felt obliged to smooth her ruffled feathers. Or it was mere habit. *I daresay he wreaks havoc with the maids.*

"*Do* you wreak havoc with the ladies' maids?" she asked.

"I beg your pardon?"

"That's why Mrs. Bullerham claimed it was a rendezvous, you know. Because you're so handsome," she said brazenly. She was rewarded. The mask of assurance faltered. She had disconcerted him. "And also, probably, because there's a devil in your eyes, Mr. Brentick."

His confusion lasted but an instant, and he flashed a wolfish grin. How white his teeth were, gleaming in his lean, tanned face.

"Your recent ordeal has overheated your imagination," he said. "She's made you see evil everywhere."

"No, not evil," she answered thoughtfully. "Krishna, rather. Are you familiar with the Hindu deities?"

"I know some of the thousand names, though I can rarely keep them straight," he said, obviously puzzled by the abrupt turn in the conversation.

"How long were you in India?" she asked.

Philip remained nearly another hour at her side. Never had they conversed for so long a time. More important, this was the first time the talk ventured near the personal, and what he learned was puzzling and troubling. He'd experienced niggling doubts before, but in recent weeks, they'd swelled to daunting proportions. He listened to her today, and watched her expressive face, and wondered whether it *was* possible she knew nothing, made no connexion at all between him and the man who'd robbed her.

He considered the evidence again later, when she'd gone. She hadn't let Jessup die, for one. Furthermore, after four months, Philip was still alive. To eliminate him without awakening suspicion would be difficult, he admitted. Still, the task was not beyond the wily Indian's powers.

But nothing. Not even a glimmer of recognition. That left a few alternative interpretations. For instance, Padji may have latched onto Miss Cavencourt for his own purposes. The Indian may have played on her kind nature and convinced her to take him to England.

He could have several reasons for doing so. Fear of the

rani's rage when she learned of the theft was one excellent reason, although it needn't drive him all the way to England. Another, more in character, was a vow of revenge upon the rani's true enemy, Hedgrave.

Philip knew the Laughing Princess was not worth fifty thousand pounds, let alone the additional thousands previously expended to retrieve it. He was aware the Falcon represented no more than a very expensive tool in an ugly game: two vicious children squabbling over a toy each wanted only to spite the other. He could not be greatly shocked to discover the game had become deadly.

In that case, Miss Cavencourt may not be, as he'd originally believed, a cunning disciple of the ruthless Rani Simhi. She might be merely another tool, though an innocent one. Or was that simply what he wanted to believe now, because he'd been trapped too long on this damnable ship? Had the long months of abstinence twisted his reason? Was he making excuses for her simply because he desired her? How absurd. He didn't need to *like* her to want to bed her—or any attractive woman.

Yet she'd played havoc with common sense from the start, hadn't she? She'd aroused him when he'd attacked her that night in Calcutta, and found himself grappling with a she-cat. Only recently, however, as he'd come to know her better, had the memory returned to haunt his dreams: the swish of silk and the tinkle of thin golden bangles . . . the scent of patchouli mingled with smoke . . . darkness . . . and a fierce struggle with a warm, slender body, lithe and so pleasingly curved.

He'd thought she was a native, until she'd cursed him in those crisp, well-bred accents. He smiled wryly. The unladylike epithets had aroused him as well. He'd known one fleeting, utterly mad urge to return, to join battle with her again . . . and conquer.

That, however, was four months ago. Now? Now, he admitted silently and with no small self-mockery, she was driving him crazy.

* * *

Despite Mrs. Bullerham, Miss Cavencourt stood conversing with Philip the following day, at their usual time and place.

"You said you ran away to be a soldier," she observed. "But you've never said why you had to run away, or what you were running from."

When he hesitated, her earnest gaze flitted away. "Or is that too personal a question? Roderick tells me I always ask awkward questions, and that's one reason I— But he's a solicitor, you know, and never likes to tell anyone anything."

"Force of habit," Philip said. "Men of law must be discreet regarding clients' affairs, and secrecy becomes a way of life. My case is no secret, though. I ran away because my father and I did not see eye to eye on my future. He'd reared and educated me to follow in his footsteps as a schoolteacher. He even sent me to public school. He had some dream I might one day soar to the dizzying heights of a university position."

"From what I've glimpsed of your knowledge, Mr. Brentick, I should say it might have been an achievable goal."

"My father had certain infallible methods for ensuring obedience and diligence." *Torture, for instance. Torture works very well*, he added silently. "These were administered sufficiently early and consistently to remain effective, even when I was away at school and no longer under his unique tutelage. I did attend to my studies. All the same, by the time I was eighteen, I knew I could no longer obey his wishes."

Papa had a perverse sense of humour, you see. That was why Lord Felkoner had forbid the military career his youngest son most desperately desired. His lordship had chosen the Church with the same fine sense of irony. Incorrigible Philip might look forward to more years of the grinding studies he detested. After would come the eternal tedium, the steady drip, drip of hypocrisy and meaningless work, years of pious chores which bore not even the saving grace of vigourous physical activity. Lord Felkoner, obviously, had wanted his son walled up permanently, and the airless catacombs of clerical life would do very nicely, thank you.

Philip saw his frown reflected in anxious eyes, and quickly smoothed his features. "Hardly unusual," he said lightly. "Hotheaded youths run away every day to become soldiers or sailors. I was lucky. I got to India, and the young officer I served led me to all the excitement and adventure my naive young heart could have wished for."

"You were lucky to survive," she said somberly. "India's is not the most amenable climate for Europeans. Even my parents, who'd lived there many years before, didn't survive the second visit."

He remembered something Mrs. Bullerham had said. "Fever?" he asked.

"I suspect my mother was dying before she ever got on the ship," she answered. "I think England had already—" She caught herself, and went on in brisker tones, "Yes, the fever took her first. Within another month, my father was gone as well."

"I'm sorry. That must have been terrible for you, especially in a strange country, away from your friends and relatives."

"I had Roderick." She was silent a moment. When she spoke again, only the slightest quaver betrayed her. "Would you be very much shocked, if I told you it was a relief?"

"No."

"I was relieved," she went on more steadily, "because I didn't have to worry any more. I didn't have to wonder what I could do, or feel helpless because I'd never find an answer. Nothing could be done. My father returned to India because he was ruined, and needed Roderick to look after us. Papa was broken, you see, and couldn't be fixed."

Her eyes glistened. As Philip watched her slim hand rise up and dash a tear away, something tightened within him.

"That is what Mrs. Bullerham meant about my lack of proper supervision," she continued. "My parents were broken. They weren't living, really. They were like a pair of smiling dolls propped up on a shelf."

To play a servant was a confounded nuisance. He ought to be able to hold her in his arms and let her cry away the hurt. He certainly wished he could stomp down to Mrs. Bullerham's cabin and choke the life out her. Sentence after sentence, she'd cut and slashed. She'd even probed what must be a very old though still tender wound. Gad, but she and Lord Felkoner would have made a splendid pair.

"Miss Cavencourt," Philip said gently.

She dashed away another tear and looked at him.

"Shall we get up a petition?" he asked. "To have Mrs. Bullerham keelhauled? It is accounted an infallible cure for digestive complaints."

A watery smile rewarded him.

"I wish yours were not such a sympathetic countenance," she said. "I'm not a watering pot. I rarely weep unless I'm thoroughly enraged."

"I thought you were enraged. You have every right. Not a syllable that woman utters but is calculated to wound, and cruelly. She deserves her liver. I hope she chokes on it."

"That's hardly charitable."

"I'm not a charitable man. Moreover, I recognise the type. My fath—my family contains a few such vipers, and I've met more than enough in India as well, native and otherwise." Too heated. He was letting words slip. Philip collected himself. "Let us not discuss these dispiriting topics. You'd promised to help me sort out some of the major Hindu deities. Let's dwell on the gods, shall we, and consign the Mrs. Bullerhams of this world to—"

"Obscurity," she quickly supplied. Then, to his relief, she laughed.

=== 8 ===

THE STORM STRUCK a few days later. It swept down suddenly upon the *Evelina* in a gale-driven, whirling mass of black clouds that swelled and churned round the lone vessel, heaving up the waters beneath her.

With startling efficiency, the crew took in the sails just as the storm roared down upon them. It was already raging when the top-gallant yards were sent down and the masts struck.

Philip, who'd never experienced a major storm at sea, stayed after the other landlubbers had fled below, but not long. A tremendous swell sent the vessel lunging perilously to port, and Philip skidding across the wet deck toward the raging waters. One of the mates grabbed him, and, in no polite language, ordered him below.

Philip staggered towards the companionway, and the heavens cracked open to light the ship blazing white for one wild instant. As he ducked below, the white flame was doused by heavy black, and a deafening crash rent the air and seemed to shake the very ocean bottom.

Another crash and heave threw him from the bottom step. He tumbled forward and cracked his head against a timber. Along with the blast of pain came an onrush of bile. He staggered on to the cabin, hurriedly unlocked the door, and dove for a basin in the very nick of time.

Though the storm was over by late morning, the sea continued violent, heaving and tossing the twelve-hundred-ton vessel as though it were a child's toy boat.

For three days Philip clung to his mattress. He scarcely possessed the strength to cross the few feet to the cabin door. He was utterly unable to do anything for Jessup, barely able to look after himself. Luckily for the sorry pair, Miss Jones was immune to *mal de mer*. The indefatigable Abigail appeared twice a day, bearing bowls of some bland but sustaining mixture. With her came a cabin boy, whose unenviable task it was to empty basins and chamber pots for the seasick landlubbers.

By the fourth day, the buffeting had subsided somewhat, and agony dwindled to mere misery. Able at last to observe with some degree of lucidity Miss Jones's nursing methods, Philip soon ascertained precisely where all her sympathies lay.

Philip she simply handed his bowl and spoon. Then, turning away, Miss Jones devoted herself to Jessup. She lovingly fed and fussed over him. She fluffed his pillows, straightened and tucked his blanket, and tenderly held his hand until he sank into a doze.

By the conclusion of this operation, Philip was again beset by doubts. Had fifteen years of India, the last five spent dodging treachery at every turn, entirely poisoned his mind? Was it possible he saw intrigue and conspiracy where none existed?

As she turned back to him at last, Miss Jones must have remarked Philip's frown, for she said comfortingly, "Don't you worry now, Mr. Brentick. This pesky weather's just set him back a bit. But I do tell you, and I hope you won't take it amiss, as you'd better help him change his ways. He can't go back like what he was, you know."

"I beg your pardon?"

She moved nearer, and spoke in lower tones.

"My pa was just like him, strong as an ox. Drank gin like it was rainwater and never felt it. Then the influenza got hold of him, and he was never the same after. The littlest chill'd keep him in bed near a fortnight. Finally, the leech just told Pa straight out if he didn't want to be a pitiful wreck all the rest of his life, he'd got to mend his ways."

"My master spent half his life in India," Philip answered defensively, as she stood, hands on her hips, fixing him with a reproachful look. "Consider the climate's effects."

"Mr. Wringle'd do better to consider his wenching and drinking and stuffing himself," Bella answered with a sniff. "Don't tell *me* that ain't a man likes his carousing, because I won't believe you. An ignorant country maid I may be, but I wasn't born yesterday. Nor I ain't seeing all my tending go for nothing, and so I mean to tell him, soon as he's feeling more himself again."

Having delivered this lecture, her face softened. "There now," she said somewhat abashedly, "don't mind me. It's just the worry. He scared me half to death when I seen him get so horrible sick again, after all these weeks doing so good, too."

"I'm sure your careful nursing will not go for naught, Miss Jones," Philip said. "My master is aware, as I am, that he owes you his life. In fact, I'm sure he owes it twice now, for I've been no good to him at all."

She blushed and attempted to make light of his quite genuine praise.

"Goodness, Mr. Brentick, it's but a bit of soup now and then, and I'd go clean mad if I'd to stay in one place all the day."

"Yet Miss Cavencourt and Mrs. Gales need your services as well," he said. "You must be exhausted, running back and forth."

"Miss Amanda don't like to be fussed over when she's sick. She gets cross, you know, and wants to be let alone. And Mrs. Gales is only the tiniest bit under the weather. When I left, she was setting up in the bed, just knitting away, like that was the only cure for anything."

"Is—is Miss Cavencourt very ill?" Philip asked.

Bella appeared to consider. "Well, she's green enough," she said after a moment. "Greener than you are, Mr. Brentick. You look a deal better than yesterday, I'm happy to say. All the same . . ." She eyed him thoughtfully. "Mr. Wringle's whiskers make him look more distinguished, but I can't say the same for yourself. You look like a sailor what's been on a five-day binge."

Philip stroked his rough chin. "Raffish, Miss Jones?"

She shrugged her plump shoulders. "Whatever that is. Where's your shaving things?"

"Thank you, but I don't feel up to shaving at the moment. Perhaps later."

"Well, don't I know that?" she answered indignantly. "I got eyes, don't I? I'll shave you," she added, to his astonishment.

His shock grew to horror as her gleaming eye lit upon the washbasin, where his neglected razor lay.

"Thank you, but that will not be necessary," he said firmly. "Nor advisable. The ship is not altogether steady at present."

"I was shaving my pa since I was twelve years old, and I done Lord Cavencourt time enough when his valet was too drunk to be trusted with even a towel. My hands is perfectly steady."

"No one has . . . *ever* . . . shaved . . . me," Philip said, picking out the words with all the cold deliberation of his sire at his intimidating best. "*No one*. Not even J—no one!"

She drew her hand back from the razor and sighed. "Oh, very well, if you're going to get all in a roar about it. I was just looking for something to do.

Swiftly recollecting himself, Philip assumed a mask of penitence. "I do beg your pardon. Illness appears to make me cross, as well. But it is a quirk of mine. I can't bear to be shaved." He thought quickly. "If you truly want something to do . . . "

"Well, didn't I just say so?"

"In that case, I would be immensely grateful if you'd sew the button back on my coat. It came loose the day of the storm. When I fell ill so suddenly, I tore my coat off, and the button came loose," he explained. "It's dangling by a thread."

Bella's round face brightened. "Well, that's more like it, then." She retrieved the coat, then glanced about. "Got anything else? I expect you don't care much for mending, and there's no tailors near to hand."

When the door at last closed behind her, a choked guffaw broke the silence. Philip's icy blue gaze fell upon his servant, whose shoulders were shaking.

"Are you experiencing convulsions, soldier?" he asked frostily. "It would serve you right, for pretending to sleep, only to eavesdrop."

"Bless me, guv, if the wench wasn't gonna shave you. *You,*" Jessup chortled. "I never heard your voice go so high like that afore. Lawd, did y' think she meant to nick up somethin' else for you?"

"You know perfectly well I let no one come near me with a razor. Not even you, you decrepit old budmash. She's taken *your* measure, hasn't she? You heard her, lad. Miss Jones means to see you mend your wicked ways. She'll do it, make no mistake, even if it kills you."

Jessup chuckled. "Well, and mebbe I might let her. She do make salvation look sweet enough, that one. And pluck to the backbone, ain't she? I seen brave soldiers near wet themselves when they heard that tone from you, and she didn't so much as blink. Damme but I thought I'd bust a gut, tryin' to stifle myself."

"Why don't you try again?" Philip answered, taking up a pillow. "Or would you rather I *helped* you?"

Bella returned to the Cavencourt cabin bearing one coat, one shirt, and two pairs of trousers.

Amanda had dragged herself up to a sitting position. She gazed dully at the pile of clothing.

"What is that, Bella?"

"Mr. Brentick decided to come off his high ropes and let

me mend his things." Bella took up her sewing box and deftly threaded a needle. "He took it ill when I asked to shave him," she added, grinning. "I was afeard he'd jump clean out of bed and whack his head on the ceiling."

"I suppose most men wouldn't trust a woman with a razor," Amanda said.

Bella's grin broadened. "I wish you could have heard him. And seen him. For a minute there, he almost had me quaking in my slippers. I never in all my life seen anyone get so high and mighty. Looking down his nose at me, he was—and there I was standing practically on top of him, as there ain't room enough in that cabin for a cat to wash its whiskers. And he got this little twitch in his jaw and his nose pinched up, and his voice just—just *dripped* out, like pieces of ice. '*No one shaves me,*' he says. And I fair near dropped a curtsey and said, 'No, Your Highness, no they don't, I'm sure.'" She giggled. "Oh, he is a one, that one."

"I expect it was being so seasick," said Amanda, baffled by the strange flutter within her. *Mal de mer.* Would it never end? "No doubt he was out of sorts."

"He was in a temper fit is what. He don't like being sick, I can tell you. Hates it worse than you do. Still, who can blame him, such a nasty little place it is, and him with them long legs." She shook out the trousers and gazed at them in shrewd appraisal. "And who'd think, skinny as he is," she said, "any man could have such a small bottom?"

Amanda's face grew unpleasantly hot. She glanced at Mrs. Gales, but that lady remained serenely asleep. The widow slept as steadily as she plied her needles and hooks. A cannon blast might wake her, but nothing less, once she'd composed herself to slumber.

"He asked after you," Bella said, after a moment. "He seemed very worried. Maybe that's why he got so grouchy. Poor man, it don't seem fair, do it? Him so fine and handsome as a prince in one of your fairy tales. Why, he might have been a gentleman, miss, and then—"

"Bella."

The maid looked up enquiringly at the unaccustomed sharp tone. "Yes, miss?"

"My head is aching like the very devil. Do you think you can mend *silently* for a little while?"

By the end of the week, though the sea continued choppy, the deck was sufficiently safe for perambulation. Late in the day, Philip made his way above.

Bella had said her mistress was fully recovered, but the mistress did not appear. He waited an hour at their customary place, then spent another two hours prowling the vessel from stem to stern. Perhaps she'd come earlier, and the exertion had tired her after the strain of illness. Perhaps she'd taken to her bed once more.

He would *not* think about beds. Not her bed. Nor was it wise to consider his own narrow mattress. That had seemed a deal too much like a coffin, and the airless cell in which it lay seemed to reek of illness and decay. So Bella must have noticed as well, for she'd arrived today with bucket, mop, and cloth, and the hapless cabin boy in tow. With Jessup alert and vigilant, Philip had happily fled, leaving the maid and her slave to scrub the living daylights out of every square inch of offending surface.

Not that her efforts could possibly make the space tolerable to Philip. Falling asleep would continue to be an ordeal. To linger there at all when it wasn't necessary was needless torture. *Ah, thank you, Papa.*

"There now, Miss Amanda, it's all right."

Amanda's eyes flew open, and she jerked upright . . . to utter darkness. Panic seized her, and she tried to shake off the hand grasping her wrist.

"It's all right, miss. You had a bad dream," Bella said soothingly.

That was all. A dream. A very long one. She must remember it. Padji ought to know. But she wouldn't forget, not this one. Not one detail.

Amanda sank back upon the pillows, and patiently accepted Bella's fussing and fluffing and tucking. "Thank you," she said softly. "I'm sorry I woke you. Do go back to sleep. I'm all right now."

In a few minutes, Bella was lightly snoring. Her mistress, however, remained painfully awake.

Amanda turned restlessly.

Seven bells. Eleven-thirty.

Eight bells. Midnight.

Squelching a sigh of exasperation, Amanda slid from the bed. She fumbled about, found her clothing, and managed to dress without waking her companions. Then she crept from the room, closing the door gently behind her.

Above, a full moon lit the deck with soft, eerie light. There were sailors about, but they were busy with their tasks, their voices muted. Amanda automatically headed for her usual place at the rail. Then she hesitated. It was one thing to wander about unattended in broad day, with Mrs. Gales at the stern keeping discreet watch. It was quite another to stroll about alone after midnight.

Amanda was about to turn back when the cool breeze carried a familiar scent to her nostrils: Tobacco smoke. She saw a tall, slim figure move from the shadows of the mizzenmast to the rail. His hair gleamed silver in the moonlight. He leaned upon the rail, half-turned from her. She could just make out the tiny red glow of his cigar when he drew upon it.

She told herself she ought to leave before Mr. Brentick became aware of her presence. She was amazed he hadn't noticed already. His senses always seemed so acute. Yet she smelled the smoke and a great, empty place seemed to open within her, and she knew only that she didn't want to be alone.

She'd taken but two steps when his posture tensed and his head swivelled in her direction. Too late to retreat.

Heart thumping, Amanda continued, though the space between them seemed to have grown to an immense stretch of cold and hostile plain.

His greeting was warm, however, when she neared. "Miss Cavencourt," he said softly, surprised. "For a moment I thought you were a ghost."

"You'd better pretend I am," she said, abashed by his wondering stare. "Or that I'm sleepwalking. I'm supposed to be slumbering like a good little girl, but I couldn't, and I thought I'd go mad trying to keep quiet about it."

"With all due respect, miss, you *are* mad, you know. We have settled that question long since."

He looked down at the cheroot he held, and frowned. As he raised his hand to toss it into the water, she cried, "Oh, don't throw it away on my account. I don't mind at all. In fact, I rather like it," she added. "It reminds me of Calcutta."

His eyebrows went up. "You miss the stench?"

She smiled and, unthinking, leaned upon the rail, and inhaled. Her entire being seemed to relax. "Not that, exactly, but the smoke. The rooms filled with incense, and the stories. My friend, the Rani Simhi, would smoke her hookah and relate myths and legends," she explained, looking away from him and towards the moon-dappled ocean. "I felt like a little girl, transported to a mysterious place where fairy tales were real."

"After what we've endured recently, I shouldn't mind being transported to mysterious places. Will you take me?" he asked. "Will you tell me a story?"

She bit her lip. "I really ought to return. I shouldn't be out at this hour."

"No, you shouldn't," he agreed, "and I shouldn't ask you." He paused a moment, his eyes very intent upon her face. "But I am monstrous selfish. I wish you would stay . . . long enough to tell me one of your stories."

She thought he must hear her heart thumping so stupidly, even above the moan of timbers and the splash of waves against the vessel. But he only looked at her in that strange, fixed way. Part of her wanted to run, for it reminded her of the steady gaze of a jungle cat, or a bird of prey. Yet another part of her—mesmerised or stunned, she knew not which—could not bear to go away. She thought she could look into his beautiful face, its chiseled planes silver and shadow in the moonlight, for all her lifetimes. "Earthly beauty is a glimpse of the Eternal," the rani had said. "Earthly love is a glimpse of transcendent love."

Eternity and transcendence, indeed. Smiling at her folly, Amanda returned her focus to the glistening blue-black water, and let her mind sink into the smoky, warm, scented rooms where the stories lived.

"When he was a young man, as I've before mentioned, Krishna was a devil with the ladies," she began. "When he was a boy, he was full of mischief. One day, he stole some butter.

Philip took the story with him when he returned to his cabin, just as he took with him her voice and scent, and the dreamy, faraway glow of her eyes. The story made him smile yet, for he saw the several characters in her mobile face, and heard their voices in hers. He'd laughed helplessly when she revealed Krishna's triumph, and her face had expressed the child-god's ineffable ennui as he learned of the miracle he'd performed. Miss Cavencourt had touched something more, though, and Philip found it uncanny she'd chosen precisely that tale.

In punishment for stealing the butter, Krishna's mama had tied him to a heavy mortar used for grinding and crushing food. When at length he grew bored with his situation, Krishna had dragged the mortar between two huge trees and heedlessly uprooted them.

In the roots of the trees were two princes an evil sorcerer had entombed. They'd been buried alive, but the child-god had inadvertently returned them to life.

Did it haunt them after, Philip wondered, as he sank back upon his pillow and closed his eyes. Or had Krishna freed their spirits as well? He wished he might have asked her. He wished he might ask her now. But if she had been with him now, he wouldn't care to talk, would he?

Numskull. If only he'd got himself a tart in Capetown. At this rate, he'd be a dithering imbecile by the time the ship entered the English Channel.

=== 9 ===

"I DREAMT OF the robbery," Amanda said. She sat this morning upon her customary cask in the blistering galley. Perspiration trickled down her neck, though she'd arrived scarcely five minutes before.

"A troubling dream," Padji said as his large hands dextrously kneaded dough. "I heard you cry out three times, and my heart ached for your trouble."

"You heard me?" she repeated incredulously. "From the other end of the ship?"

"I lay by your door, O beloved, as I do each night. So I slept by the door of the great Lioness. Such is my duty."

"By my door? But you couldn't have been. . . . You must have been dreaming as well, because—"

"I moved from the place when you rose," Padji said, "lest you stumble over my lowly person."

"Where did you go then?"

"Above. The hour was late. The mistress must move where she chooses, fearlessly, in confidence her servant is near to protect her. I was near, O daughter of the sun and of the moon."

"Indeed. You are . . . most conscientious, Padji."

He shrugged. "It is my *dharma*. I am of no significance. Tell me of this dream that so troubles you."

"I know it was only a dream," she said uncomfortably, "yet I remembered what the rani told me."

"The eye observes mere appearance, which the mind

gives name to. The heart sees into the darkness and discerns truth. In dreams, the heart speaks to the eye and mind. So she tells us in her endless wisdom."

"So she tells us." Amanda sighed. "In any case, a great deal of it seemed obvious, but part of it—well, I didn't know what to think."

"Tell me the whole of it."

"It was the robbery," she said in Hindustani. "Just as it happened, except at the last. The thief had knocked me down and run off with the Laughing Princess. But this time, I jumped up and chased him. Miles, it seemed, down one long passage, then a turning, then another passage. The night was utterly still and black."

"You saw no moon?" Padji asked.

"No moon, no stars. It was like a maze in a great void. Then I came to the final turning, and felt the breeze, which carried the scent of the sea. I stopped suddenly and looked down, and saw the sea beneath me, churning and sparkling, coal-black. I screamed."

"That was your first cry," Padji said, nodding.

"A voice answered me," Amanda went on. "The moon, enormous, white and full, broke past the clouds and shone down upon him. He wore a jewelled turban, and the rich garb of a prince, but his face remained in darkness. His voice was the robber's voice."

Padji gave her one brief glance before he returned to his kneading. "He called to you?"

"He said, 'Come to me. My boat will bear you safely.' But I was afraid of him," Amanda said, looking down at her hands. "I turned to run away, but the passage had vanished, and I stood on a narrow ledge, the sea before me and the sea behind me. Then the ledge itself vanished, and I fell a great way. That, I expect, was the second time I cried out in my sleep. He caught me, and his cloak enfolded me." She paused, her cheeks burning. "I had rather not describe the details."

"He took you as a lover," Padji said without looking up from his work.

"Certainly not!" Amanda's cheeks flamed anew. "I would never dream such a thing."

He shrugged, and she recommenced. "I struggled, *needless to say*," she added, glaring at him, "and he laughed. When the laughter died, he'd vanished. I was chilled. I picked up his cloak to put around me, and found the Laughing Princess at my feet. I tried to pick it up, but it was too heavy. I was weary and hungry and cold, and all alone on this great, black sea, so I wept, and called to the moon—to Anumati—to help me. Then the breeze blew. It came warm this time, filled with the scent of agarwood. The air grew thick with smoke. I raised my hand," Amanda said, lifting her arm as she had in the dream. "A dark form swept down from the heavens. It was a falcon. It circled my head three times, then alit upon my wrist. 'I will serve you,' he said."

Padji paused, his brown eyes alert. "The hunting falcon is female. This spoke to you in man's voice?"

"The robber's voice, again. At least, so I believed in the dream, because I told him he was false, and a thief. I shook my wrist, but his talons gripped painfully, and I cried out."

"The third time."

Amanda nodded. "That last cry must have wakened Bella, because she woke me. I was too agitated to go back to sleep. That's why I went above," she added without meeting Padji's gaze.

Padji threw the dough into a bowl and placed a cloth over it. "The dream is plain enough," he said. "Anumati sent it to you. She knows you grow anxious and impatient. She warns you the statue cannot be moved until you are no longer upon the endless sea. You understood that wisdom, for we spoke of it many weeks ago."

"Of course I understand. That isn't what bothers me." Her finger traced the outline of a bud embroidered on her skirt. "I only want back what's mine. But sometimes, when I think about what must be done, I wonder if it's wrong." She glanced up. "You promised not to—not to hurt anybody, you know."

"I obey your wishes in all things, my golden one."

"I am not . . . convinced Mr. Brentick knows anything about it," she said, unconsciously lapsing into English. "It's possible his master has not confided in him. Mr. Brentick has not been long in his employ and—and men of law are very secretive. My brother certainly doesn't confide in *his* valet. It's even possible Mr. Wringle objected to his own role, but hadn't any choice. Or maybe he doesn't know the statue was stolen. It may have come through another intermediary. Lud, even Randall Groves."

"One cannot know. One cannot look into another's heart," Padji agreed.

"In fact," Amanda went on with more assurance, "if either were truly dangerous men, Anumati would have warned me, wouldn't she, in the dream?"

"You did not see the man's face in the dream."

"But I heard his voice," Amanda reminded. "It was not Mr. Brentick's. And Mr. Wringle hasn't the same form. He's too short and square." She glanced away, frowning. "Why did I dream of a prince and a falcon, though? Can there be some other on this ship? But that doesn't make sense at all. What the devil did it mean?"

"Thrice he changed his form," Padji said reflectively. "A thief, a prince, a falcon, each held you by turns. One robbed, one loved, one brought pain." He shrugged. "Most strange. A prophecy, perhaps."

Amanda shook her head. "No. Dreams may help explain what is, but I am still too English to believe they can tell what will be. I am certainly no oracle. Nor do I wish to be." She shivered, despite the heat.

Amanda certainly never *intended* to return to the upper deck at night. The trouble was, the closer they got to England, the more anxious she became.

Two months passed, during which more than one night lengthened into morning while she lay broad awake in her bed. She didn't venture above every time she was restless, only when it became intolerable. That added up to a mere half-dozen late night rambles. She found Mr. Brentick there every time.

Still, he could not possibly get the wrong impression. Amanda had let him know, the second time she'd crept above, that Padji was lurking about. Padji must have let others know as well, and in his own inimitable way, solicited discretion. Certainly, not one whisper of Miss Cavencourt's nocturnal wanderings reached Mrs. Gales's ears, even though Captain Blayton told her everything.

The *Evelina* was at long last approaching the Channel. She'd probably be sailing up the Thames in a matter of days, if the winds held favourable. In a matter of days, the Laughing Princess would be Amanda's at last . . . if all went well. But she would not think about that, she chided herself this night as, for the seventh and positively last time, she escaped her cabin and sneaked up to the deck.

Mr. Brentick looked round at her approach, his countenance half surprised, half—was it pleased? Amanda recollected that in a matter of days, he would be out of her life forever. Well, what did she expect, she asked herself crossly. Did she think that, like Padji, the valet would suddenly develop an irresistible need to abandon his employer and follow her to Yorkshire? If he looked pleased, it was because he liked her Indian stories.

"Another difficult night, Miss Cavencourt?" he enquired sympathetically. "I suppose you long to be home, and its being so near makes you restless."

"It's good to hear some rational excuse," she said. "I simply felt wild to get out of the cabin. Now I shall sleep the morning away again." She glanced up. "Are you always here?" she asked. "Are we seized by similar demons at the same time? Or do you never sleep?"

"Old habits die hard. In the military, I grew accustomed to a few hours' rest snatched here and there."

"Oh."

He glanced about. "I suppose Padji is of similar habits."

"I wonder if he sleeps at all." She, too, looked around her. "Where is he? I told him there was no need to skulk about. Everyone knows he's there."

"Evidently, he's well schooled in discretion."

"Yes."

"He's been with you a long time, I take it."

She considered briefly how to answer. Perhaps it wasn't wise, but if she told the truth, Mr. Brentick's response might tell her something. She wanted reassurance. Not that it mattered, really, whether he was innocent. She'd never see him again. But how unpleasant to part, suspecting him, feeling unsure . . .

"I might as well speak frankly," she said. "We're nearly home and I doubt the captain would have Padji tossed over at this late date, even if he could find anyone audacious enough to attempt it." She stood a bit straighter, her posture half-defiant. "Padji wasn't my servant. He ran away from the Rani Simhi. He'd committed an offence, and was terrified of what she'd do to him. You may find that difficult to credit, considering his size and strength. So did I. But I got on this ship and there he was . . . and so I told the captain a clanker."

"What hideous crime did the fellow commit?" Mr. Brentick asked.

With some relief she discerned only genuine curiosity in his tones. "I was attacked . . . and robbed one night, and he was supposed to be protecting me."

"The rani sounds monstrous unforgiving."

"That's what Padji would have one believe. Nonetheless, I'm happy to have him with me. He *is* an excellent cook."

"And an excellent watchdog." He sounded peeved.

"Does he make you uneasy, Mr. Brentick?"

"My dear lady, the fellow is over six feet tall, big as an ox, and strong as one. Only a nitwit would not be uneasy." After a short pause, he went on, "Do you know, I'm terrified to move a muscle when you're by, lest it be interpreted as an unfriendly act, and result in my immediate demise."

"Padji is big, but he's not stupid," she defended. "I'm sure he can distinguish an unfriendly gesture from a friendly one."

"Can he distinguish friendly from too friendly, Miss Cavencourt?" he asked.

Her face grew warm. "I don't think I wish to know what you mean," she answered firmly. "You're getting that tone in your voice, Mr. Brentick."

"What tone is that?"

"Your flirting one."

"And you find it disagreeable."

She threw him a sidelong glance. "You know perfectly well that women find it agreeable. I'm sure you practised for years to get it just right."

"Practised? For *years?*" he echoed aggrievedly. "You make me out to be thoroughly unscrupulous."

"Not at all. You told me you'd developed diligent habits of study. One might naturally assume you applied them to more than Cicero's orations."

"Natural philosophy, for instance?"

"Call it what you like. I only request you not do it with me," she said nervously. "I know I shouldn't be here, but you needn't make me feel I've sneaked off to an assignation. I realise flirting is practically an addiction with you, Mr. Brentick, but you must try to show it who is master. If I were a man," she added in earnest tones, "you wouldn't try to flirt with me, would you? Why not just pretend I'm a man?"

He gazed at her a moment, then laughed.

"Miss Cavencourt, the moon offers little light tonight, but even in this near Stygian darkness, the task you propose is quite impossible."

Amanda raised her chin and turned her own gaze to the black water. "Then you shall just have to flirt all by yourself, because I most assuredly will not help you."

"You are exceedingly kind," he murmured. "*That* task is merely onerous."

"Excuse me. I am not well-versed in these matters. I was under the impression that flirting, like quarrelling, takes two."

"I said it was onerous," he answered gravely. "Yet I am not frightened by the enormity of the challenge. On the contrary, if I don't flirt, and very soon, something terrible might happen. I'm filled to bursting with double entendres and leading questions. If I don't let them out, I might . . . explode. I don't mind exploding, really, if I must, but you might be struck by a flying limb, and that would be most *improper*. Not at all the thing. Mrs. Bullerham would never countenance it."

A half-strangled laugh escaped her, floated upon the sea breeze . . . and sank into a taut silence. She hadn't noticed he'd moved, but he was much nearer now. His presence, dark and oppressively masculine, seemed to enclose her.

"You don't know you're provocative, do you?" he asked, his voice low, puzzled.

Alarmed, Amanda swung round sharply. That was a mistake. She came up short mere inches from his chest. Her glance flew to his face. It seemed a long way up. She felt very small, vulnerable, and trapped. "What are you doing?" she demanded.

"Flirting. All by myself."

"You are not. It's—it's something else entirely." Where the devil was Padji, confound him? The air was quite cool. Amanda felt feverish, and her heart seemed to shrink very tight in her breast.

Shadows veiled the valet's expression, and in the darkness his blue eyes gleamed black, unreadable. Yet her other senses had grown painfully acute. She was conscious of a faint, lingering aroma of tobacco and some light cologne or soap. Her ears caught the quickened sound of his breathing. Or was that her own? She retreated, and felt the rail dig into her back.

"It *is* something else," he said, more softly still. "I'm trying to pretend you're a man." He face bent closer. "I'm trying to remember my place." His arms brushed hers as his hands clamped down on the rail on either side of her. "It's not working," he whispered, his breath warm on her face as his mouth descended to hers.

A hairsbreadth from contact, his head jerked back abruptly. Amanda blinked, then saw two large brown hands gripping the valet's shoulders.

"The mistress is sleepy," Padji said sweetly. "It is time for her to retire."

Nearly seven curst months, Philip raged silently while he stood at the rail and pretended not to watch Miss Cavencourt chatting with her companion. Seven months and not even one miserable kiss. Seven months on this vessel with the same woman, and he hadn't so much as touched her. Nor would he. He'd seen to that, hadn't he?

Two days had passed since his ill-fated attempt, and Amanda Cavencourt had not come within fifty feet of him, curse her. But he couldn't curse her, really. Though she might break a few rules, ignore a few conventions, she wouldn't break them all. India and the rani hadn't possessed her entirely. England's oppressive morality maintained a hold.

Philip ought, actually, be grateful he was still alive. He didn't deserve to be. An unforgivable lapse, that. He'd known the Indian was standing guard, and the Falcon had simply . . . forgotten. One moment he was aware, as always, of every detail of his surroundings, of every sound. The next, he was aware only of her, of her husky voice and unconsciously sensuous movements and the maddening scent of patchouli. He'd wanted to lose himself there, in her.

Now she wouldn't even speak to him.

"Portsmouth," Padji repeated stubbornly.

"He said Gravesend. Even Captain Blayton said Gravesend. Mr. Wringle and Mr. Brentick will disembark there with the rest of us," Amanda said, for the fifth time.

"The mistress troubles her mind with the duties of her slave," Padji reproached. "I speak to the sailors. They tell me many things of England. They are patient with the ignorant black man and draw him maps. The two will leave us at Portsmouth, for that way is quicker."

It was quicker, Amanda had to admit. Lord Hedgrave lived in Wiltshire. "Then you are saying Mr. Brentick lied to me."

Padji shrugged. "Sometimes the servant must say what the master tells him to say. Sometimes the servant is told lies, and believes them. I am fortunate. My mistress utters only golden truth to me."

Amanda gazed unhappily about the galley. "Do you realise what you're saying?" she asked. "The captain expects to reach Portsmouth *tomorrow morning*."

"I have told the maid. She is prepared. There is naught for you to trouble with, mistress. All is in readiness."

"All? What about me?" she demanded. "Am I supposed to stand about idly the whole time?"

"Yes, O beloved daughter of the great Lioness."

Nothing to do. Nothing to say. Not a word. Not even good-bye. All the same, it was better she said nothing. After the other night . . . when he'd almost kissed her.

Amanda knew she was not the most decorous woman. She would never be altogether a lady—at least not the conventional sort. Still, she wasn't a lightskirts. It was one thing to treat servants as human beings and friends, for her servants had always been her friends. It was quite another to be kissing someone else's servant. One was not supposed to kiss any man, even a gentleman, unless one were betrothed to him.

So it needn't have anything to do with rank at all, rather with what was right and what was wrong. Except, Amanda reflected sadly, she'd never entirely accepted all her culture's rights and wrongs. Except, she added more sadly, she had wanted that beautiful, naughty man to kiss her, more than anything else in the world.

==10==

"WELL, LASS, WHAT'S this?" Jessup asked as Bella set the tray down. "Not spirits, is it?"

Bella grinned. "My mistress don't know, and she'll be fit to be tied if she finds out. But you been complaining how thirsty you was, so I thought, no harm in a drop. But mind," she added, shaking a finger at him, "only a drop. You don't want to end up a sick old wreck like my poor pa, do you? Like I told you, Providence gave you another chance to mend your wicked ways."

"I was hopin' I didn't have to mend *all* of 'em," he said meaningfully. "A man needs somethin' to look forwards to. Like a bit of a cuddle now and then with a pretty lass," he added with a wink.

"Well, I can't think what pretty lasses you could find just now," Bella answered, eyes downcast.

"Can't you?" he asked. He took hold of her hand. "Mebbe you'll think clearer when you're not so thirsty."

"Only a taste for me, Mr. Wringle," was the prim answer. "Spirits always make me act so foolish."

"Do they now?" he answered cheerfully as he released her hand to take up the bottle.

The crew members who weren't sensibly sleeping were very non-sensibly engaged in jollity upon the forecastle. The noise carried but faintly to the stern, where Philip stood.

He was half tempted to join them, to spend this last night blind drunk.

It was the first night of the full moon, which was partially veiled now by a thin cloud. Yet it shed light enough to dance upon the water, which shimmered blue-black in the night. The Indians, Philip recalled, attached some deity to every phase of the moon. Whose night was this? *She* would know, of course. Miss Cavencourt meant to write a book about the myths and legends she'd so assiduously collected during her sojourn in Calcutta. Perhaps he'd read it one day. By then he'd have forgotten her, very likely, or would recall just enough to make him wonder at how susceptible a long voyage could make one. He doubted he'd remember later how very much he wished for her company now.

Her hair was merely brown, he reminded himself, and hazel was an apt enough label for her eyes. She wasn't pretty, nor even attractive, really, unless one had cultivated a taste for the darkly exotic. Nor was she so fascinating a companion . . . unless one preferred contradiction and secrets and was helplessly drawn to a woman who must be unravelled, like an endless puzzle.

His muscles tensed, conscious of an approach. Barely audible, the footsteps, yet he recognised them immediately. Philip didn't move, didn't so much as turn his head. He didn't want to look at her when it must be only to watch her walk on past as though he didn't exist.

The footsteps drew nearer. A few feet away, they paused. A moment later, she stood beside him, her hands upon the rail.

"Several deities are connected with the full moon," Miss Cavencourt said, just as though they'd been speaking this last hour. "Anumati personifies the first day. She and the others are fertility deities. She in particular, though, brings her worshippers inspiration and insight, wealth and longevity, as well as offspring."

Slowly, disbelieving, Philip let his eyes turn to her at

last. She was gazing at the moon, and in the silvery light her uplifted profile seemed to belong to some ancient goddess.

"Does she bring me a pardon?" he asked. "I'm rather in need of one."

He waited through what seemed an interminable silence.

"The trouble with you, Mr. Brentick, is that you don't understand me," she said at last. "When I talk, I talk. When I take a walk, no matter what time it is, I take a walk. It's quite simple. There's no need to make it complicated. That's so—so curst *English*." She turned to meet his bemused gaze squarely. "I know I don't behave altogether properly. That doesn't mean *I'm* improper. Only that sometimes I do what I like. Do you understand?"

"I understand perfectly, Miss Cavencourt."

"Are you sure?"

"Yes. The trouble is, sometimes I do what *I* like. Regrettably, I not only behave improperly, but I *am* improper. Sometimes."

She considered this, and must have comprehended, for her expression grew exasperated. "Then what am I supposed to do?"

"I doubt you need worry yourself about that. Whatever need be done, we can be quite certain Padji will do it," he said mournfully. "I'm only amazed I'm not at present the main course at some aquatic family's dinner."

She gave a soft chuckle. "Then I may take it you've learned your lesson."

"Yes, miss," he answered meekly.

"Because I'd rather continue friends, you know."

Something seemed to squeeze his heart. "Are we friends?"

"Something like, don't you think?" she said, her gaze earnest. "You're so easy to talk to, and your stories are quite as good as my own."

"That is high praise, indeed, coming from you. If you write a fraction as well as you speak, the British public will be enchanted with your tales. I am," he added. "When you tell a story, I'm transported to my boyhood. Every adult care vanishes, and the world becomes the world you reveal. You have a remarkable gift."

"Perhaps that's because I never altogether grew up." A hint of mischief curled her mouth, and she looked back to the sea. "Like a child, I am also partial to being terrified. Shall I tell you a gruesome tale tonight?"

He grinned. "I should like that above all things."

"Very well—but only because you've flattered me." She glanced up at the moon, as though for inspiration, then back at him. "Once upon a time," she began, "a group of pleasure-seeking travellers ran aground off the Indian coast."

She gave each traveller a character, and detailed with relish the charms of the alluring maidens who rescued them. She described the feast these beauties served, and made his mouth water. She made him long to sip the magical wine the guests tasted. Philip could hear the whisper of silk and the tinkle of bangles, smell incense and jasmine, feel the velvet softness of the sirens' skin.

Just as the travellers were seduced by their hostesses, Philip was seduced by his companion's low, sensuous voice. He heard her voice bidding him sample the food and wine, just as he felt her hands caressing his face and playing in his hair, her arms encircling his neck, her mouth, soft and ripe, warming and teasing his. He sank, with the guests, upon silken cushions, and gave himself up to pleasure.

"On through the golden afternoon into twilight, the guests dwelt in this garden of earthly delights. At last, darkness crept upon them." Miss Cavencourt's throaty voice dropped and cracked, grew raspy, and a tiny, delicious chill of anticipation crept up his neck. "The first of the guests, lying in the arms of one beautiful maiden, opened his eyes to gaze into those of his lover. . . and saw hers . . . cold as ice. Before his horrified gaze, she changed. Her skin darkened and shrivelled. Her thick, silken hair frizzled up as though a flame had been set to it. She laughed, and the horrible, hungry sound froze his heart. Then she smiled, and that was more ghastly still. Her hands, like claws, grasped a gleaming blade. He, immobile with terror, could only watch helplessly as the knife descended, ever . . . so . . . slowly . . . to his throat."

The smiling sidelong glance she threw Philip was quite evil. She was enjoying herself, bloodthirsty wench.

"She cut his throat," Miss Cavencourt went on in sepulchral tones, "and drank the blood. Every one of the travellers met the same fate. You see, this was not a paradise of sensual pleasure, but a demons' lair. The alluring maidens were ogresses, who seduced men only to feed on them." She shook her head sadly and sighed. "The wages of sin."

He'd remained a respectful distance away, though his lounging stance as he leaned back upon the rail, his body half-turned to her, was hardly decorous.

Nonetheless, he remained as he was, taking her in, trying to drink his fill of her, all the while knowing this could not possibly be enough. He told himself it must be enough. The enchantingly evil story was her farewell gift to him, though she couldn't know it was farewell. Nor should she. He made himself speak normally.

"A moral tale," he said. "Yet puzzling. I'd always thought the Hindus celebrated pleasure. What of your favourite, the blue-skinned Krishna, who played his flute and drew women by the score?"

"Earthly love, in all its many forms, offers us a glimpse of transcendent, spiritual love. That, apparently, is how the Hindus accommodate it, as they seem to accommodate all aspects of life. This story was probably some sort of warning not to let physical pleasure blind one to evil. Or, the tale may simply have been composed by a misogynist," she added, grinning. "Actually, it's rather mild, when you compare it to Adam and Eve's fall from grace. *All* our earthly woes are blamed on one naive female."

He laughed. "You lived too long in India. It's made you a skeptic."

"And a heretic and a cynic. But not consistently. My brain is not nearly well-regulated enough."

"Consistency is boring. To me it bespeaks a narrow mind. There are far too many predictable people in this world, Miss Cavencourt. Be thankful you are not one of them. I am." He paused a moment. "I shall miss you."

"I shall miss you as well," she said lightly. "You're an exceptionally good listener. Still, I have a few days left to tax your patience, have I not? I promise to treat you to one or two more grisly tales, for you seemed quite taken with tonight's."

"I was a soldier. Murder and mayhem are quite in my line."

"Then murder and mayhem it shall be." She stepped back from the rail. "Now, however, it's time to say good night. I got away early because Mrs. Gales was dining with the captain. I'd best return before she does. She rarely lectures, but I should hate for her to discover how disreputably I've been behaving."

"Others may consider it disreputable. I consider it kind." Philip straightened and moved a pace nearer. "You were especially kind to pardon me. You don't know how grateful I am."

She smiled. "To be alive, certainly. Still, it wasn't all kindness, Mr. Brentick. To encounter a kindred spirit is rare, and I hated to lose the few days we have left. I wanted us to part with pleasant memories. As friends," she said, putting out her hand.

So simple a gesture. So trusting. She thought him a servant, yet she offered her hand to him as a friend. Even the Falcon's cynical heart was touched. Because she was so very alone, he realised. What a pity that was.

He took the proffered hand, and as he felt the cool, soft, slim fingers close about his, his heart constricted within him. His hand tightened as well. *Good-bye*, he said silently.

Then, because a polite handshake could not be enough, he held it a moment longer, and another. His eyes scanned her moonlit countenance, memorizing her as she was this last night, all silver and shadow, her eyes widening in surprise or perhaps alarm, he knew not which. It hardly mattered. He raised her hand to his lips, and heard her sharp intake of breath, but more important was the light tease of patchouli about him, the scent and velvet softness of her skin against his mouth. He felt her hand tremble. Reluctantly, he released it.

"Good n-night, Mr. Brentick," she said in a tiny voice.

"Good night, Miss Cavencourt." *Good-bye, Amanda.*

She turned and began to move away.

No.

No.

"Damnation, not like this," he muttered.

In one swift flash of movement, like the Falcon he was, he'd closed the distance between them, lightly caught her shoulder to turn her back to him, and pulled her into his arms. One sure hand clasped her neck, the other pressed her back, preventing escape. Swiftly, too, his mouth descended to hers, covering it before she could cry out, and taking before she could think not to give.

He was a thief, after all, and he'd steal this, too, if he must.

Four bells. Ten o'clock. Amanda heard the sound distinctly just as she was moving away. After that, nothing was clear. She was aware of a blur of motion, a hand on her shoulder. Then the world, or some mad wind, sent her spinning into his arms.

It could not be happening.

Automatically, her hands went out to break free, but they were trapped against his chest, and she was imprisoned in the hard strength of his arms. She looked up, alarmed and confused, only to watch his face blur into darkness as his mouth crashed down on hers.

It was not happening.

Her trapped hands knotted into fists, and she squirmed

against the unrelenting snare of his body, only to strike muscle and heat. Shocked to the core, she shuddered and ceased struggling.

She didn't know what to do. And then she didn't want to do anything, because the insistent pressure of his mouth eased. The kiss grew gentler, more coaxing . . . and more dangerous. Far more dangerous, for he tasted of the sea, yet more of himself, and that was sweet and heady like opium. Her lips answered and, like a drug, the taste and scent of him stole through her in a stream of languorous warmth that sapped the strength from her muscles and left longing in its wake.

Her hands opened against his coat, crept up the sea-tinged wool to his shoulders, and on, to curl around his neck. The air was filled with the salt sea, and with the scent of him, of smoke and spicy soap, and she nestled into the warmth and the strength of him. It wasn't happening. It was a dream. She'd dreamt it before.

Helplessly, her muscles answered every light pressure of his hands, turning into each caress as though his touch were music. Mad, sweet music, irresistible. She became a serpent in his arms, a cobra moving to some enchanted flute. Dark and dangerous the spell, too, for at its edges something wild waited.

His fingers tangled in her hair. His tongue, cool and feather light, teased her lips, tempting and tantalising until they parted.

The waiting, wild demon sprang then, and the dream became another world, fierce and dark and hungry. His tongue invaded and demanded, sending fiery shocks through her. Her fingers tightened about his neck, while her body strained against his, and her heart raced so she thought it would burst from her.

His lips left hers to trail teasing kisses upon her brow, then down along the bones of her cheek, and on to her neck and the hollows of her ear, where he lingered to torment until she moaned. Then his mouth found hers again, and drank possessively, while his hands dragged from her shoulders down the length of her body to her waist and hips, moulding her to him.

That was when it crackled within her, the fear. She heard a low, choked cry—her own. Yet it was not happening. It was a dream.

He broke the kiss, but his hands moved to clasp her waist tightly. His breathing was laboured, as hers was. When he spoke, his voice was low, hoarse.

"I really . . . don't want . . . to let you go," he said, striving for breath between words. "But you are driving me mad and . . . " His eyes were dark, hot, intent. Damp tendrils clung to his forehead. The hands at her waist gripped harder.

Numbly, she looked about her. Not a dream. Good God.

She snatched her hands from his neck.

"Stay with me," he whispered.

She pushed frantically, then pulled at his fingers, trying to loosen his grip of her waist. "Let me go," she gasped. "Please. Oh, Lord, please let me go."

He exhaled a long sigh and his hands released her.

Tears sprang to her eyes. "I'm sorry," she blurted out. "I didn't mean—oh—" Then she fled.

Philip watched her slip away into the shadows, and willed himself not to pursue her. He couldn't bring her back. Even the Falcon could not swoop down and make off with this prize. He smiled ruefully. Make off where? He hadn't any place to take her. What had he thought—that he might ravish her here, on the deck, in some dark corner amid the casks and ropes? *Idiot*.

He returned to his eternal position at the rail and stared down at the water.

Any lingering doubts he'd entertained had vanished the instant he'd kissed her. She was innocent. Her mouth had told him so. Hers was not the response of a practised seductress—he'd had enough of that kind to know—but of the child she partly was, utterly untutored in lovemaking.

Shocked, he'd very nearly stopped it as soon as it had begun. Another moment's struggle, surely, and he'd have released her, for unwilling women were not to his taste. He would have stopped it, certainly, were it not for those confiding hands, creeping up to his neck, and were it not for her ripe, trusting mouth's willingness to follow his lead. That had quite undone him.

She'd succumbed too quickly, and so sweetly. Her slim, beautiful body had curved so naturally and so warmly to his. He'd wanted to wrap her around him, to lose himself in her erotic innocence, even as he taught her.

Oh, he'd lost himself all right, in needless torment. He knew perfectly well he couldn't seduce a naive gentlewoman, yet that was exactly what he'd commenced to do. The temptation had been, quite simply, quite completely, irresistible.

Even now, his heartbeats refused to steady. Even now, the taste of her mouth, of her skin, lingered, along with the scent of patchouli and the sweet heat of her slim body. He glanced down at his fingers, white-knuckled, clutching the rail.

He told himself it was but a kiss. A prolonged one, admittedly, but at most no more than a passionate embrace. He'd embraced countless women, Asian as well as European, and bedded scores of them. This painful arousal was simply the result of seven months' enforced abstinence.

Tomorrow he'd be free of this accursed ship, and of her, and there would be other women. He could buy half a dozen tomorrow, in Portsmouth. He need simply endure this one night, a few hours, and it would be over at last.

Accordingly, since only a few hours remained, the intrepid Falcon headed for the forecastle, with the very sensible intention of drinking them away.

Amanda felt reasonably steady by the time she entered

the cabin, though she rested her back against the closed door for a moment.

Mrs. Gales looked up from her needlework. A shadow of concern swept her calm countenance, and she rose.

"Are you ill, my dear?" She crossed the cabin to take Amanda's arm.

"N-no."

"You were above?"

"Y-yes. Talking to Mr. Brentick. I thought it best to—to keep him occupied."

"Poor dear, you must have been quite uneasy."

"I'm fine," Amanda said. Her glance flew to the cot, where Bella lay, snoring. "Is *she* all right?"

"Certainly. It was only a bit of laudanum, after all, and I'm sure she was careful how much she drank."

"And Padji?"

"He carried her in, then said he was going above," Mrs. Gales answered, as composedly as though Padji's carrying in an unconscious Bella were an everyday event. "He did not want to be absent overlong."

"D-did he get it?"

"I presume so. He was grinning like a naughty boy."

"Where is it?" Amanda's legs would support her no longer. Shakily, she lowered herself onto the banquette.

"I don't know. He only put her on the cot and left, with that smug grin on his face."

Never one to waste words herself, when action was more efficient, Mrs. Gales quickly found her brandy flask and pressed it into Amanda's hand. "There's no more to be done now, my dear," she said gently, "and no point in worrying. Have a sip. You'll feel better. Then you must try to get some sleep. We have an anxious morning ahead of us, I daresay."

═══11═══

PHILIP DID NOT return to the cabin until shortly before daybreak. Getting dead drunk had taken an unconscionably long time.

He'd scarcely fallen asleep when a cannon blast shot him upright, and twin blasts of pain shot through his eyeballs. He gazed wildly about. Seeing no evidence of destruction, he finally realised that what he'd heard was some inconsiderate brute banging on the door and shouting.

Philip dragged himself from the mattress. An anchor had, apparently, fallen repeatedly upon his head, and his mouth was redolent of low tide. He'd not brought himself to so revolting a state in years.

The knocking and shouting recommenced with renewed vigour. Philip staggered to the door and unlocked it.

One of the mates with whom he'd dissipated stood in the passage looking abominably fresh and alert.

"Time to be off," the mate announced. "Captain's on fire to be gone, and I better warn you—in his mood he's not like to give you more than a quarter-hour."

Philip bit back a profane retort. The commander had not taken yestereve's last-minute request well. In wartime, East India men customarily stopped at Portsmouth, for they travelled in convoy. England was not at war at the moment, however. The wind having risen briskly, Captain Blayton had adamantly refused to make the unscheduled stop.

Philip had been forced to invoke the Marquess of

Hedgrave's power and, this receiving scant respect, had finally thrust the last of the documents into the captain's hands. According to these, Messrs Wringle and Brentick were on a secret government mission. Captain Blayton at last, and with very ill grace, had consented to drop his unwelcome passengers at Portsmouth. Evidently, that meant he would drop them into the harbour if they could not disembark within the next fifteen minutes.

"A quarter-hour it is, then," Philip said. He fumbled in his coat—in which he'd slept, or tried to sleep—and found his purse. He thrust a pile of coins into the mate's hand, asking for help with the baggage.

The hefty bribe elicited the assistance of four strong seamen, which was fortunate, as it turned out, for Jessup proved to be in worse state than his master. A brawny sailor had to carry him down the ladder onto the boat waiting to take them ashore. Throughout the short trip, Jessup's head hung miserably over the rowboat's side.

After depositing their passengers and flinging their belongings haphazardly about them, the crew members hopped back into their boat and rowed feverishly for the *Evelina*.

Jessup dutifully took up one carpetbag. Clutching it with both hands, he managed to stagger about three feet. Then he slumped down upon a trunk and gazed blearily about while Philip took his own throbbing head and aching body in search of transportation.

Some hours later, after being jolted in a stinking coach from one low hostelry to another—and arguing with the driver at each stop—the two were at last comfortably disposed in the large chambers of a commodious inn.

Jessup immediately fell upon his bed, where he sprawled, groaning.

Philip glared at him. "What the devil's the matter with you? You weren't up roistering with the rest of us, and you seemed well enough all yesterday." His eyes narrowed. "May I take it Miss Jones stopped in for one of her visits?"

Jessup moaned.

"What in blazes did the wench do to you?"

"Nuthin', guv." Jessup dragged his hand over his face. "Leastways, I don't remember. I must've had a drop too much. She brung a bottle and—"

"And you haven't touched liquor in seven months. Damned fool. You know your liver isn't what it was. Didn't I tell you that, a score of times? Confound it, didn't your chubby reformer tell you?"

"Aye, she tole me."

"But you didn't listen. I suppose you emptied most of the bottle yourself."

Jessup nodded wretchedly.

"Oh, good work. Very intelligent," Philip said. "After what your poor belly's been through, you're lucky it didn't kill you."

A tap at the door interrupted the lecture. Philip answered it, to learn from one of the inn servants that his bath awaited him in the adjoining chamber. His mood instantly lightened.

"That's what I like," he said, turning back to Jessup. "Prompt service. Fawning attention. Someone bowing and scraping to me, for a change. Gad, seven months, and never a proper wash the whole time. Don't look for me for at least a week, soldier," he said as he headed for the connecting door.

Jessup grumbled something unintelligible, then buried his face in his pillow.

Philip chuckled. "I do hope you got some pleasure from her last night," he said, shaking his head, "seeing you're paying so handsomely today."

Soap, gallons of fresh, hot water, towels that weren't damp and scratchy with salt: paradise, Philip thought as he sank into his bath. The throbbing in his head subsided and his taut muscles at last began to relax.

More than half an hour later he climbed out, dried himself off, and went to the trunk to unearth the dressing gown he'd forgotten to take out before. It was near the bottom, for he hadn't bothered with it during the voyage. He'd not felt inclined to linger in the tiny, stale cabin, even if life aboard ship had accommodated a long morning's dawdle over newspapers and coffee.

The dressing gown lay carelessly folded upon the rolled-up rug which contained the Laughing Princess.

Philip stared at the robe, then at the open door between the two rooms.

Wine. Jessup drunk, unconscious. And Philip above, lost in an embrace . . . that never should have been allowed to begin. Where had Padji been?

The heavy haze which had filled Philip's mind all morning abruptly cleared, and an unpleasantly familiar warning chill trickled down his neck.

In that moment, every piece of the game came together in his brain.

He took out the rug, though he didn't need to. He unrolled it, though he knew what he wouldn't find.

Naked, he knelt by the trunk, gazing down at the rug's contents: a jar of incense.

He closed his eyes and laughed. It was an ugly sound that made Jessup jump up from his bed and hurry to the open doorway to stare at his master.

"That bitch," Philip said softly. "That treacherous, scheming bitch. Seven months." He turned to meet Jessup's baffled gaze. "Seven months," Philip repeated. His mouth warped into something like a smile. "Is that not Oriental patience for you, soldier?"

"What—" Jessup stopped short as his employer held up the jar of incense.

"Seven months they've played us for a pair of fools. Whored her maid. Whored herself—or would have, I've no doubt. I hope you got a tumble out of the maid, my lad. I, you see, was too much the gentleman to attempt the mistress . . . because she's a *lady*," Philip spat out.

Jessup moved into the room, his horrified gaze fixed upon the jar of incense.

122

"You see it now, don't you?" Philip said in deceptively cool tones. "Why should you suspect her that last night, after all those days and nights, weeks, months? No one knew—or so we smugly believed—it *was* our last night. Why should you dream there was anything in the wine? Did it taste odd in any way, soldier? Would you have noticed? Or would you have put it down to your ailment, and going so long without?"

"But she drunk it, too," Jessup said, dazed. "I seen her. I wanted to get her drunk."

"Of course Miss Jones drank it. Why shouldn't she? She might lie there in a stupor, for she'd no more to do. The Indian slips in, picks the lock as neat as you please, takes out the statue, throws the maid over his shoulder, goes out and, moments later, deposits maid and statue at the feet of his mistress. Then he proceeds to the forecastle to join our dissipations and watch me drink myself into stupefaction." Philip's fingers closed about the neck of the jar. "I couldn't have done it neater myself . . . if I'd such a pair of clodpates to deal with."

Abruptly he flung down the jar, then ripped a shirt and a pair of trousers from the trunk. "Sorry," he muttered. "Aye, you'll be sorry, sweetheart."

Five minutes later, he was dressed and out the door.

An hour after, he stood at the pier, clenching his fists in impotent fury. The *Evelina* was long gone, driven swiftly by the most accommodating wind she'd encountered since leaving Calcutta.

One might hire a speedier vessel, and very possibly overtake her. But then what? Board the ship and demand that Lord Cavencourt's sister be flogged? Keelhauled? Tried and hanged as a thief? What the devil had he been thinking of?

Murder, Philip answered silently. A nice, satisfying little murder. He would take her smooth, slim neck in his hands . . . and choke the life out of her. He merely wanted to strangle her, that was all. With his bare hands.

"But that would never do, miss, would it?" he murmured.

"What would Mrs. Bullerham think? Most improper."

Stories. All those lovely stories. The seductive voice and scent. The ridiculous, contradictory innocence and vulnerability, and the pity he'd felt because she was so utterly alone.

"Oh, Amanda," he whispered. "You miserable . . . little . . . scheming . . . *bitch.*"

In one particular, the Falcon had erred. Padji had not placed the statue at his mistress's feet. He had concealed it for the remainder of the journey in an exceedingly elaborate and lofty arrangement of turban.

He did not reveal this until they were all safely ensconced in their hotel in London. Only then did he present to his mistress, with all appropriate ceremony, the Laughing Princess. In the event the theft had been discovered too soon, he explained, it was best the statue not be in his mistress's possession. Equally important, she ought not know where it was. Thus, only Padji would suffer for the crime.

Amanda was far too weary to point out that she'd never have let Padji be punished in her place. She'd barely the strength to thank him. She'd spent these last days in a frenzy of anxiety and guilt. Even in Gravesend, she'd expected Mr. Wringle to pop out of every door and alley, screaming for a constable. More appalling was the prospect of seeing Mr. Brentick's shocked, reproachful face. He would have concluded Amanda Cavencourt had toyed with his affections purely for her own criminal ends.

Which was absurd, she told herself now, as she crawled into bed and pulled the blankets up over her head. She was quite certain he could know no more of the Laughing Princess at present than he ever had. Even if he did, she could not be the only suspect.

As to what had occurred that last night—well, that had nothing to do with his affections, did it? Such things were not unheard of. Lady Tewkshead had eloped with Sir Rodger Crawford's groom. Miss Flora Perquat had been exiled to

Calcutta because she'd had a child by her father's gardener. Mr. Brentick must have kissed any number of gently bred ladies—and bedded at least some of them. One embrace would mean little to him. Furthermore, he'd kissed Amanda only because there was no one else conveniently at hand.

He would not break his heart on her account. Men had a different attitude about physical intimacy than women did. It was laughable to imagine she'd led him astray. Men went astray by nature. The difficulty was in leading them otherwise.

Amanda's hand slipped under her pillow and closed around the sandalwood figure. It didn't matter, she told herself. It was done and the princess was safe. Nonetheless, long hours passed before the tears abated, and Amanda Cavencourt, thief, fell asleep.

═12═

CAVENCOURT? THE ELDERLY solicitor mumbled, while his trembling hands sought to make order of the documents his visitor had exasperatedly flung back upon the desk.

"Lord Cavencourt's sister," Philip repeated, for the third time. "She lives in Yorkshire. I want to know where."

Coming here, clearly, was a mistake. Mr. Brewell had nearly succumbed to apoplexy at the sight of him. The old lawyer had no sooner recovered from the shock than the argument had commenced, and with it a blizzard of legal documents that might have papered the dome of St. Paul's, with plenty to spare for Westminster Abbey.

Unfortunately, when one had been out of one's native country for fifteen years, and had scarcely set foot in London previous to that, useful acquaintances were few and far between. When, moreover, one preferred one's presence not be known, the list of possible information sources shrank even further.

The Falcon had contacts in virtually every corner of India, persons whose discretion could be relied upon in the interests of the Crown or, more often, Profit. London, on the other hand, might have been the moon, so alien it was. Actually, one might have tracked down Miss Cavencourt a deal more easily on the moon than in the chaos of this infernal city.

Three weeks he'd wasted, searching on his own, hanging about hotels and inns and questioning tradesmen. He'd gone in disguise to clubs and gaming hells, even managed without invitation a few visits to Society affairs. He'd learned little.

He heard no mention of the Cavencourts in the gossip he eavesdropped upon. Not wishing to draw attention to himself, he'd dared do little more than listen. As it was, he encountered far too many former fellow officers and company men. To attract their notice was to court recognition, and word might easily reach Hedgrave.

The Falcon had far rather have slivers of bamboo jammed under his fingernails and set on fire than find himself under examination by Hedgrave or any of his colleagues. Only yesterday, in Bond Street, Philip had narrowly escaped Danbridge's shrewd scrutiny . . . and the inevitable humiliation of admitting that yes, the intrepid Falcon, whose name was feared throughout India, had got the statue . . . and had it stolen from him. By a twenty-six-year-old spinster.

All of which left Philip with his family solicitor. At present, Philip could have cheerfully applied the bamboo method to Mr. Brewell. The lawyer was older than Methuselah, and his chambers had most likely been built— and not cleaned since—the Flood. One glimpse at the musty old office, and Miss Jones would have flown at it with mop and brush. Very likely she'd have taken the dusty old lawyer, in his rusty black coat and breeches, out of doors and given him a vigourous shaking.

"Cavencourt. Cavencourt." The watery grey eyes looked up from the papers. "Would that be the Baron Cavencourt? The eighth, isn't it? Or is it tenth? Odd family. Something about his—or was that the other one? But they're in India," he concluded, much befuddled.

"Lord Cavencourt lives in Calcutta," Philip said patiently. "His sister is recently returned to England. We were on the same ship. She mentioned Yorkshire. What I want to know is *where*."

Mr. Brewell shook his head sadly, and his wrinkled, grey face assumed an expression of reproach. "With all due respect, this is hardly the time to be racketing about the countryside after women. There is a great deal to be settled. In any case, you ought think first of going home. The family—"

"Can go to blazes," Philip snapped. "We've discussed all that at unnecessary length."

"But at least—"

"I owe them nothing. They've lived quite comfortably without me more than fifteen years. I daresay they'll manage to endure another few days. I came for information," he continued in taut tones. "If you can't provide it, I shall seek elsewhere. Good day." He turned and headed for the door.

"But my—"

"And not a word," Philip ordered. "Not one word."

"That will considerably complicate matters."

"I don't give a damn."

"Might one at least mention you're alive?" the solicitor pleaded. "I need only say I received word from trustworthy sources."

Philip paused, his fingers on the handle. "Very well. But no more than that." Then he left.

Philip returned to the inn to find his bags packed, and Jessup reading a sporting journal.

"What the devil is all this?" Philip demanded.

"I thought you'd want to be goin'. You was just complainin' this mornin' how we'd been wastin' time and you was sick o' the sight o' London."

"I've spent the better part of three weeks scouring every inn and alley of the curst place. You think I want to try the same exercise through all of Yorkshire? Brewell, like everyone else in this confounded warren, hadn't the foggiest idea where the Cavencourts reside," he added angrily. "I daresay he'll be another ten years muddling and stumbling about, trying to find out. If he does try. Which he'd rather not. He doesn't approve my racketing after women, you see."

Jessup picked up a valise. "Kirkby Glenham," he said.

"What?"

"She lives in Kirkby Glenham," Jessup said expressionlessly. "I've paid our shot and hired a carriage. Did you want to have a bite before we go?"

Philip stared at him. "Are you sure? How did you find out?"

Jessup looked away and mumbled something.

"What?"

"Debretts, sir. I looked 'em up in Debretts. Kirkby Glenham. Lived there since the time of the second Baron. There's a map on the table." Jessup nodded in that direction. "It's a manor house on the moors."

Mr. Thurston, the Cavencourts' London solicitor, had warned Amanda that the manor house was not quite ready for her, because his agent had been unable to fully staff it. She, however, had no wish to linger in Town, where she might collide any moment with an irate Mr. Wringle or a murderous Lord Hedgrave.

Thus she arrived at her family home to find the interior entirely shrouded in dust covers, and mould and mildew growing everywhere. In addition to an apparently competent bailiff and an elderly gardener, she found one maid of all work feigning, in a lackadaisical manner, to do the work of a staff of twelve.

At the end of a fortnight, thanks mainly to Bella, dust, mould, and mildew had been scoured away. During this same period, thanks to Padji, the maid of all work had fled, and the gardener threatened to do likewise. After three weeks, Miss Cavencourt had acquired one housekeeper and one scullery maid, while the bailiff had given notice. During this period, a number of servants had come, and quickly gone. They came because the wages were good. They left—usually within twenty-four hours— because Padji was not.

"I have told him a hundred times," Amanda complained to Mrs. Gales, "but he won't listen, or he doesn't understand."

They were in the estate office. Seated in her father's

huge, ugly chair, her elbows on the great desk, Amanda gazed mournfully at a ledger. Opposite her, Mrs. Gales calmly knitted.

"It is a considerable adjustment for him," the widow said.

"But he expects everyone to adjust to *him*. How is one to make him comprehend that English servants do not, and are not expected to, behave as Indians do? No one is humble enough or attentive enough, he thinks. Why in blazes must Mrs. Swanslow taste my food for poison when Padji himself has cooked it?"

Amanda closed the ledger with a thump. "He has her in such a tremble, I cannot make heads or tales of her writing. I cannot tell if these are household accounts or Persian songs of prayer. And now I must replace the bailiff, which is Padji's fault again. He had no business shadowing Mr. Corker about the grounds."

Mrs. Gales laid her knitting aside. "You want a cup of tea, my dear."

"I want a bailiff," Amanda wailed, "and a butler, and maids. Bella should not be looking after the chambers, and the scullery maid should not be doing the laundry."

"Jane had better not do the laundry," Mrs. Gales said. "She doesn't know the first thing about it, and all your lovely frocks will be ruined." She rose. "Do quit this room, Amanda. You only upset yourself here. I shall see about the tea and bring it to the library."

When Amanda hesitated, the widow added, "We shall go to the employment agent in York tomorrow. Until then, there's no point fretting yourself. It will all come about in time, dear. We must be patient."

Amanda obediently trailed after her into the hallway, while wondering, not for the first time, how the widow managed to remain so consistently unruffled. A full eight hours' sound sleep each night no doubt contributed. Amanda slept, but not soundly. Hours passed before she could drive her worries back into the recesses of her mind.

The library was a sensible idea. Amanda would read, and blot out this whole dreadful morning—these last wretched weeks, preferably—with one of the half-dozen bloodcurdling Gothic novels she'd got from York. Chains and dungeons and headless corpses were just what she needed. Come to think of it, a dungeon and chains might be just what Padji needed, bless his interfering heart.

She'd hardly settled into her favourite chair when the door-knocker crashed. With a sigh, she rose to answer it. The employment agent knew she was desperate. He may have sent along an applicant. Mrs. Swanslow had gone to the market, and it would be best if Padji were not the one to open the door. One prospective laundry maid had fled at the first glimpse of him.

Padji, fortunately, was nowhere in sight when Amanda reached the vestibule.

Belatedly, she realised a servant would not come to the front door. Who could possibly be calling? Not any of her neighbours, certainly. She'd given up expecting any sort of welcome from them, not that she had, really—

Amanda's meditations came to an abrupt halt as she opened the door and looked up . . . into the stony, blue-eyed countenance of Mr. Brentick.

"Oh," she gasped. Then, her brain offering no further help to her tongue, she simply stared at him.

"I beg your pardon, miss," he said. "I was not welcome at the servants' entrance, and so, had no choice."

"N-not welcome?"

"Not to put too fine a point on it, Padji closed the door in my face. Very firmly."

"You mean he slammed it, I suppose." The first shock subsided, only to be swamped by chilling anxiety and confusion. "I cannot think why he would be so rude—but he—he's not himself—quite—lately—at least, I hope not. He is not—adjusting. Oh, dear." She backed away. "Please come in."

He threw her a searching look as he stepped over the

threshold. "I expect you're surprised to see me," he said.

"Surprise is hardly adequate to the occasion." Desperately she tried to collect her wits. She'd almost forgotten how very blue and piercing his eyes were, and how tall he was. Or did it merely *seem* that he towered over her? "What on earth are you doing in Yorkshire, Mr. Brentick?" She glanced past him at the empty doorway. "Where is Mr. Wringle?"

This earned her another searching glance.

"Is something wrong?" she asked.

"Yes," he said. "Something is very wrong."

Amanda's face went hot and cold as the colour rushed over it and drained away.

At this moment, a shadow darkened the hallway. She glanced behind her, to see Padji's massive bulk advancing.

"Never fear, mistress," he growled. "I shall see to him."

"Miss Cavencourt, I must speak with you," the valet said quickly. "I am in great difficulty and—" He sidestepped neatly as Padji's huge hand shot towards him.

Amanda hastily stepped in Padji's way. "Enough!" she said. "Did I ask for your assistance, Padji?"

"I only anticipate, mistress," came the low Hindustani response.

"There is no need to manhandle visitors," she answered in the same tongue. "Everyone who comes to the door is not an assassin."

"Actually, your competent assassin rarely comes to the front door," Mr. Brentick politely pointed out. In response to her startled look, he added, "I am acquainted with the language, miss. Fifteen years in India, recollect."

She glanced from him to Padji, her mind working as rapidly as it could in the circumstances. "Padji is surprised to see you, as I am. I'm afraid he doesn't care overmuch for surprises."

"There is a perfectly reasonable explanation, Miss Cavencourt, if you'd be so kind as to indulge me a hearing."

Padji's eyes narrowed. "Send him away, mistress. This man is trouble for you. Also, he stinks like a pig."

Mr. Brentick's blue eyes flashed in his pale face. Unnaturally pale, Amanda now realised. He looked ill, despite his fiery gaze. And thin.

"I beg your pardon," he said stiffly. "I have been upon the road nearly four days, and my lodgings have not been of the most luxurious. I should never have presented myself in this condition, had I any other choice. I spent the last of my funds on coach fare, and came here on foot from the last posting inn."

Amanda's hand flew to her breast. "Good heavens, what on earth has happened?"

His blue gaze seemed to skewer her. "I have been discharged," he said. "Without notice, without a character, without a farthing."

"Oh, no."

"Also, I may add, without explanation. We were in Portsmouth scarce two hours, when my employer flew into a rage. I have no idea what set him off. I know only that he called me an irresponsible incompetent—among other names I shall not sully your ears with—and discharged me."

Padji gave a disdainful snort.

"That is monstrous," Amanda said, disregarding her watchdog. A suffocating wave of guilt washed over her. She knew what had happened. Mr. Wringle had discovered the theft, and taken out his rage on his hapless servant.

"I cannot apologise sufficiently for intruding in this inexcusable way, miss." The valet shot one darkling glance at Padji before returning to the mistress. "I should never have dreamt of doing such a thing, but I had nowhere else to turn."

A low, rumbling sound came from Padji's throat.

"Stop growling," Amanda snapped. "You are not a savage, I hope, and in any case, you are not blind. It's obvious Mr. Brentick is tired—and hungry as well, I'm sure. Take him down to the servants' hall and— No, on second thought, I shall come with you." To the valet she said, "Let us find you something to eat. Then, when you're feeling better, we'll discuss this further.

* * *

They'd found Mrs. Gales in the kitchen and, luckily for Philip, the widow had supervised his meal. Padji, he had little doubt, would have blithely poisoned the unwanted visitor, if left to his own devices—and if, that is, Philip were halfwit enough to remain alone with him. Padji had not troubled to disguise his hostility. Miss Cavencourt's reaction was far more puzzling.

The Falcon had, as was his custom, arrived armed with several strategies. For instance, he'd fully expected Padji's attack. Which meant a quick move to grab Miss Cavencourt and hold a knife to her throat, and thus obtain the statue under most undesirable circumstances. As soon as she'd stepped between him and Padji, Philip deduced that the lady was a most incautious and inefficient adversary. Accordingly, he'd mentally shredded Plan A. In another few minutes, he'd begun to feel disagreeably inefficient himself, because she did not react properly.

Philip warily eyed his nemesis now, as he followed her into her office. Padji stood in the open doorway, arms folded across his chest, his round, brown face eloquent with disapproval.

"Mr. Wringle's behaviour seems most unaccountable," Miss Cavencourt began slowly.

He watched her flit past him to take up her position behind the great barricade of a desk. In her pale blue frock, amid the dark, masculine surroundings, she seemed smaller and more fragile than Philip remembered. Not quite real. But that was because she was so false.

"Also most ungrateful," she added, "when one considers your devotion during his long illness. He gave you no explanation beyond what you mentioned?"

"No, miss. At the time I suspected something else displeased him." He hesitated.

"Yes?"

"I regret to say he was beside himself," Philip continued

carefully. "He tore through all my belongings— as though he believed I'd *stolen* something." He lowered his gaze from Miss Cavencourt's startled golden one. "Of course you have only my word I hadn't."

Padji sniffed.

Miss Cavencourt's face grew paler.

"Do you think something *was* stolen, Mr. Brentick?"

He pretended to think hard before answering, "It's possible, though I can't imagine what. He had clothes and legal papers, and a few trinkets and souvenirs—some carved objects, that sort of thing. Nothing of value to a thief, as far as I could tell. He had money, naturally, but he never searched my pockets, and he had plenty to toss about at the inn. It's a puzzle to me, miss."

"If you had taken anything of value," she said, "you'd hardly have arrived here on foot, half-starved." She moved a piece of paper from the right side of the blotter to the left. "I collect you need a loan," she said without looking at him.

Padji scowled.

Philip transformed his expression of innocence to one of embarrassment. "I didn't come for charity—not of that sort," he answered. "I need employment. I've been trying to find work nearly a month now, but with neither references nor friends, there's nothing. Except, that is, to take the King's shilling. I'm no coward, miss, and I'll do that if I must, but—"

"So you must," Padji averred, nodding his head. "So it is fated."

"It most certainly is not!" said Amanda. "Mr. Brentick has served his country near half his life. He seeks work. I do not see why we should not assist him." Her gaze returned to Philip. "The trouble is, I don't know any gentlemen hereabouts you might serve."

"I don't expect the same position, miss," Philip said with appropriate humility. "I'd take anything, so long as it's honest work."

She moved the sheet of paper from the left side of the

blotter back to the right. Then she pushed the inkwell one half inch to the left. She picked up a pen and laid it down again. She bit her lip, and a tiny crease appeared between her brows. Philip waited patiently through the growing silence.

She was a terrible actress. Her guilt, for instance, was too clearly evident, even now. Everything was too evident. Her surprise and curiosity in response to his hints about the theft were too obviously feigned. Her pity for the ill-used valet, in contrast, was unnervingly genuine. Gad, for a moment, she'd even made him feel guilty about the lies he told. Only for a moment, though. Matters were not precisely as he'd assumed, perhaps. Nonetheless, he had no doubt she had the statue, and that was all he need concern himself with.

Thus he waited, his brain ready to provide a suitably manipulative response to whatever her ineptly lying tongue uttered next.

"Would you be willing to accept the work of ten people?" she said at last in a hesitant voice.

His brain screeched to a halt. "I beg your pardon, miss?"

"I am short staffed," she said more firmly. "We're having a devil of a time finding employees . . . and keeping those we do find. My bailiff has given notice and I need a replacement. I also need—oh, lud, *everybody*."

The gears began grinding again. Philip assumed a mask of sympathy while Miss Cavencourt proceeded to pour out her domestic anxieties, with Padji interjecting his own opinions every few sentences.

When she was done, Philip neatly simplified the issues. "What you want first of all, are two reliable people: one to manage matters out of doors, and one for indoors. I am not properly equipped to handle the former, but I'd be grateful for a chance to take on the latter."

"The mistress is confused," said Padji. "Her slave is by, to see to all her wishes. She has no need—"

"I need a staff," Miss Cavencourt said sharply. "I realise

this house is not half the size of the rani's palace. Even so, it wants servants, and *you* certainly don't manage them. You overset everyone who comes. You have driven even Mr. Corker—the most forbearing man I've ever met—to give notice. Whatever possessed you to ask him where I bury the servants who displease me?"

Philip's mouth twitched. He quickly frowned instead.

"Well, he did," Miss Cavencourt told him aggrievedly. "And just this morning, Jane—that's the poor scullery maid—dropped into hysterics because he found a cobweb in the pantry, and threatened to cut off her finger."

"A mild rebuke," Padji said, "for so grievous an offence to the mistress's sight."

Exhaling a sigh of exasperation, Miss Cavencourt sank into her chair. Sank quite literally, that is, for the enormous carved monstrosity swallowed her up. She appeared about ten years old. "Oh, Padji, I am at my wits' end with you."

Padji gazed sorrowfully at her. "My golden beloved is displeased," he said. "I have offended. I shall cut off my own worthless finger to appease her." His hand closed over the knife at his sash, and Philip tensed.

"You most certainly will not, you wicked creature," she said crisply. "I will not have you bleeding all over the carpet. Put your knife away and behave yourself. You have distracted me from my discussion."

"But, mistress, you cannot wish this false, stinking creature in your sublime abode."

Squelching an insane urge to draw his own knife, Philip calmly intervened before the beloved mistress could respond.

"If Miss Cavencourt would be kind enough to outline her needs and direct me to my quarters, I should be happy to clean my offensive person to everyone's satisfaction."

She stared at him. "Are you quite sure, Mr. Brentick? That is, you must be aware what a Herculean task I propose—and we haven't discussed it, really—"

"If you are willing to try me, miss, I am willing to do whatever you require. As I've indicated, I need work."

She coloured, and got that irritatingly guilty look in her eyes again.

"Yes, of course. And I need help, obviously."

"But, mistress—"

"Please hold your tongue, Padji."

"But this man is a vile seducer!" Padji cried. "Not once, but—"

A wash of brilliant rose spread over the lady's cheeks and neck. "That is quite enough," she snapped. "Please leave this room, Padji, and close the door after you. I wish to have a private word with Mr. Brentick."

Padji folded his arms over his chest and stood firm. "It is unseemly. This man is not to be trusted."

Seducer? Was that all? Impossible, Philip decided. That was merely the Indian's excuse for his hostility. But why need he make excuses . . . unless the mistress didn't know the whole truth. Was it possible she believed Brentick ignorant of the whole business? Could she possibly be so naive.

Ten minutes later, Padji had finally retired in high dudgeon. With his exit came rising panic. Still, Amanda chided herself, the thing must be got out of the way now.

Accordingly, she stood up, raised her chin, and plunged headlong at the mortifying subject. "I know you are not a seducer," she said, "and I will not accuse you of behaving improperly when I gave you so much reason to think that I—well, that I was not—that I was *fast*."

Mr. Brentick's blue eyes opened very wide, and he blinked. Twice.

Amanda went on doggedly, "I've had time to reflect upon my actions, and now see that for all my protests and so-called explanations, they would lead people to—to certain conclusions. The voyage was long and the company limited. It was a circumstance conducive to intimacy and—and . . . confusion. We were both confused, apparently." She paused.

He said nothing.

"And so, we made a mistake," she said.

"A mistake," he repeated.

"But I am not fast, and you are not the villainous seducer Padji thinks you, and so we shall not repeat the error, naturally."

"Naturally."

"Then you understand?" She tried to read his expression, but all she found were fathomless blue depths.

"Yes, miss. Quite. The entire episode is to be forgotten."

"Yes." Oh, certainly. That embrace—had it been only a few weeks ago?—was merely carved into her memory like an inscription upon a marble tombstone. It would wear away in a millennium or two. Sooner, if she could remember not to look at his mouth. Or his hands. Sooner still if he'd only stop gazing at her in that watchful, intent way.

=13=

THE FOLLOWING DAY, Philip met with Jessup in a York public house.

"It's going to be difficult," Philip admitted. "She's deposited the thing in a bank vault, drat her."

"You sure?" Jessup asked in dismay. "How'd you find out so quick?"

Philip dropped him a disdainful look. "Have you forgotten who I am, soldier?"

"Not likely, guv. But I been wonderin' now and again if *you* forgot," was the blunt reply. "Been wonderin' if you picked up a touch of fever."

Philip ignored this tactless slur on his abilities.

"I had a thorough tour of the house yesterday," he said patiently. "The statue wasn't displayed. Which means Miss Cavencourt believes someone may come after it."

"Which he done."

"Naturally, being the vexatious female she is, she must make my task as difficult as possible. Accordingly, the first place I visited today was the bank, where a talkative clerk confirmed my worst suspicions. I swear," he said exasperatedly, "the Old Nick himself set that woman in my path."

"Then it's gone," said Jessup. "And I say good riddance. Nothin' but trouble since we started on this business."

"For fifty thousand quid, one expects trouble."

"You don't need the money. You done good enough these last five years. Enough to set yourself up like a proper gentleman. And I done good enough with you. Let the lady keep her piece of wood. She worked hard enough for it. She deserves somethin'—no one ever outsmarted the Falcon afore."

Philip glared into his ale mug. "I'm not outdone yet."

"Oh, give it over, guv," Jessup urged. "Ain't you had enough? I have. The jolliest armful I ever run across, and so sweet and kind she was, fussin' over me like I was a baby. She done for me, that one. I ain't goin' near another female, long as I live," he added sorrowfully. "I could've swore she liked me. Why, I'd watch her tidyin' and dustin', and listen to her scold, and I thought I could do that all the rest o' my days. She got me thinkin' 'bout a little cottage, and flowers, and a square of vegetable garden . . . and fat babes, squallin' and crawlin' on the floor. And everythin' would shine and smell so clean. And her with them snappin' black eyes, layin' out my supper—"

"You're maudlin," Philip interrupted. "Get a grip on yourself."

"I do. I had enough. It were a damn fool job to take in the first place, on account of some damn fool lord with a maggot on his brain. It never were your kind of job. One thing to work for king and country, but this— it's just common thievin'," Jessup said, dropping his voice. "Besides, the lady stole it back, fair and square, and never done neither of us no harm. Which she could of, which you know good as I do. Leave her alone, guv."

"I will not," Philip gritted out, "leave her alone. I agreed to a job—whether it's entirely in my style or not—and I have *never* failed anybody, at any time. You think I can retire with this humiliating fiasco as the last act of my career?"

Jessup sighed. "You stole it, didn't you? She just stole it back is all. You didn't fail, exactly."

"One either fails or succeeds. There's no part-way about it. I'll get it back," Philip said tightly, "however long it takes. Meanwhile, I've work for you."

* * *

Like the long-suffering Jessup, Mrs. Gales, too, experienced qualms. Hers, however, were of a more delicate nature, and thus more cautiously expressed.

She and Amanda sat in the library.

"My dear, do you think this altogether wise?" the widow asked as she handed Amanda her tea. "You really don't know the man. It is possible, is it not, that Mr. Wringle sent him to recover the statue?"

"I thought of that," Amanda answered. She took her cup and carried it to the window seat, so she could gaze out at the withered garden. "Padji was so hostile, I supposed he was thinking the same thing. But he wasn't. He'd got it into his head that Mr. Brentick had come for the sole purpose of ravishing me." She smiled faintly. "Which is thoroughly absurd, even if the poor man hadn't been too weak and hungry for such an exertion. You saw him, Leticia."

"Yes." The widow sighed.

"Besides, the statue is quite safe now. I'm the only one who can claim it. Poor Princess, locked away in a cold, dark vault," Amanda said wistfully. "It hardly seems worth all the trouble and anxiety, when I can't even look at her or touch her. I'd wanted to keep her here, nearby while I worked on my book, as . . . well, as inspiration, perhaps. Instead, all I can do is travel into York occasionally to visit her. Poor princess."

"Only for a while, dear," Mrs. Gales consoled. "Just until we feel reasonably certain the marquess hasn't traced it to you. Not that I think for a moment he could," she added in hasty reassurance. "If I were Mr. Wringle, I certainly should not wish to inform his lordship that the statue mysteriously vanished—in Portsmouth, of all places. If Mr. Wringle has any common sense at all, he'll make for the West Indies, or New South Wales, with all due celerity."

Amanda turned to look at her. "Now that might explain it," she said thoughtfully. "If Mr. Wringle wanted to disappear, he must get rid of his servant. Mr. Brentick is far too striking not to be remarked."

"Indeed," Mrs. Gales murmured. "Far too striking."

Amanda returned to the dreary landscape. "Still, he ought at least have *paid* him. But then I should not have a butler. He may not have all the necessary experience, but at least Padji doesn't intimidate him. Perhaps Mr. Brentick will remain more than twenty-four hours."

Mr. Brentick could boast nothing remotely approaching the necessary experience. His ideas of a butler's duties were vague, to say the least. He'd quickly ascertained, however, that his new employer's comprehension of the position was equally dim. A master storyteller Miss Cavencourt might be. A household manager she decidedly was not. She must make all the servants her friends, and setting friends to the weary business of domestic drudgery presented a contradiction her intellect could not untangle. Oddly enough, the only servant she commanded with anything like authority was that great Indian hippopotamus, and that was only when Padji had vexed her past all bearing.

This much Philip had discovered long before he'd swung into his saddle to ride to York. A subtly probing discussion with the employment agent clarified numerous other domestic issues.

Philip returned to the remote manor house armed with some basic information. For the rest, he'd rely upon his natural resourcefulness.

At eighteen, dismissed and disowned, he'd left Felkonwood with but five pounds in his pocket. Three months later, by a combination of work and wagers, he'd acquired the money to purchase his commission. He'd not, as his father confidently assumed, entered the military in the lowly position of an enlisted man, but as an officer. From that point on, Philip Astonley had proved to himself, repeatedly, that he was fully capable of achieving any object he set his sights upon.

When he'd proved to his satisfaction and his superiors' astonishment his genius for command, Philip soon sought a new and more dangerous proving ground. In the last five years, he'd astonished all of India. He'd become a legend.

Now he need only prove himself as a servant, overlord of a handful of men and women. One who'd commanded regiments could certainly command one small household. As to his inept general—he'd merely to win her trust.

With smooth military efficiency, Philip set to work.

Immediately upon his return from York, he met with the bailiff and persuaded Mr. Corker to stay on.

The following day, a parade of maids appeared before Mrs. Swanslow. Padji stalked in to scrutinise them. Two of the maids shrieked, and one fainted. Mr. Brentick entered and revived the unconscious girl, then calmly introduced Padji as a brilliant though temperamental *French* cook.

Thus reduced from supernatural monster to mere Gallic lunatic, Padji was endured with a proper British stoicism. Nobody fainted again, no one even threw her apron over her head. A few giggled—then quickly stifled themselves as their eyes met the butler's imperious blue gaze. With his subtle guidance, Mrs. Swanslow selected two housemaids.

By the end of the week, with the acquisition of some daily servants and one footman, James, the house was adequately staffed, though certainly not as fully as it had been in the last baron's time. Still, Miss Cavencourt expressed no desire to entertain—rather the opposite—and her butler saw no benefit in accumulating a pack of idlers, merely for appearances' sake. The lady had a book to write. She needed quiet and calm, not an army of minions stumbling about the place and quarrelling in the corridors.

Accordingly, Mr. Brentick ordered the library cleaned first thing each morning, hours before the mistress arrived to work. After that, no one but Mrs. Gales or Bella was permitted to intrude upon her. Mr. Brentick noiselessly carried in her tea, and noiselessly took away the remains. He slipped in like an efficient, well-mannered ghost, and vanished in the same manner.

Within a month, his staff became ghosts as well: smiling, cheerful, but quiet and quick. In a month, he'd converted an assortment of sturdy Yorkshire workers into an army of amiable, discreetly attentive wraiths.

Thus a damp October passed, to be succeeded by a wet and cold November. Fortunately for its India-acclimated inhabitants, the manor house was of modest proportions. It would, in fact, have nestled quite comfortably in the east wing of Felkonwood Castle, with room to spare. Years before, Miss Cavencourt's grandfather had enlarged and modernized the manor with an eye to comfort rather than grandeur. Here, no great hallways swept chilling draughts into vast, echoing, chambers. Once properly cleaned, the chimneys performed flawlessly. Even in late autumn, the rooms were snug enough.

The intimate dining room and cozy library faced west, looking out onto a sadly neglected garden. Twigs and dead leaves clogged the ornamental pond at its centre, for, despite Philip's efforts, Padji and the gardener had collided once too often. The latter had departed in a huff several weeks ago. Still, the garden would be restored in the spring.

The house nestled in a shallow dale. Beyond the garden, dark, wooded slopes reached towards the brooding moorland beyond. Nonetheless, even now, at twilight, he did not find the world beyond the library windows altogether dreary. Dark it was, this place, cold and remote, yet with the darkness and remoteness of a secret, quiet in its moody mystery.

Philip stood, the drape pull forgotten in his hand as he drank in the lowering night.

"I suppose it must seem very gloomy to you," came Miss Cavencourt's low voice, startling him.

He quickly pulled the drapes closed.

"All the better, miss," he answered. "In contrast to the chill and gloom out of doors, indoors seems the warmer and brighter." He frowned at the small figure huddled over the writing table. "Your tea will grow cold. Tomorrow we must move your table. I do believe you are working in the draughtiest corner of the room."

She looked up. Miss Cavencourt's method of composing her thoughts, he'd learned, was to discompose her coiffure. Over and over again, while she worked, her nervous fingers would rake back her hair, heedlessly loosening pins and steadily reducing her businesslike chignon to a wanton tangle of coffee-coloured tresses.

Her butler's hands itched to make all tidy and efficient again, so that he might view her coolly as a professional problem. At present, unfortunately, she presented another sort of riddle—an old one, which he was strongly tempted to solve in the time-honoured manner of his gender.

When he'd first arrived, seduction was the very last thing on his mind. In a matter of weeks, it had relentlessly thrust its way forward again. Occasionally, it did reach first place, whence he found it increasingly difficult to dislodge.

"I think it's better this way," she said. "The fire is too cozy and inviting, and the warmth would probably make me drowsy. I find it hard enough to concentrate as it is."

Philip told himself he experienced not the least difficulty concentrating. If she appeared a lonely waif, sadly in want of someone to take her in hand, that was not his problem. He didn't care if her aristocratic nose turned red and her fingers blue with cold. She could freeze if she liked. It was nothing to him.

He removed the tray from the small table by the fire and carried it to the large one where she worked. Finding no clear surface space available, Philip simply set the entire tray upon the manuscript page before her.

"Mr. Brentick, I was working on that!"

"Yes, miss," he said. "I discerned no other method of persuading you to stop."

Her amber eyes lit with annoyance. "Does this not strike you as a shade overbearing? To drop the entire tray under my nose?"

"You ate nothing at midday," he said. "If I bring back another untouched tray, Padji will commence to weeping, and that inevitably throws Mrs. Swanslow into one of her spasms. Then Jane, in sympathy, will go off in one of her fits. We are of tender sensibilities belowstairs. When the mistress neglects her tea, we are inconsolable, and consequently, break out in violence. I realise your work has precedence over such mundane matters as rest and nourishment, miss. Regrettably, the rest of the staff lack my philosophical detachment. What are we two," he concluded, sadly shaking his head, "against so many?"

"We two, indeed," she said with a sniff as she watched him pour. "I can see whose side you are on."

He handed her the cup. "As I understand it, a butler's primary aim in life is the maintenance of domestic order and peace. It wants a firm hand to sustain the battle against chaos," he said, with a meaningful glance at the disaster representing Miss Cavencourt's literary masterpiece.

Ink-spattered pages lay strewn about in gay abandon. Upon table and floor scores of books—most with bits of paper sticking from their pages—stood in forlorn heaps.

She followed his gaze and flushed. "I am not very organised, I'm afraid," she said.

She was not organised at all. Her working methods were as tumbled and disordered as her hair. Ink smudged her fingers. He observed a dark smudge between her fine eyebrows. He wanted to rub it away with his thumb. He wanted to repair her hair. Then she looked up, and the defensive embarrassment in her countenance made him want more than anything else to kiss her.

"Yours is a creative soul," he said, manfully ignoring the patchouli scent teasing his nostrils. "Neatness and organisation want a more pedestrian intelligence."

"I suppose that is a kind way of telling me I'm addled," she muttered.

"No, miss. I was about to provide an unanswerable argument for your acquiring a secretary's services."

"Of course I need a secretary," she said indignantly. "I'm not that addled, Mr. Brentick. Naturally, the idea occurred to me. But you forget that many of the works I consult are in Sanskrit, and the rani's notes are all in Hindustani. I should have to scour the entire kingdom for the kind of secretary I need, though it's far more likely he or she lives in India. Furthermore, by the time I did find this paragon, I might have already finished the book, even in my *chaotic* manner."

He sighed and took up her copy of the *Bhagavad-Gita*.

" 'There never was a time when I was not,' " he translated, " 'nor thou, nor these princes were not; there never will be a time when we shall cease to be.' "

"Oh, dear," she murmured.

He looked at her and grinned.

Mr. Brentick assumed the role of secretary in the same quietly efficient manner he'd assumed every other responsibility connected with his employer. The following morning, he accompanied her to the library, where he devised a system for organising her notes. Then he collected the reference works she'd need that day, placed markers in the appropriate pages, and arranged them neatly within easy reach.

He remained with her until noon, reviewing what she'd written previously, and making notes. He stood by patiently to answer every question, fetch books or papers, mend quills, and clean up ink spills. In that curious way he had, he made himself invisible, for the most part, though he became visible the instant she needed him. Every morning thereafter he spent in the same fashion.

Mrs. Gales joined them at the outset. Invisibility, she soon found, was not nearly so much to her liking as it was to the butler's, and the mornings passed slowly indeed, though she had her needlework to keep her busy.

One morning, after a week of this quiet chaperonage, Mrs. Gales rose from her usual seat by the fire and, quite unnoticed, left the room, rubbing her aching head. She met up with Bella in the hallway, and frowned.

Bella nodded in quick understanding, and led the widow to the servants' hall, which at this hour was deserted.

Over a pot of tea, Mrs. Gales expressed her disquiet.

"Sometimes," she said, "a body can be *too* perfect, Bella."

"Well, I don't like 'em quite so skinny myself," said Bella, "but I'd say his face is perfect enough."

Mrs. Gales raised her eyebrows. "I referred to his behaviour. He has made himself indispensable to an alarming extent."

"He do have a way about him, don't he? Not a one of us but does exactly what Mr. Brentick wants—and he don't have to say a word, do he? Only has to look at you and, I declare, whatever he's got in mind, why, it gets right into yours, too—and sticks there pretty tight."

"Indeed." Mrs. Gales refilled her cup. "The question is, what is he putting into *her* mind?"

Bella considered. "Just them heathen gods, I expect," she said. "They don't talk about nothing else, do they?"

"No. That wicked Krishna it was today, and his legion of females. Small wonder she can't keep track of the wives and mistresses. Other men's wives, no less," Mrs. Gales added disapprovingly. "Yet they discuss it in so scholarly a fashion, one feels a fool to intrude."

"It's only for the book, ma'am."

"Yes. I suppose these so-called gods' doings are quite tame compared to the Rani Simhi's biography. Still, *he* will never hint that Amanda ought know nothing of these matters, let alone write of them. All he ever corrects is her syntax. Really," the widow added in vexation, "the man is a deal too much an enigma for my tastes. And I am not at all easy about the way he looks at her." She rubbed her head again. "Bella, I do fear . . . yet he is so very *attentive*," she said helplessly. "So kind, so considerate. He makes her laugh. He makes her—"

"Happy," Bella finished for her. "There's the nub of it, ma'am. Maybe there's more in it and maybe not, and maybe it ain't the properest sort of doings. But all I can think is how things was before. She had to grow up too fast—and Lord knows nobody ever laughed much here."

Mrs. Gales sighed. "Yes, I imagine it must have been so. Her mother was ill many years, was she not?"

"She weren't never right, ma'am. Not since Miss Amanda was a babe. Leastways, that's what my ma told me. I was hardly more than a babe myself then, so I never knew her ladyship when she wasn't . . . sick."

The hesitation in the maid's tones made Mrs. Gales look at her sharply. "What ailed her, Bella? Amanda seldom mentions her mama, and I never met the lady."

"I weren't no lady's maid then, ma'am, and folks wasn't like to tell me everything, now, was they?" came the evasive answer.

Loyalty Mrs. Gales respected. If Bella disliked to gossip about the family's past, the widow possessed sufficient loyalty herself to refrain from pressing.

==14==

THE LIBRARY WAS still, but for the scratching of Miss Cavencourt's pen and the hiss of coals in the grate. Philip stood at the window, his white-gloved hands clasped behind him, his attention fixed upon the wooded slope that rose at the garden's edge. Yesterday's dark blanket of sky had lightened this morning to pearl grey. Here and there faint rays of light struggled through to drop fitful sparkles upon the pond. Trees and shrubs trembled in the wind, and dry leaves danced feebly upon water and ground.

The scratching stopped, and a muttered oath broke the quiet.

Philip turned. "That is your fifth 'damnation' this morning," he said. "I'm not surprised. You might spend your next five lifetimes explaining the *shakta* cults."

She looked up. "If I talk about Kali, I ought to explain that she's just one of the manifestations of Shiva's wife. Everyone thinks the worst of Kali, yet she's simply one element—like one personality trait among many. Personalities are not always consistent."

"You want to defend her because you are partial to bloodthirsty females, miss."

"She is the most important goddess for Calcutta," Miss Cavencourt returned. "You know perfectly well the city's original name was Kalikata. I can hardly ignore her. Besides, if I speak only of agreeable matters, the book will be boring."

He shot her a smile. "Certainly it will—to those with a penchant for severed heads and ghastly vengeances."

He moved to the worktable, which, in less than an hour, his employer had reduced to mind-numbing disorder. "You work too hard and take no rest. Once, I recollect, you sternly recommended exercise to me, miss. I think you ought heed your own advice." He gestured towards the windows. "The wind is not nearly so sharp today. A walk will do you good."

He listened patiently while she fussed that she could not afford to give up time now, when she very nearly had the thing in hand, and that, furthermore, she was quite well and didn't need exercise—not to mention it was *freezing* out there.

Philip let her sputter on. When she had done explaining the error of his ways, and taken up her pen once more, he left the room.

A quarter of an hour later he returned, carrying a woolen cloak and scarf, a thick bonnet, gloves, and sturdy shoes. He had donned a dashing black, many-caped coat.

Miss Cavencourt looked at his coat and the heap of clothing in his arms and sighed. "I collect you mean to haul me out of doors, whether I will or no. I might have known, when I got not a whisper of argument. You are very managing."

"And you are cross from spending too much time in one overheated room, with your nose stuck in a heap of papers," he said disrespectfully.

"My nose, for your information—"

"Has a spot of ink upon it." He produced a large, brilliantly white handkerchief.

Her butler having expressed a desire to tramp upon the moors, Amanda led him up a familiar though barely discernible path through the wood to the top of the slope. Away from the valley's shelter, the wind blew fiercely, but the slow climb up the hill stirred her sluggish blood, and she found the cold exhilarating.

Amanda inhaled gratefully as they paused at the top to survey the surrounding scene. Occasional scatterings of stunted trees dotted a landscape composed mostly of furze and jagged rock. The land rose and fell roughly, divided by stone walls into large, irregular rectangles.

"Is it all yours?" he asked.

"It was. If it hadn't been for Roderick, we'd have lost everything. Yet the acres we managed to keep are productive enough," she said. "I could get by on the income, but Roderick wouldn't hear of that. If he could, he'd have me living permanently in London in idle luxury."

Mr. Brentick threw her a curious glance, then looked away again. "Still, you'll want to spend time in Town eventually, at least after you finish your book. I realise Society would be too distracting now."

"I'm not going to London."

"Not even for the Season?"

"No," she said firmly. "I want no more Seasons."

"That's a pity," he said. "I rather fancy the challenge of managing a host of lazy, untrustworthy, city-bred domestics. These Yorkshire labourers are so very conscientious," he complained.

"That is your fault, Mr. Brentick. I left all the hiring to you. There was no one to prevent your employing a pack of idlers and thieves if you liked. If you are bored, or lonely for company . . ."

"I am not bored, miss. I am learning that solitude and loneliness are not the same thing."

It was disconcerting to discover that he seemed to recall every syllable she'd ever uttered to him. Equally disconcerting was his mention of London. He had a knack for coaxing people to do precisely as he wished. He changed others' minds as easily as he changed the wine goblets at dinner. But not in this, Amanda hastily reassured herself. She would never again, for as long as she lived, spend another Season in London.

"You understand, then, how and where I acquired my

taste for solitude," she responded calmly. She made a sweeping movement with her hand.

"Yes, the place broods and yearns before us, dark and mute. It does not distract us with pretty, idle chatter. Yet in its own unassuming way, it is treacherous." He glanced round and smiled at her. "For instance, if we remain much longer, mesmerised by the romantically moody landscape, you will freeze into a solid block."

He took her hand to help her down the steep, rough incline, only to release it as soon as the way became easier. Another mile's walk brought them into a corner of the dale sheltered from the winds' force by rocks and a stand of scarred trees.

After investigating the rough boulders, Mr. Brentick selected a suitable resting place. He withdrew from his pockets two flasks and two linen-wrapped bundles. Then he removed his coat and, quite deaf to Amanda's protests, spread it out for her to sit upon. The flasks, she discovered, contained cider. In the bundles nestled neat slices of cheese and thick hunks of freshly baked bread.

"You think of everything," she said.

"I was concerned you might faint of hunger on the way back. While you are fashionably slender, miss, I could not view with equanimity the prospect of carrying you home over nearly four miles of rough terrain."

Amanda hastily averted her gaze, and the warmth blossoming in her face subsided.

They dawdled over their meal with the easy camaraderie they'd enjoyed aboard ship, and had only recently revived during the weeks of working together in the library. Not until she'd consumed the last crumbs of bread and cheese did Amanda realise how probing his questions had become. She glanced up warily when he asked where she'd played as a child.

"Not here," she said quickly. "I seldom ventured so far from the house, except when Roderick was home. He and I rode here often. While he was at school, though, I had to keep within the garden bounds."

"That was wise. If you fell and hurt yourself, you might not be found for hours. I only wondered who your playmates were. You must have had to travel a good distance to visit one another."

She snapped the cap of her flask back into place. "Roderick was here," she said tightly. "He spent every holiday at home."

Mentally she braced herself to deflect the inevitable questions, but none came. Mr. Brentick merely nodded, and neatly gathered up the remnants of their picnic. As they turned homeward, the conversation turned as well, she found with relief. They spoke of Kali.

One day in late November, Philip accompanied his employer and Mrs. Gales to York. Miss Cavencourt had business at the bank, she said. He fully understood she meant to visit her statue, though she'd never once uttered a word about the Laughing Princess.

While entertaining small hope she'd actually take it home with her, Philip was prepared, in the event she did, to relieve her of it. As usual, he'd devised a foolproof plan for doing so without arousing suspicion.

The plan dropped into his mental ashbin when, after half an hour, his employer left the bank empty-handed.

Nevertheless, not a glimmer of frustration ruffled his polite demeanour as, like a lowly footman, he followed her down the street and on to the bookseller's. There he awaited the summons to carry her parcels. Miss Cavencourt spent as much on books as other ladies did on bonnets.

Philip stood by the door, his hands clasped at his back, his countenance blank and incurious as he gazed upon the passing scene. Miss Cavencourt's general factotum did not wear livery. This doubtless explained why more than one passing lady required more than a fleeting glance to ascertain that the fellow by the bookshop door was a mere servant. Some continued gazing, even after settling this matter to their satisfaction. The butler, however, very properly reserved his acknowledging nods for females of the lower orders, who rewarded him with blushes and an occasional giggle.

He'd been amusing himself in this fashion for twenty minutes when a gentleman stopped nearby to glance into the shop window. He was as tall as Philip, his build a degree broader, yet trim and athletic. The hair beneath the elegant beaver was black, and the visage dark and rugged. Philip guessed the man's age at near forty, though the dissolute eyes and mouth may have added a few years.

Though Philip kept his eyes fixed, ostensibly, upon the street, he was aware of the stranger's scrutiny moving to him. At that moment, a signal flashed to Philip's brain, eliciting a response common among the lower species when a rival male trespasses territorial boundaries. His heartbeat quickened and his muscles tensed for battle.

The stranger coolly strode past him to enter the shop.

With stiff fingers, Philip withdrew his pocket watch and stared blindly at it a moment before turning slightly to peer into the window.

The stranger, hat in hand, was speaking to Miss Cavencourt. Clutching a book to her chest, she stared at him. She appeared to answer, then turned away, dropped the book upon the counter, and hurried to the door.

She darted through the entrance and on down the street, utterly oblivious to Philip, who hastened after her. Her mysterious accoster made no attempt to follow, Philip saw with a backward glance, yet she continued hurrying down the street. She was about to cross— directly into the path of an oncoming cart—when Philip ran up and grabbed her arm. He pulled her back from the road and into a narrow alley.

Her bosom was heaving and her face was flushed, her eyes sparkling with unshed tears. He drew her deeper into the shadows, lest curious passersby remark her agitation.

"I want to go home now," she said quaveringly. "I want to go *home*, Mr. Br—" The rest caught on a sob.

She turned to him and pressed her hot face to his chest.

Automatically, his arms went around her, to hold her as her control broke and the sobs racked her slim body.

Philip stared over her bonnet at the grimy wall opposite. He tried to make his mind blank and hard, because that must harden his heart as well. He silently prayed she'd calm soon, before he weakened.

He could not kiss her tears away, nor permit his hands to stroke her back. That sort of unservantlike behaviour would, when she was herself again, create difficulties. He'd spent too much time winning her trust, making her dependent upon him, to risk any awkwardness now. He would not let himself succumb to pity . . . or to the coaxing warmth of her slender body.

Drat her. If she didn't stop soon—

To his unutterable relief, she abruptly drew back. He released her and produced his handkerchief.

"You think I'm mad," she said brokenly into the linen.

"That's nothing new," he said. "I've always thought so."

Her automatic but feeble attempt at a smile sent a darting ache through him.

"Who was the blackguard?" he asked.

"Nobody. One of my moth—my parents' friends."

"A friend, I take it, you didn't like overmuch."

She stared at the handkerchief she was twisting into knots. "No, I didn't—don't."

"I hope he was not disrespectful, miss."

"Oh, no, not at all. Mr. Fenthill is the very soul of courtesy," she said tightly. "But I am not. It is very difficult for me to behave politely with people I—I dislike. Impossible, actually. And so—and so I made a cake of myself. Really, I am sorry. Now all of York will pity you for having a lunatic as your employer." She thrust the crumpled handkerchief into her reticule.

"Not if they learn how grossly you overpay me," he said with feigned lightness. "Are you sufficiently composed to depart this filthy alleyway, miss?"

She nodded, refusing to meet his gaze.

"Very good. Let us extricate Mrs. Gales—forcibly, if need be—from her debate with the linen draper, shall we? You will both want a cup of tea and a bite to eat before we start back."

The night was cold, but he'd become accustomed to that. Or perhaps Philip merely ignored it, just as he'd ignored the noisome heat of Calcutta. Idly he paced the garden walkway, smoking his cheroot while he turned the puzzle over in his mind. He perceived a problem, a major obstacle, and he was certain today's episode formed a part.

No one visited Miss Cavencourt except the vicar, who had called once only. The villagers Philip had encountered were wary and tight-lipped. The few who asked after her employed the mournful tones of those enquiring after the mortally ill. He scented scandal or tragedy of some kind, yet none of his spy's skills could elicit the information he wanted. The villagers might gossip among themselves, but with strangers they were stubbornly aloof.

Exceedingly frustrating that was. Until he had the facts, he could not deal with the problem, and until he dealt with it, she'd remain here, hidden, while her statue remained inaccessible in the York bank.

Philip was aware of the light before he actually saw it. He glanced back at the house, his quick survey showing none but darkened windows until . . . ah, the old schoolroom.

"Oh, miss," said Bella softly as she closed the schoolroom door behind her. "I knowed you was restless. Another bad dream, was it?"

Amanda sat huddled in a child-sized chair. She pulled her dressing gown more tightly about her. "No. At least, not tonight. It was today, and I was wide awake."

"Miss?" Her round face creased in bafflement, Bella crossed the room to join her mistress. The abigail pulled a low stool forward, sat, and took Amanda's hand. "Lawd, you're cold as ice," she said as she chafed the frigid fingers.

"I saw Mr. Fenthill."

Bella's busy hands stilled.

"Actually, it was more than seeing him," Amanda said. "He spoke to me."

"Oh, miss, how could he? But there, ain't that just like him?" the maid added indignantly. "Never did think of anybody's feelings but his. No wonder you come home so pale and not like yourself at all. And hardly touched your dinner, either, Mrs. Gales said. She thought it was—" Bella caught herself up short. "Well, you was working too hard, is what she thought."

Amanda's fingers tightened round her maid's. "She doesn't know, does she? I know you'd never tell her, but she may have heard from others."

"She don't know, miss, and she's too much a lady to pry, so don't you go worrying yourself. Not that you should, anyhow. Because she's likewise too much a lady to judge you on account of what your poor ma did."

"But it wasn't Mama's fault, either." Amanda disengaged her hand, then rose and moved to the window. After a moment she said, "It wasn't. I don't think it was anyone's fault."

"Mebbe so," was the doubtful response, "but he could of let her alone, couldn't he? Her a married woman, a mother, and old enough to be *his* ma."

"She could not have been a mother at the age of ten, Bella. In any case, perhaps if he had been more mature, Mr. Fenthill might have found the will to keep away." Amanda sighed. "But that's all 'if,' and Mama was all 'ifs' and 'might have beens.' If only she'd had an easier time bearing me, if only she hadn't had the accidents . . . Lud, sometimes I think, if only Papa had let her go when she begged him. She was so miserable, and there was the opium to make everything go away. If he'd let her go, and Mr. Fenthill had taken her away and made her happy, she might have found the strength to break her terrible habit. Mr. Fenthill loved her. He might have helped her."

"He only helped her to more of her poison, Miss Amanda, which you know as well as I do. Don't you be making excuses for him. I declare, you'd find some excuse for the Devil himself."

=15=

THE FALCON STOOD motionless by the door, his body poised for flight, his ears alert to sound on every side, even as he concentrated upon the conversation within.

So that was it, simple and sordid. Her mother an opium addict and adultress. The affair with a man ten years her junior had evidently been neither the first nor discreet. A long and ugly series of scandals explained Miss Cavencourt's firm refusal to reenter Society.

Gad, she'd not been blessed in her parents, had she? What had she said so many months ago? She'd told him her parents were broken. Philip understood now that financial ruin had simply struck the final blow. He could only marvel that her wretched life hadn't broken her as well.

In the room beyond, the two low, feminine voices continued. Or rather, it was mainly Bella's voice now, gently scolding and comforting by turns. She was quite right. Amanda was too soft-hearted. Nothing was her mama's fault, or her papa's, or the doctors', or even that scurvy Fenthill's, according to her. The next you knew, she'd be inviting the filthy libertine to tea.

Why not? Her dearest friend in Calcutta had been the notorious Rani Simhi. Her devoted cook was one of the deadliest men in all India. Her butler was a master spy and thief. Amanda Cavencourt befriended the people most likely to use and betray her. She was a trusting little fool. A hard life had taught her nothing.

On the other hand, Philip hastily reminded himself as his conscience made ominous noises, she had stolen the statue. Never mind that she'd stolen it *back*. She'd been as deceitful and underhand as the rani, had even employed accomplices. Hardly the behaviour of a helpless victim.

Philip had just got his conscience in a stranglehold when he heard soft footsteps ascending the stairs. For all his bulk, Padji could tread lightly enough when he chose. Drat the fellow! The Indian spent most of his nights roaming the countryside. Tonight, of all nights, he'd decided to skulk at home instead.

The schoolroom was tucked into the far end of the dark hall. Padji was swiftly climbing the main staircase, which meant one must pass him to reach the backstairs.

Philip moved to the wall opposite the schoolroom and found a door handle. He opened the door and slipped inside, just as Padji reached the head of the stairs.

Philip heard the light tread approach, then pause inches away. He held his breath as the door handle moved. An instant later, he sensed the Indian moving away, then heard the tap upon the schoolroom door.

"Come out, mistress," Padji said. "Why does the foolish maid keep you in that cold place?"

Philip heard the door squeal faintly as she opened it. James should have oiled it, he thought automatically.

"She doesn't keep me," came Miss Cavencourt's annoyed voice. "Don't blame Bella for my odd starts. What are you doing, skulking about the house at this hour?"

Padji answered he'd thought he'd heard intruders.

"Well, it was just us, and we were about to return to bed anyhow."

The three passed Philip's hiding place. Their low voices faded to a murmur as they descended the stairs.

He waited several minutes after the house fell silent again, then drew a long breath of relief. He'd not moved, had scarcely breathed the whole time Padji had stood by, for the Indian's senses were as acute as his own.

Now that he could breathe properly, Philip found the air in the room exceedingly close and stale. He stepped back a pace and encountered a solid wall. Gad, no wonder. He'd entered a closet of some sort.

His heart was already pounding when he grabbed the door handle. It didn't budge. He tried again. Nothing. The latch was stuck—or some part was stuck. In the utter blackness he couldn't see, and his agile fingers played over the parts to no avail.

Fighting down panic, he reached into his coat for his trusty lock picks . . . and found nothing. He'd changed coats on his return from York, and neglected to transfer his tools. Bloody hell. Not even his knife. What the devil was wrong with him? He'd never been so careless before, never.

This was all her curst fault. He'd been so preoccupied with that swine in York and her hysteria—

He couldn't breathe. Not enough air here for a mouse, let alone a grown man. A man, he reminded himself, as panic rose in a chilling wave. A man, not a child.

Any fool could deal with a closet door. One need simply think it through in a calm, logical fashion. He'd find a way out. He must. He would not be trapped here all night. Good God, not all night!

He raised a fist to pound on the door, then stopped. He couldn't scream for help. He wanted another deep breath to steady himself, but didn't dare. Soon no air would remain. He'd suffocate. Better to scream and let them release him. He needn't explain. Let her discharge him. He'd find another way. Another way, but that would take time— weeks, months perhaps, and all these past weeks' work would go for naught.

He tore his neckcloth from his throat. He could always throttle himself, he thought wildly. But that was madness. *Think, Astonley.*

He couldn't think. He never could when this one un- reasoning terror caught hold. He couldn't think and he couldn't scream, and he would just die here by inches.

No, he would not. Of course he could breathe. He was trapped only. He would go mad, but he would endure.

He leaned back into the corner and slid slowly to the floor. Then he drew his knees up to his chest, just as he had so many times so many years ago, and lay his pounding head upon them.

Amanda gritted her teeth, set down the candelabra, and inserted the key in the lock. She had to twist it back and forth a few times before it caught properly. Then she yanked the door open, and her heart wrenched so sharply she had to cling to the frame for support.

For one chilling instant she beheld a death's head. His face cold white and rigid, Mr. Brentick stared unseeingly straight ahead as though she weren't there. She wanted to hug him, hold him close, and comfort him. She knew, though, she must not, for that would shame him. She knelt to meet his blank gaze and tried to pretend she found nothing out of the way.

"Mr. Brentick," she said gently. Her hand crept out to touch his, to call him back to the world.

He blinked, and looked down in a puzzled way at her hand.

"How long have you been here?" she asked.

"I don't know." His voice was weak, distant, a stranger's.

"Do you think you can move your limbs? If you can, I can probably help you up."

He pulled his arms away from his knees and slowly, with obvious pain, straightened his legs. "It's all right," he said. "They've merely gone to sleep." He shook off whatever had seized him and managed a rueful smile. "Not rigor mortis, as I'd thought."

"Don't joke about such things," she said sharply. "You've frightened me half to death."

After a few failed attempts, she managed to pull him upright.

"My legs are like jelly," he muttered.

"Just lean on me." She caught him tight about the waist. He was practically a dead weight, but somehow she got him the few feet across the hall to the schoolroom, then onto the window seat. He slumped against the window and bit his lip. He was definitely in pain.

"Muscle cramps," she said, making her tones firm and matter-of-fact, though she could have wept for him. Wept for him and killed the monster who'd so cruelly tortured a helpless little boy.

With businesslike resolution, she took hold of one leg and began kneading the knotted muscles.

He gasped.

"Trust me, Mr. Brentick. I've had years of practice. Mama suffered terrible muscle spasms. They made her scream. This always helped."

She determinedly wrestled first one, then the other taut calf into submission. When she was done, she looked up to find him gazing warily at her.

"How did you come to rescue me?" he asked.

"I will tell you that," she said, stepping away from him, "after you explain how you came to be in the closet."

"I suppose it's no good to say I was sleepwalking?"

She shook her head.

He swung his feet to the floor, but did not stand up. He simply sat there, studying the floor. She was just opening her mouth to demand an answer when he spoke.

"I was in the garden, smoking, as I do every night, weather permitting. You know I'm not a great one for sleep."

She didn't respond.

"I saw the light in this room. It was one o'clock in the morning, so I thought I'd best investigate."

"I see. Padji suspected intruders as well."

"Just so. I crept up as quietly as I could," he went on. "Hearing only your and Miss Jones's voices, I was about to leave, when I heard someone else coming. I was standing in front of the closet door—not that I knew it was a closet— and so, I slipped behind it, thinking to take the intruder unawares. When I realised it was only Padji, I felt a perfect fool, hiding there. I waited until you'd all gone—then I couldn't get the door open."

"You should have called for help."

"I didn't want to alarm the household."

"Indeed? You had rather spend the night in a very small closet?"

"Perhaps I was not thinking clearly," he said.

She sighed. They could go on this way forever, skipping about the subject, and that she couldn't bear.

"Padji thought you were spying on me," she said bluntly. "He said he locked you in to teach you a lesson."

In the tight ensuing silence she heard his breath quicken. Her heart ached for him, for his masculine pride. Yet she had her pride, too. She knew he'd overheard—perhaps intentionally, perhaps not. In any case, it was too late for pretense on either side.

"He doesn't know," she said, "but I guessed. That day on the ship when you fell ill, you were delirious. Without realising, you told me a secret. I didn't entirely understand then, but tonight, when Padji told me what he'd done, I guessed that's what your father had done and . . . well, I didn't want Padji to be the one to release you."

He turned his head away slightly, to the window. The flickering candlelight threw fitful shadows over the rigid planes of his face.

"Thank you," he said, his voice barely audible.

She understood what it cost him to say that, and hastened to salvage his pride as well as her own. "I imagine you couldn't help overhearing tonight any more than I could that day," she said. "I don't know what you heard, but it must have been quite enough, else you'd not have hidden. I suppose you wanted to spare me embarrassment. You didn't want me to guess you'd heard my—our family secret. Not that it's much of a secret. I should have told you the truth today. I'm not ashamed, not really. I just . . . I didn't want you to pity me. I've had enough of that to last seven lifetimes, I think."

Another lifetime seemed to pass before he looked towards her. His mouth eased into a faint smile. "In the circumstances, Miss Cavencourt, I don't dare pity you. You might retaliate in kind. I've never been pitied, yet I suspect it must be worse even than that curst closet." He rose. "The truth is, I was an incorrigible child. A birching only made me laugh. I was afraid of nothing, you see—except, that is, being trapped in a small, closed space. It was the only punishment that worked."

"I'm not surprised," she said calmly, though the very matter-of-factness of his explanation made her heart ache. "I'd guessed you were a little devil. Still, that is a monstrous cruel way to discipline a little boy, no matter how wicked."

"What would you have done?" He moved closer, and in the unsteady light she discerned a familiar, intent gaze. "I know you'd have tried to understand me, because you try to understand everybody, from the great god Shiva to Jane, the scullery maid. Still, you'd have to *do* something. What, then?"

Too easy to answer. She knew she would have covered that troubled, angry little boy's face with kisses, cosseted him, spoiled him, loved him with all her heart.

"I should not have tried to make a scholar of you," she said carefully. "If you were a very restless child, you'd have been happier boxing, fencing, riding. There's discipline in sports, for both mind and body. Also, vigourous physical activity would have tired you too much for mischief. Your papa tried to make you what you were not. Children should be permitted to be what they are."

"You think my mischief was the common sort," he said. "It wasn't. In addition to the usual boyish pranks, I was insolent, told lies constantly, and *stole*."

She ought to be shocked. She wasn't. The moment she'd opened the closet door and seen his face, she'd understood. "Because you were angry and unhappy."

He was still studying her face. "You are bound to find a kind excuse, Miss Cavencourt. Can't you believe a human being might be born bad?"

"I can believe that, but not of you. Surely that must be obvious," she added hastily. "If I'd thought you intended any ill, I should have left you in the closet, or to Padji's tender mercies. I know everyone thinks me too forgiving, Mr. Brentick. All the same, I do not always turn the other cheek. Martyrdom is not in my style."

"No," he said softly. "I realise you're not a saint."

His tone made her face heat. Belatedly she became aware of her bedtime attire. Despite a flannel nightdress and a robe of serviceable wool, she felt undressed and unsafe. He seemed too near, and also too much undressed. His neckcloth was gone, and his shirt had fallen open to reveal a triangle of flesh that gleamed bronze in the candlelight. She wanted to move to him, touch him. She wanted to hold him, and be held. She shivered.

"You must be chilled to the bone," he said. He began to pull off his coat.

"No!" She quickly retreated. "I don't need it. I'm going back to bed. You can take the candles. I know my way blindfolded." She moved to the door. "Good night, Mr. Brentick," she said. Then she fled.

Philip could have spent the night merely writhing in mortification, but Miss Cavencourt's knowledge of his weakness seemed the least of his troubles as he climbed into bed.

He sat back, rubbing his throbbing temples, wondering how she'd managed to make everything so deuced complicated.

Delirious, she'd said. He felt delirious now. He could not believe he'd admitted the truth, so much truth. He could have simply pretended not to understand what she was talking about. If pressed, he need only deny.

Yet he'd found himself trapped once again, entangled in undeserved kindness and compassion. She'd rescued him herself to spare his pride, and had not left until she'd made him well again. She'd lifted him out of the chilling darkness into sanity. With her own surprisingly strong hands she'd even wrestled the pain from his frozen body.

Gratitude had weakened him and made him incautious. Stunned and grateful, he'd found himself unable to deny, scarcely able to manufacture a fraction of a lie.

That wasn't the worst, though. She'd not only explained and absolved him, but dressed him in shining armour. Of course Mr. Brentick hadn't been spying on her. He'd bravely come to battle intruders, had accidentally overheard, and then sacrificed his own peace of mind to spare hers.

"Oh, Amanda," he muttered. "How could you believe that? Was there ever such a trusting little fool?" He'd wanted to shake her, had tried to do so verbally. Yet even the truth about his character only elicited more of her unendurable *understanding*. "Angry and unhappy," she'd said. *Fool*, he'd answered silently. Bella was right. Miss Cavencourt would make excuses for the Devil himself.

Perhaps she was not entirely credulous, though, Philip thought, as he sank back upon his pillow. She hadn't altogether spared his feelings, had she, for all her compassion? She'd told him plain enough she knew not only what he'd suffered in the closet, but why, and where the terror came from. Gently though she'd worded the admission, Philip had perceived her warning as well. For now, she sympathised. Should he lose her sympathy, however, she'd not hesitate to use his weakness against him. Or rather, she'd let Padji use it. She was not naive in every way. She knew the Indian's character and his uses. Hadn't she used him before?

Very well. The game had grown a shade more complicated and dangerous. He'd need to revise his plans.

Unless someone persuaded Miss Cavencourt to end her self-imposed exile, the Laughing Princess would remain in the York bank indefinitely. She must be got to leave, and take the statue with her.

Her ever-so-kind and understanding knight, Brentick, would *never* venture upon the tender subject of London Seasons again. Knowing the sordid truth, he'd respect her wishes to remain hidden in this remote place.

Yes, she'd tied his hands in that. Frustrating it was, for he could have persuaded her easily enough in a matter of weeks. Now he must manipulate others to do the job for him.

Cool and calculating once more, Philip clasped his hands behind his head, and prepared to spend the remaining night contemplating the tools currently at his disposal.

===16===

NOVEMBER SWEPT AWAY on icy winds and December whirled in amid a snowstorm that transformed the harsh, grey landscape to shimmering white.

The snow brought Amanda mixed relief and disappointment. She and Mr. Brentick had taken long walks through the moors nearly every day of the last month. She knew the exercise did her good, for when she returned to her manuscript, she always felt fresh and clearheaded.

On the other hand, to spend so much time privately with him boded ill for her peace of mind. Away from the house, he relaxed, and their conversations were those of friends, rather than mistress and servant. This was what she preferred, usually; she'd always disliked the barriers rank created. Nevertheless, she found herself wishing, in this one case, for the safety of such barriers. Feelings warmer than mere friendship had again surged to the surface. As the days passed, she found it increasingly difficult to maintain a levelheaded detachment. The snow would bring a few days' respite, time in which she might talk herself round to common sense.

On the afternoon following the storm, therefore, Amanda beheld with surprised dismay her butler's entrance into the library. He wore a woolen overcoat, and carried in his arms a heap of clothing. Also boots, she saw with foreboding. Her boots.

"I am not setting foot out of doors," she said resolutely, "until *June*."

Half an hour later, she was trudging up the path that led to the moors. Mr. Brentick followed, dragging a sled.

When they reached the top, one large, vivid anxiety immediately swamped all Amanda's other worries. She looked at the sled, then down at the incline before them. This side of the hill seemed to have grown exceedingly steep since their last walk. She turned her panicked gaze up to him, while her heart churned with terror.

"Haven't you ever gone sledding before?" he asked.

She shook her head and darted another glance at the endless, nearly perpendicular drop.

"There's nothing to be afraid of, Miss Cavencourt."

"I'll watch," she offered.

"You'll freeze, standing here."

Mr. Brentick positioned the sled, then, very firmly, himself upon it. When he took up his place behind her, fear compounded with a flood of other sensations. Two people could share a sled in only one way, apparently, and that placed her between his legs, her back against his chest. Her heart crashed crazily at her ribs, and every muscle in her body petrified into hard knots.

As the sled began to move, a scream rose in her throat, but caught there. She could no more scream than she could breathe. Then the world went whipping past in a flash of white and dark, while the wind blasted her face, making her eyes stream.

Terrified, she leaned back into the hard security of his chest, her mittened hands frozen to the sides of the sled. It was awful. It was . . . wonderful, she discovered in the very next instant.

This was rapture—to fly down the hillside, the cold beating at her, while the warm, strong, reassuring body held her safe and secure. Her scream broke free, but it broke into a cry of joy and breathless laughter.

She heard his shout of laughter mingle with hers, and she felt as though he surrounded her with happiness. He seemed to vibrate with her in the wild joy of wind and speed, as they plunged headlong into the dale's depths.

They reached the bottom an instant or a lifetime later, and the sled glided gently to a stop. Amanda was still laughing. Her body tingled yet with the sheer joy and excitement of the ride. She gloried in the warmth of her quickened blood, and relished the delicious stinging in her cheeks.

As their merriment subsided, she felt his chin drop to the top of her muffler-wrapped head. His arms tightened about her. Unthinkingly, she let go of the sled to relax against him while she caught her breath.

She felt him tense. Turning her head, she saw the laughter ebb from cobalt-blue eyes and a darker emotion take its place.

Amanda knew an instant's flash of recognition, then came an ache within that built swiftly to unendurable pressure. The white haze of their breath mingled in the narrow space between them. His head bent lower, his eyes dark as midnight, intent and mesmerising. His mouth was a breath away . . . and an eternity away.

She turned quickly, and pulled herself forward.

After a brief hesitation, he rose and helped her up.

He became himself again in that moment, ironically polite as he brushed snow from her coat and mittens. Amanda could not collect herself so quickly. They'd nearly reached the top of the hill before her churning brain had quieted, and her pulse steadied.

When they reached the summit and it appeared Mr. Brentick intended to continue towards home, Amanda ought, certainly, have been eager to return to the safety of the library. But her gaze reverted to the steep incline, and she remembered the rush of joy and the thrilling speed. She'd never before experienced anything like it. She heard herself cry out, like a child, "Oh, Mr. Brentick, aren't we going to do it again?"

He'd got ahead of her. He stopped abruptly and waited

until she'd caught up. "Haven't you had enough for one day?" he asked.

She shook her head.

He grinned. "Very well, miss." He dragged the sled round.

They'd climbed up and sledded down that curst hill at least fifteen times before Miss Cavencourt would admit she'd had enough. Thank Providence for the climb, Philip thought. Had any alternate means of ascending offered itself, they'd likely be sledding until Judgement Day.

He threw her an exasperated glance as they staggered through the garden. Four times her weary legs had given out, tripping her headlong or sideways or backwards into the snow. Four times she'd tumbled, and each time she simply lay there and laughed. He'd wanted to strangle her. He'd wanted to close his hands around her lovely throat . . . and kiss her senseless.

Idiot. Sledding, he'd thought in all his sublime smugness, would keep her amused while also keeping her far from the house. Mrs. Gales wouldn't like it. The widow was hardly lunatic enough to chaperon them, and risk frostbite while she stood and watched them play. No, she wouldn't like it, and must eventually grow sufficiently alarmed to separate the pair. She'd have to take Miss Cavencourt away from Kirkby Glenham.

A perfect plan it had seemed, better even than the long walks. He'd believed so until the end of today's first descent.

He'd known she was terrified, yet knew as well she'd trust him to keep her safe. Consequently, he was not surprised when she'd succumbed almost immediately to the thrill of speed and danger. It was the rest undid him. She'd hurtled down with him, shrieking, laughing, and the sound of her happy excitement had made him wish they'd never reach the bottom. For those moments, he'd wanted only to plunge recklessly and endlessly through eternity with her. All the same, there was an end—there must be—and at the end was a woman snuggled trustingly against him: Amanda, rosy cheeked and breathless in his arms. She'd looked up at him, her eyes shining pleasure and gratitude, golden trust and . . .

He wouldn't think about that, Philip told himself as he held the door open and answered automatically whatever it was she said. He'd forgotten himself, but only the once, and only for a moment. It wasn't such a terrible plan, as long as one were fully prepared.

"She has missed tea again," Mrs. Gales said grimly as she moved away from the sitting-room window. "There is still no sign of them, and it will be dark soon."

Bella flicked a speck of lint from the chair, and plumped up the cushion. "Your own tea'll get cold, ma'am, and worrying won't bring her home any faster."

Mrs. Gales sighed and took her seat. "They've gone out nearly every single day this month. Yesterday, again, she came home soaking wet. It's a wonder she hasn't caught her death."

"Yes, ma'am, but I heard Mr. Brentick scold her about that himself. And he did send her right up to get dry and change her clothes."

"Why must she spend so much time out of doors in the first place?" was the sharp response. "Sledding, indeed. What on earth possessed him?"

Bella took the seat opposite. This was not the first time in recent weeks that the widow had invited her up to share a pot of tea and Padji's delectable sandwiches. The usually imperturbable Mrs. Gales had grown increasingly agitated as the days passed and Miss Cavencourt's intimacy with her butler increased.

"It ain't healthy for her to spend the whole day hunched over her papers, he says," the abigail responded. "I do think he's got the right of it, ma'am. Why, she looks so bright and rosy, I'd hardly know it was the same Miss Amanda. And for all she do come back fairly dripping, she's laughing, too."

Mrs. Gales's lips tightened into a rigid line as she poured

a cup of tea and handed it to the maid. "She gave him a silver cigar case for Christmas," she muttered.

"Yes, ma'am, but she always was generous that way, you know. Not enough to load me up with frocks and underthings, but she give me a gold bracelet, she did, just as if I was a fine lady had somewheres to wear it."

"Also cigars," Mrs. Gales continued as though she hadn't heard. "And permission to smoke in the library."

"She found out he was going outside at night, ma'am, and said there was no point his freezing. Her pa always liked to smoke his cigar in the library."

"Brentick is not her father, or her brother, or even a gentleman caller. He is her *servant*." The widow set her cup down. "I don't like to interfere. She is no green girl, but an independent young woman, and I am not her governess. I have tried to drop a hint, but she refuses to understand me."

"Well, ma'am, Padji talks plain enough, and she don't want to understand him, either. Not but what it ain't his place to say anything, no more than it's mine. Now she won't hardly speak to him, and the way he looks at Mr. Brentick—I declare, it gives me goose shivers, is what."

Mrs. Gales frowned at the tea sandwiches. "It's not how Padji looks at him that worries me, Bella."

"Not there," Amanda said, horrified. "I won't have the entire household watching me stumbling about and falling on my—"

"Ornamental pond," he finished for her as he wrapped the muffler about her head. "Very well. But it's a good hike to the next nearest one."

"Can't we go sledding instead?" she begged. "I had much rather sit and let you do all the work."

"You'll like skating," he promised. "It's like dancing."

"On ice. Balancing on a couple of blades. I was never a good dancer."

"Obviously, you never had a good partner."

"But suppose the ice breaks? It's been warmer, hasn't it? Suppose it breaks and swallows me up and—"

"It is a very shallow pond, miss. Furthermore, the temperature has soared nearly to the freezing point. Hardly a heat wave."

She fussed and worried as usual, and as usual, Mr. Brentick ignored her. Still, Amanda reminded herself, she'd been frightened of sledding at first. Now he had to devote all his energies to persuading her home again, because she couldn't get enough of it. Winter sports had played no part in her childhood—playing formed virtually no part—and she'd no inkling what she'd missed. She felt as though she'd never been truly alive before, never, certainly, so tinglingly, vibrantly alive as this man made her feel.

Yes, he made her feel like a child again, but not the child she'd been. Instead of that wistful, lonely little girl, he'd conjured up a noisy, giggling brat who always demanded more, and *more*.

All the same, when they reached the pond, Amanda wasn't certain she wanted *any*, let alone more.

"Perhaps Mrs. Gales was right," she said. "I really ought not keep you so much from your duties. Perhaps we should return."

He was kneeling before her, fastening her skates. "Mrs. Gales objects to my idling, I take it," he said without looking up.

"Good heavens, not at all. She says I expect far too much of you. I think she's right. You should not have to entertain me, in addition to everything else."

"Please quiet your conscience, miss. I'd far rather play than work. In any case, I haven't nearly enough to do." He sat beside her to fasten his own skates.

Amanda folded her gloved hands and watched him in silence. So quick and capable he was, always, his hands deft and efficient at every task. Never a wasted motion. He was bound to be an excellent skater. She wished she might simply watch him. He moved so beautifully, so lean and lithe he was, easy and assured, smooth and graceful as a cat. To look at him, to hear his voice . . . She suppressed a sigh. She'd commanded herself a thousand times to be content with what he gave.

He stood and held out his hand.

"Maybe I should just watch first," she said. "Can't you give me a demonstration?"

He shook his head. "It's too cold for you to sit still."

"Please?"

He grinned, his beautiful blue eyes teasing. "Coward."

"Well, yes, I am," she admitted ruefully. "I really hate falling down."

"You love falling down, Miss Cavencourt. You think it's quite the most hilarious experience in all the world."

She stared mistrustfully at her skates.

"Don't just stand there, Mr. Brentick," she heard him cry in a familiar feminine voice. "Help me up."

Amanda's head shot up.

"Oh, lud, how stupid," he continued in the same voice. Then her tall, capable, *manly* butler broke into girlish giggles.

Her mouth fell open.

He stared blankly back.

"That was *me*," she said wonderingly. "How the devil did you do it?"

He shrugged. "A skill I was apparently born with. I thought it might divert you from your unreasoning terror."

"Can you imitate anybody you want to?"

"Virtually anybody. Women are difficult, but your voice is low enough." He put out his hand. "No more procrastinating."

She ignored the hand. "How clever you are," she said. "Do someone else."

"Miss Cavencourt, I haven't come to perform tricks. We have a skating lesson ahead of us."

"I'd rather a lesson in mimicry," she coaxed.

"That will not get your blood circulating. Nor will you

find it nearly so amusing as skating."

He grasped her hands and hauled her upright. Her ankles wobbled ominously.

She looked down at her feet, then up at him.

"Just so," he said soberly. "We are in for a most diverting afternoon."

"You see?" said Amanda. "He'd rather be outdoors. He insists it doesn't make more work for him. He says the house runs so smoothly he has too much time on his hands."

Mrs. Gales set her knitting aside and folded her hands in her lap. They'd retired upstairs to Amanda's sitting-room after dinner. The chilly January afternoon had turned into a bitter cold evening. Upstairs was warmer, cozier, and, Mrs. Gales may have silently added, farther from the omnipresent butler.

"Why, do you think, my dear, he devotes virtually all his time to you?" the widow asked quietly. "He works with you all the morning, then he spends all the afternoon, far from the house, alone with you. He seems to have a most peculiar notion of a butler's responsibilities."

Amanda flushed. "What are you driving at, Leticia?"

"Need you ask me, dear? Doesn't your own heart tell you what troubles me, and all those who care for you?"

Amanda looked away, to the fire. "I see," she said. "Padji has been talking to you now. That doesn't surprise me. But I am astonished you'd credit what he suggests. You know he's disliked Mr. Brentick from the start."

"I have not discussed you with Padji. I observe with my own faculties, Amanda. You are falling in love with your butler," was the blunt conclusion.

The world went black, but only for a moment. The tiny, sharp ache in Amanda's breast vanished in a moment as well. Even when she lay in her bed, defenseless because the night offered no distraction, the ache eventually subsided. Her days were full and busy, and longing had simply come to be a part of them, a trickle of sadness amid the joy. The night loomed empty, though, empty and hopeless because he was not by to light and fill it for her, to make her come alive as he did by day.

Falling in love . . . if it were merely that, she'd stand a chance. But she must have fallen in love lifetimes ago. Now she simply lived with it by day, and died a little of it, by inches, every night.

She turned bleak eyes to her companion. "It's all right, Leticia," she said calmly. "I promise you've no reason to be uneasy. I'm quite safe with him. We've had all the privacy anyone could want, and he's never tried to take advantage. He doesn't want me, you see. But he is too kind to hurt me."

Mrs. Gales's look of shock quieted to compassion. "Amanda, my dear—"

Amanda put out her hand to stop further words. "Please, let it be. Just let me be as happy as I can for a bit longer. Let me live with it my own way, please."

She rose and left the room.

═══ 17 ═══

THE LETTER ARRIVED on the first of February.

Philip found it in a locked drawer of the estate office desk. The lock was an utterly futile precaution, and another testament to Miss Cavencourt's credulity. He might have picked it in twenty seconds. Sometimes, just to keep in practice, he did, though a duplicate key reposed in his pocket.

This day he used the key, though he certainly wasn't in any hurry. Mrs. Gales had prevailed upon Amanda to accompany her to the village, and Padji had gone as well, claiming business with the blacksmith.

Fearing no interruption, Philip leaned back in the huge, ugly chair to peruse the letter at his leisure. He'd no sooner scanned the greeting than he sat up sharply. He flipped the sheet over to check the signature, and uttered a low series of oaths.

The epistle came from the Rani Simhi and, as one might expect, constituted a fascinating mixture of truth, lies, and needless evasions.

She claimed she'd received a note from the Falcon, thanking her for the Laughing Princess. He'd never written such a note, curse her. The Falcon would never behave in such an adolescent way.

The rani also maintained that she'd sent her agents in pursuit, but the thief eluded them. It was believed he'd left India altogether. Then she offered several lines of apology for 'unwittingly'—oh, very likely—placing her 'beloved daughter' in danger.

Philip turned the sheet over and frowned. Padji's departure a shock, was it? He quickly scanned the next paragraph. She forgave Padji . . . she was comforted, knowing he'd guard Amanda with his life . . . utterly devoted . . . to be trusted implicitly . . . fated to be.

Then an interesting switch, from submission to Fate, forgiveness, and loving kindness to narrative a deal more in character:

> All the same, I know the Laughing Princess cannot be fated to remain in the hands of my betrayer. I have prayed to Anumati and begged help. She answered at last in a dream: the man who possesses her statue will become but half a man, incapable of taking pleasure with a woman. So she has promised me, beloved daughter of my heart, and Anumati has always fulfilled her promises. The curse will not be lifted until the Laughing Princess is restored to you or to a daughter of your blood. The princess is a woman's gift and a man's curse. Remember this, and be comforted.

Philip returned the letter to its place, closed the drawer, and turned the key in the lock.

By the time the rani had written, she must have obtained an accurate description of him. She'd have learned he and Jessup had boarded the *Evelina*. She would have deduced exactly what had happened—except, of course, for the second theft. Amanda's first letter could not have reached the Indian woman before this one was written.

The Rani Simhi knew, yet didn't describe him. Why not? Why keep her "beloved daughter" in the dark?

Philip drew a deep breath. Suppose she *had* described him? Where would he be now? Slowly asphyxiating somewhere, no doubt. From now on, he'd better have a look at the post before his employer did.

* * *

"This is not Calcutta," Philip patiently repeated. "Collecting the post is a lower servant's duty. You lose face with the others when you so demean yourself."

"So have I done from the beginning," Padji answered. He poured steaming broth into a saucepan. "To lose face is nothing. I am an insect beneath the heel of my mistress."

He stirred the rice briefly, sprinkled in some seasoning, then added vegetables, and covered the saucepan. He turned to face Philip. "If it is nothing to me, Brentick sahib, I beg you will not trouble your tender heart with the matter."

Philip elected another tack. "It isn't my heart that's troubled, but our footman's. If you won't consider your pride, you might consider his. James has been with us more than four months. He'll think we don't trust him."

"No other menservants did you hire but this ignorant boy. You trust him with nothing that concerns the mistress. Always it is Brentick sahib who arranges the fire. Brentick sahib who carries the tray. Brentick sahib who lights the candles. Always it is Brentick sahib who follows her about like a little dog." Padji folded his arms across his chest and surveyed Philip from head to toe. "Or perhaps like a lovesick little boy."

"Very amusing," Philip said calmly, though the blood rushed to his face. "I see this is no time for a rational conversation. You are in one of your perverse humours."

He turned to walk away.

"Poor Brentick sahib," Padji said sadly. "What can be in these letters that troubles him so? Tender words from a lover, perhaps, a noble prince who is *worthy* of the mistress? Or perhaps her brother writes of a fine match he has arranged? What will become of you when she weds?"

The world grew dark, suddenly, and wild, as though knocked from its axis. Philip's fingers fell away from the door handle as he caught his breath and his balance. The sick sensation passed in a moment, though, and he answered with forced lightness, "In that case, I should find a less arduous position."

"Indeed, that is so. Brentick sahib labours so hard, and the night gives him no rest. All in this house see how he burns for the mistress, and all pity him."

Philip turned abruptly. "Pity?"

"Even Padji's heart aches," the Indian said charitably. "I have heard you cry out her name in the night, begging her to come to you—"

"You filthy swine!"

"Pitiful, like a lovesick boy—"

In a flash, Philip leapt, with force enough to hurl any other adversary to the ground.

Padji never flinched. He pulled Philip's hands from his throat as easily as if they'd been bonnet ribbons. Instantly, the giant had him in a stranglehold.

"I know you, Brentick sahib," Padji whispered while Philip fought for breath. "Not a garden snake, but a cobra. Yet you must strike more quickly to strike me. We understand each other, I think?" His forearm pressed a degree more firmly against Philip's throat.

"I would have killed you long since," Padji went on in the same soft, sweet tones, "but the mistress would not permit it. She is a child in many ways and, foolish like a child, she trusts you. Do you give her any pain, little cobra, and you die . . . slowly."

He let go, and Philip crumpled to the floor.

Amanda gazed in blank astonishment at the brown giant as he carried the soup tureen into the dining room.

"What are you doing here?" she demanded, disliking the innocent expression on his face. The more cherubic Padji looked, the greater the mischief he'd perpetrated. "Where is Mr. Brentick?"

He calmly ladled soup into her bowl. "Brentick sahib is indisposed."

"Ill?" Mrs. Gales enquired. "How odd. He seemed fully in health this afternoon."

"The ailment came upon him suddenly, memsahib."

Amanda leapt from her chair. "What have you done to him, you wicked creature?"

"Amanda!"

Ignoring the widow, Amanda ran to the door, but Padji backed up, blocking it.

"Let me by!" she shouted. She tried to push him out of her way. She might as well have tried to move a stone mountain. Tears sprang to her eyes. "What is the matter with you?" she cried. "Who is mistress here? Get out of my way!"

She started to move to the other doorway, but Padji clasped her arm.

"No, mistress. It is unseemly."

"He's quite right, for once," Mrs. Gales put in before Amanda could retort. "You cannot go to the man's room, my dear. Brentick would be mortified."

"For God's sake, Leticia, he might be dead, for all we know—and you speak of *embarrassment*?"

"He is not dead, mistress. Did you ask me to kill him?" Padji enquired gravely. "No, you did not desire this."

Mrs. Gales threw him a baleful look.

"Then what's wrong with him?" Amanda asked, forcing steadiness into her voice. Her hands were shaking. "Why won't you let me see him?"

"He would not like it," said Padji. "The memsahib Gales speaks true. He would be ashamed to be seen, weak and ill, by the mistress."

"Drat you, I've already seen him weak and ill."

Padji shrugged. Amanda turned pleading eyes to Mrs. Gales.

The widow rose and crossed the room to release Amanda from Padji's custody. "If you wish," she said calmly, "we shall send James to check on Brentick. There is no need for you to go yourself." She dropped her voice to add, "My dear, you cannot go to the man's bedchamber."

Amanda did not care for "cannot" and "ought not." Over the past few weeks, Padji's cool distrust of her butler had swelled to black hostility. Tonight, Mr. Brentick, who was never ill, always by, was ill and absent. Meanwhile, Padji wore an ominously innocent expression. In these observations Amanda found quite enough to overcome any absurd notions of propriety.

On the other hand, Mrs. Gales's pitying expression gave Amanda pause. She flushed, and though she did agree to sending James, she insisted on a note from Mr. Brentick. If he was too ill to write, she'd go to him.

The footman went, and the note duly arrived a short while later. Mr. Brentick assured her he simply had a sore throat. He preferred to keep away from the rest of the household until he felt certain it was not a symptom of a contagious ailment.

Two hours after a dinner only the widow tasted, and following a frustrating conversation with Padji, Amanda joined Mrs. Gales in the drawing room.

"They did quarrel," Amanda said as she dropped wearily onto the sofa. "Padji admitted they both lost their tempers. He says he *may* have hurt Mr. Brentick a little, but only enough to calm him down. I can't believe Mr. Brentick would be so rash as to fight with Padji."

"I understand tempers have flared more than once belowstairs," said Mrs. Gales. "Bella says Padji has been teasing Brentick unmercifully from the start. Recently, he has taken to humiliation. Only yesterday, she says, Padji peered down at the man's head, and there before all the staff, very amiably offered to remove the *lice*."

"Lice?" Amanda echoed blankly. "But that is insane. You know how fastidious Mr. Brentick is."

"I'm afraid Padji knows as well. It is just the sort of comment to make Brentick quite wild."

Amanda nodded. She remembered how upset he'd become the day he'd arrived, when Padji had complained that Mr. Brentick stank like a pig.

"I collect your cook is bent on driving him away, Amanda. If, that is, he doesn't drive him mad, first." The widow hesitated briefly before adding, "I think you know why, my dear."

Amanda turned away. She knew why. Padji was convinced Mr. Brentick meant her ill. He claimed the butler flattered and bewitched her, day by day stealing her trust and affection, only to satisfy his base male appetite. When Amanda argued that her butler had been a thorough gentleman for more than four months, Padji only sneered. Brentick sahib was cunning. He wanted the mistress completely in his power. By the time he made himself her lover, his besotted victim would have given over all control to him. All her wealth would fall into his hands. Then, when he'd stripped her of reason, honour, and worldly goods, he'd abandon her. Padji declared he could no longer stand idly by, watching her make the same mistake his former mistress had made with Richard Whitestone.

"I know why," Amanda answered at last. "Padji has decided he must save me from myself."

"I daresay you could discharge him."

"How could I? He believes he's protecting me, which is his duty, his *dharma*. In any case, Padji chooses his employers. They don't choose him."

Amanda rose from the sofa to take a restless turn about the room, as though she'd find some other answer there. Yet she knew there was but one answer. Padji wouldn't kill Mr. Brentick outright, because that, for some inscrutable reason, required his mistress's command. He would, however, make the man's life hell.

"Padji wouldn't go, even if I discharged him," she said, pausing by Mrs. Gales's chair. "I owe him far too much to attempt that anyhow. Yet if he stays, he won't leave Mr. Brentick alone. It's my fault. The way I've behaved . . . because I wanted as much of Mr. Brentick's company as I could get. It was enough for me, truly it was—much more than I'd ever hoped for."

Mrs. Gales took her hand and patted it. "My dear," she said simply.

"I suppose this is what the rani meant when she spoke of

a love beyond reason," Amanda continued. "It had already taken hold of me, long before I realised, and so I was beyond thinking, even when I knew the truth. I wanted only to be with him. I would have done whatever he asked, I think. No wonder you were so worried, all of you. I gave you reason enough. Yet you've been so kind and patient, Leticia." She squeezed the widow's hand. "I wish I'd listened, if only to spare you anxiety."

"I'm afraid I've not been terribly helpful."

"Because you don't like to interfere or nag. In any case, I wouldn't have listened. But the madness is done now," Amanda said. Her voice shook as she added, "We'll go to London, and take Padji with us. That will be best. London will keep us busy enough. We'll go to parties, Leticia, and— and we'll drive in the Park. They shall have to endure me this time, because I have money. Not 'poor Miss Cavencourt' any longer, am I, thanks to Roderick. Even respectable now, after a fashion. You don't know about—about before, do you? That's all right. I'll tell you. Not tonight, but tomorrow, perhaps, and you will tell me how to go on. You always know, Leticia. I should have listened to you, long ago."

She bent and hugged her companion. "I wish I had listened," she whispered. "You said he was too handsome, didn't you?"

She gave an unsteady laugh, and hurried from the room.

By the following day Philip had recovered sufficiently to attend his employer in the library. His neckcloth concealed the bruises on his throat, and his hoarseness was easily explained as the aftereffects of a sore throat. If he staggered slightly when Miss Cavencourt outlined her plans to depart for London in early March, that, too, could be blamed on aftereffects.

"We shall probably return at the end of the Season," she said composedly, though she averted her gaze. "I daresay you'll manage with Mrs. Swanslow and Jane."

So, she did not intend to take him with her? This must be Padji's doing. What had the curst Indian told her? Gad, what the devil was he thinking? What did it matter? Philip would not have gone with her in any case. This was a pose, not a bloody career!

"Certainly, miss," he said meekly.

"I shall keep you apprised of our needs." She took up her pen. "That will be all," she added dismissively.

"I beg your pardon?"

She looked up, but still not directly at him.

"You aren't intending to work on your manuscript, miss?"

"Yes, I am, but I shan't trouble you today. You and Mrs. Swanslow will have enough to do, with preparations."

"We do have nearly a month," he said stubbornly.

"I wish to work alone today, Mr. Brentick," came the chilly reply.

Disagreeably chilly. The cold seemed to enter his bloodstream and trace frost patterns about his heart.

She was shutting him out. Small wonder, if Padji had been smearing his character. Very well. The Falcon was not about to beg for explanations.

Philip bowed and headed for the door. His fingers closed upon the handle, then froze there, his rage smothered in a flood of numbing desolation.

He swung round, saw her dark head bent over her work, and heard another man's voice—it could not be his—low, sharp, demanding—"For God's sake, what have I done?"

Her head shot up, and he saw her eyes glittering. Anger, he thought, as he returned to the worktable. When he neared, the glitter resolved to golden mist. Tears.

"What have I done?" he repeated. "What's wrong?"

"Nothing." She brushed hastily at her eyes. "I have a headache."

"I shall ask Padji to make up one of his herbal teas," he said.

"No! Oh, Mr. Brentick—" She flung the pen down. "Just keep away from him, will you? Stay out of the kitchen.

That is an order. Stay out of his way."

"I see," he said tightly. "Stay out of his way, stay out of your way. May I ask, miss, where you propose I take myself?"

She was staring at him now, her golden gaze wide and wondering as it darted from his face to his tightly clenched hands. He unclenched them.

"Gad, but you *do* have a temper," she said softly.

He swallowed. "I beg your pardon, Miss Cavencourt."

"You needn't apologise. I've heard Padji's kept you at boiling point. That's why I ordered you to keep out of his way. He told me you quarrelled yesterday, and he drove you to violence."

"We had a misunderstanding, miss," Philip said. "I was ill and out of sorts and—"

"And he might have killed you." She looked away, to the fire. "We'll be gone in less than a month. Surely you can keep away for that time."

"Yes, miss. Certainly, miss."

For the second time, Philip bowed himself out of the room, enlightened, yet no more satisfied than before.

A long day loomed ahead of him. He hadn't lied about not having enough to do. He'd trained his staff so well, they rarely needed his supervision. They had merely two ladies to tend, and no entertainments to clean up after. The scrubbing, dusting, and polishing was always done by early morning. He'd arranged all, in fact, to leave him free to keep his employer company most of the day.

Now she didn't want his company.

Now he discovered he wanted hers.

Philip returned to his room—carefully avoiding the kitchen en route—collected his coat and his cigar case, and headed for the garden.

Two cheroots later, Philip had left the garden and wandered out to the moors. The snow had melted and the air, though still cold, carried a faint promise of spring. He found the boulders where he and his employer had enjoyed their first picnic. There he sat, staring at the silver case she'd given him.

She was leaving, finally, and he was relieved, naturally. One long maddening year it had been, maddening even at the last. After all the Falcon's clever plans and manipulations, it was Padji who'd changed her mind, not the sensible widow. All those long walks, the sledding, the skating—all unnecessary.

Brentick had aroused Mrs. Gales's suspicions, as he'd intended, but in the end it was Padji who'd served him. Miss Cavencourt was returning to the world in order to keep her cook from killing her butler.

A waste of time, all those hours spent alone together, here in the brooding hills. A waste of time, fighting temptation, day after day. A dangerous waste of time. They'd grown too close, and he'd come to know her too well. She'd come to live within him, a part of him, just as her voice and scent formed some part of the air he breathed. Today the world about him was wrong somehow, dislocated, because she was missing.

It was the same wrongness and dislocation he'd felt when she dismissed him from the library. They were supposed to be together. *Together, Amanda. You need me to look after you. You're supposed to be with me. I made it so.*

He gazed about the bleak landscape and saw regret. He closed his eyes and tried to force the demoralising truth back into its dark closet, but it would not be stifled. The Falcon could lie to everyone but himself. He loved her . . . and in a month, he'd betray her.

===18===

Miss Cavencourt never locked up the receipt for the Laughing Princess because she didn't need to. The bank staff knew her. Only she could claim her statue. Thus, one week before her scheduled departure, Philip had merely to slip the receipt among the clutter of estate office documents he was organising into tidy piles. It was equally simple, a short while later, to pretend to find it for the first time.

"An item of value, it says, miss," he said, handing her the piece of paper. "Jewellery, I daresay. I presume you'll wish to take it to London."

She stared at it, then up at him. "Oh, I don't know. Do you think—" She caught herself and flushed.

"Yes, miss? May I be of assistance?"

Miss Cavencourt bit her lip, stared once more at the paper, then shook her head.

Unperturbed, Philip left the room. She'd call him back. She'd survived without him a mere three days before summoning him to assist with the book once more. Within a week, they'd fallen into old habits—or near enough. Their long afternoon activities had ended. When Miss Cavencourt wanted exercise, Padji accompanied her.

All the same, she was too accustomed to relying on her butler's judgement. She'd call him back. If not, he'd simply discard Plan A. Plan B or C would do as well.

An hour later, he was summoned to the library. Miss Cavencourt could not make out one of his notes.

When he'd done translating what was perfectly clear in

the first place, the lady asked with studied nonchalance whether he'd heard anything of Mr. Wringle. Bella had mentioned him just this morning. Bella, evidently, cherished hopes of meeting the fellow in London.

That, Philip knew, was a fabrication. Bella had nothing to do with it. He knew exactly what troubled his employer: she wanted to be sure it was safe to take the statue with her.

He affected astonishment. "In London? Doesn't she—" He stopped short. "Didn't I tell you?"

"Tell me what?" Her fingers gripped the table's edge.

"Good heavens," he said, shaking his head. "I believe I never *did* tell you. Though how it could have —"

"Tell me *what*, Mr. Brentick?" she demanded.

"I do beg your pardon, miss. I should have told you, but in the press of domestic crises, it must have slipped my mind. Later, no doubt, I assumed I *had* told you." He paused briefly. "Mr. Wringle was taken up."

Miss Cavencourt's golden eyes opened very wide. "Taken up?" she echoed. "By whom, for what?"

"By Bow Street officers. I had it from the employment agent, the first day I met with him. Evidently all York was buzzing about it. Mr. Forbish was most excited, having observed the arrest himself."

Miss Cavencourt appeared so utterly lost that her butler was strongly tempted to lift her out of her chair and carry her to safety. The trouble was, he couldn't take her anywhere she'd be safe from him.

"But that is very strange," she said after a moment. "What was Mr. Wringle doing in York? I thought he worked for a respectable London law firm."

"So it appeared, miss."

"But you said you'd been acquainted with him—and Randall Groves helped you get the position."

"I daresay Mr. Groves found no more reason to doubt the man than I did. I noticed nothing out of the way in Mr. Wringle's behaviour. That is, not until the regrettable incident in Portsmouth."

"I see." Her amber gaze dropped to the table. "Do you know what the charge was against him?"

In low tones her butler informed her that Mr. Wringle had been trafficking in stolen goods, among other felonies. Most shocking it was.

"Astonishing, to be sure," she answered slowly, as she digested the news and reached precisely the conclusion Philip intended. "Bella will be distressed." She looked up. "But we needn't tell her right away. I should hate to upset her now, when she has so much to do."

"Most considerate of you, miss. I only hope I haven't distressed *you*," he said, frowning in concern.

"Oh, no. I'm just . . . surprised. Well, not altogether, for this does explain his inexcusable behaviour to you, Mr. Brentick. The man is a hardened villain. Once he was home, safe and well," she said indignantly, "he had no more need for you. He must have feared you'd discover his true self. Certainly you would, because you are so clever and—and perceptive."

Philip had to drop his own gaze then. He wished she wouldn't look at him so. Her guileless golden eyes told him far too much. She not only believed every word, she believed in *him*.

It was a pity, really. So quick and capable her mind was, as she glided through the labyrinths of Hindu mythology and philosophy. So sadly inept, on the other hand, when it came to comprehending her faithless butler.

He heard her tell him she'd go to York the day after tomorrow to collect her "jewellery," just as he heard himself nod and answer calmly. This, after all, was precisely what he'd worked so hard to accomplish. Yet it seemed another man composedly acceded to her wishes, while Philip Astonley wanted to shake her and scream at her not to be such a beautiful, trusting little fool.

Padji rarely slept. He usually spent some part of the night prowling the house and another part roaming the countryside. As Philip had discovered the night he'd ended up in the closet, the Indian followed no predictable routine. Sometimes Padji never left the house at all. At other times he vanished before midnight and did not return until near daybreak. Twice he'd not turned up until after breakfast, leaving the meal to an irate Mrs. Swanslow. When he did go out, moreover, one could not be certain whether he lurked near the house or roamed miles away. The Falcon had therefore contrived several different schemes to accommodate all eventualities.

On the night before the planned trip to York, Padji chose to wander abroad. He returned shortly before dawn and headed for his sleeping quarters, a small room off the kitchen. Philip gave him time to settle in, then crept out to the kitchen.

"Hush," he said in a drunken whisper. He needn't raise his voice. Padji's ears were prodigious sharp. "We don't want to wake everyone."

He answered himself with a feminine giggle. Miss Cavencourt's giggle, to be precise.

A short, amorous conversation ensued, the Falcon playing both drunken servant and the tipsy mistress he enticed out of the kitchen and down the hall to his room.

He'd scarcely closed the door when he heard Padji in stealthy pursuit. Damp cloth in one hand and heavy saucepan in the other, Philip leapt upon the chair he'd previously placed by the door, and flattened himself against the wall.

The door flew open, Padji swung through, and Philip slammed the saucepan against the Indian's skull. The giant sank to his knees, and Philip swiftly pressed the cloth to his face. Padji collapsed.

Moments later, Philip was hauling the cook's inert body through the butler's pantry, then down the steps to the cellars.

He deposited Padji in the outermost wine cellar, tied him up, and gagged him. Then he locked the door, stuffed a few shards of metal into the lock, and began building a barricade of casks.

This labour done, he quickly put into place the dozen

booby traps he'd prepared days before. The Indian shouldn't come to for several hours, and he'd have a devil of a time untying himself, then breaking down the door, but it was best to create as many hindrances as possible. Every minute could count.

Philip returned upstairs, locked the cellar door, and speedily erased all signs of recent events. He checked his pocket watch and smiled grimly.

Knowing he could delay her if that proved necessary, he'd persuaded Miss Cavencourt to make a very early start. He'd already packed and stowed in the carriage his few belongings. He'd plenty of time to bathe and shave, time even to breakfast leisurely—if he'd had any appetite.

A thief, a prince, a falcon. . . . A prophecy, perhaps. Padji's words came back to Amanda as she sat, silently fretting, in the curricle beside her butler.

She'd felt uneasy all day because she hadn't told Padji her plans. He of all people was entitled to know she was retrieving the Laughing Princess. The trouble was, he'd want to guard her, and if Padji accompanied her to York, Mr. Brentick could not. She had not wanted to give up these last few precious hours.

Now, as they drove homeward, Amanda wished she hadn't been so stupidly sentimental. The disturbing dream had visited her again last night, leaving her anxious when she woke. She'd wanted to speak to Padji of that at least, but he'd gone wandering again. He was nowhere to be found this morning when she'd come down.

To compound these previous vexations, her butler had been behaving oddly all day. When she tried to make conversation, he answered absently, or with the polite detachment of the early days of his employment.

Their discourse en route to York had been desultory at best. Once there, he'd taken her briskly from shop to shop. He'd claimed business of his own when she stopped for refreshment, and left her to eat her meal alone. After that, she'd retrieved her statue from the bank, and they'd left. No, the day had not passed as she'd hoped.

She threw him a sidelong glance. He seemed very pale. Faint, grim lines at his eyes and mouth made his face taut and hard. This was not the laughing, boyish countenance of her teasing playfellow, or even the amused, ironic visage of her efficient secretary. He seemed another man, a chilling stranger.

Abruptly it occurred to her that they'd left York an hour ago, home waited nearly another hour's drive ahead, and they travelled at present upon a desolate stretch of a little-used country road.

What nonsense, she chided herself. She knew perfectly well this was the shorter route to Kirkby Glenham. Mr. Brentick's countenance was tired, that was all. She had no reason to be uneasy. She'd been alone with him countless times, in equally uninhabited locales.

It was the bundle at her feet that made her so irrationally anxious—that, the distressing dream, a poor night's sleep, and a devilish conscience. Not to mention a pathetic case of unrequited love which had long since robbed her of her reasoning power. *Idiot.*

She'd no sooner succeeded in talking herself round to sense, when the carriage stopped.

"Miss Cavencourt, I must speak to you," he said.

Her anxiety instantly resurged. "That's hardly reason to stop," she said. "It's growing late, and I promised Mrs. Gales I'd be home for tea. You *can* talk and drive at the same time, Mr. Brentick."

"Not this time."

She darted him a nervous glance. His expression had softened somewhat, and he did appear merely tired, or troubled. Lud, what a ninnyhammer she was!

She folded her hands in her lap. "What is it, then?"

He turned slightly toward her. "Miss Cavencourt, I'm afraid I can't continue working for you any longer."

Her heart chilled and sank within her, though she told

herself she'd expected this. She'd known a message would come one day while she languished in London. He'd grow bored. He'd want a more challenging and convivial position. He deserved better than the dull isolation of Kirkby Glenham. Still, she'd not expected the break so soon. She couldn't speak. She nodded stiffly.

A warm, gloved hand closed over hers.

"Look at me," he said. "Look at me, Amanda."

Amanda. Her head flew up. She looked square into blue, stormy eyes, and her heart wrenched painfully.

"I must leave. You'll know in a moment. Damn, I'm so sorry—yet I can't be. It's just not in my nature. *Bloody hell*," he growled.

He pulled her into his arms and dragged her close against him, as though she'd try to run away, when of course she never would. He held her so a long moment while his hands moved over her back and shoulders in hard caresses. "I'm not a gentleman," he murmured into her hair, "and it's been hell pretending, Amanda. I've always wanted you."

Wanted her. Tentatively, her hand crept up his coat to rest over his heart, and she leaned back in his arms to gaze into his beautiful, troubled eyes.

"I want you, too," she whispered. "I—"

"Don't."

"But I—"

His mouth crushed the rest, and the words she'd meant to utter melted in the first hot taste of him.

Her hand slid up the fine wool of his coat, past the starched linen neckcloth and up, to curl about his neck. She'd wanted him so long, waited so long for this. His mouth was bruising and his tongue impatiently seeking, yet she wasn't afraid. She loved him. She wanted all he'd give, and would gladly give all he wanted.

He plundered her mouth, an easy conquest, for the taste of him, wild and sweet, was a tantalising liquor racing through her veins. Happily she surrendered to the warm prison of his body, the hot, hard trap of his arms and the punishment of his restless hands. His mouth moved to her neck, to taste and tease until aching pleasure made her moan. Under his ravaging hands, her body strained eagerly for his. Her hands caught in his hair and pulled his face back to hers. More. She wanted more.

Time vanished, and all the world, leaving only endless yearning and heat. Black and glittering, it churned hotly about them, an eternal, fathomless sea. Only their two souls existed. They were prince and princess of the dark sea, as they had been in the dream. So like the dream. Even the Laughing Princess, lying at her feet . . .

Amanda's heart chilled, lurched wildly, and her eyes flew open. She jerked free of his mouth.

"Don't move," he said.

She became aware of something cold and hard pressed against her neck. Metal. A pistol.

She didn't move. Only her glance dropped . . . to the bundle at her feet. *A thief, a prince, a falcon. A prophecy, perhaps.* With a burst of glaring clarity, she understood. And then she realised she'd always known.

"You filthy bastard," she said softly as she looked up again into his clear blue eyes. Clear and blue and false.

"I see I was not an instant too soon." His voice was strained, hoarse. "You've a devilish way of piercing to the heart of an issue. The trouble is, you're devilish inconsistent about it."

"Bloody, thieving swine."

His mouth curled slightly. "You've called me that before, as I recollect. At the time, I wished I could see the expression on your face. Now I rather wish I couldn't. I wish a great many things, love, but it's no good." The cold gun barrel left her neck. "You'd better get down. I'll be needing the vehicle for a bit, I'm afraid."

"You'd better shoot me," she answered. "Go ahead. Murder me. For a piece of wood. I want to watch you do it. I want to carry that image with me into my next life."

He sighed. "In the first place, I'm a thief, not a murderer. In the second, you know I could never kill you. In any case, I don't have to. A tap with the handle will do well enough—but I'd rather not hurt you, Amanda."

"You already have."

"I know," he said quietly. "Please get down. I can't give you a hand, because I can't trust you now. Just get down."

She threw him one disdainful glance, then climbed down. She'd left her reticule on the seat. He tossed it down to her. She let it fall into the road.

"Amanda."

She kept her face cool and rigid as she gazed up at him. Her throat was aching, but she would not cry. She would not give him one single tear.

"I imagine you'll be paid a great deal of money," she said. "You've certainly earned it. Risking your life that night in Calcutta was nothing to the hard labour of catering to me five long months. How you must hate me for the trouble I've given you. To think—I had the temerity to steal from the legendary Falcon."

"That was very well done, Amanda. I shall always admire you for it."

"You hated me for it, because I made a fool of you," she said. "That was unforgivable, wasn't it?"

"I did admire you, dear. All the same, one has a reputation to uphold."

"Oh, I understand," she said very softly. "The Falcon always gets the job done, regardless what it takes. You lied because you had to make me trust you completely. I understand that. But you accomplished that early on. You made a fool of me in a matter of days—weeks at most. Wasn't that enough? Did you have to make me love you, too?"

She turned her back to the carriage, to him, and stared blindly at the brooding pasture land beyond.

She heard his muttered oath, but she didn't move. If she moved now, or said another word, she'd break down. She wouldn't. She wouldn't cry and she wouldn't beg.

"Follow that path to your right," he said. "Once you

pass the rise, you'll see a cottage. It's inhabited. I've checked. Someone there will take you home." A short silence followed, while she remained rigid, unmoving.

"Good-bye, darling," came the last, choked words.

She closed her eyes tight. *Go, damn you.*

She heard the curt command to the horses, the light lash of the whip, hoofbeats, and the rattle of wheels. She waited until the sounds had faded far into the distance. Then she dragged her drained body to the nearest boulder, sank down, and burst into tears.

She was still sobbing hysterically when Padji rode up an hour later, leading a second horse. He dismounted, tethered the animals, and hurried to her.

As she took in his appearance, Amanda's sobs ebbed to astonished hiccups. He'd abandoned his traditional Indian attire for the garb of a groom. In stableman's dress, he appeared larger and more intimidating than ever. Or perhaps that was on account of the black scowl contorting his round face.

He dropped a bundle of clothing in her lap. "Go into the bushes, and dress quickly," he said. "We have no time to lose."

Dazed, she took up the garments. "These are boy's clothes," she said.

"Your mount bears a man's saddle, that we may travel more swiftly," he said impatiently. "Ah, mistress, do not delay with foolish questions. I might have pursued the fiend myself, for I know the way he will take. Yet I feared he had harmed you. My heart rejoices to find you safe. Now you must gather your courage and do, this once, as Padji commands, or the Princess is lost to us forever."

Though Amanda obediently rose, desolation had long since overcome her. She shook her head. "Let it be. The statue has done enough harm. I begin to believe it *is* cursed. It makes us all mad."

Padji folded his arms over his broad chest. "Is this the

daughter of the Great Lioness?" he asked reproachfully. "Does such a goddess speak so pitifully, content to remain weak and helpless like other women?"

"I'm not her daughter, and I'm certainly no goddess. I'm exactly like other women. I've let a man rule my mind and heart and—"

"Bah, he is but a pretty fellow who has betrayed you, just as his master betrayed the great rani. She wept, as you do now, yet she exacted her price. Will you abide quietly, O my golden one, when you might avenge her fully, and yourself as well?"

"Are you insane?" Amanda cried. "It's just a carved wooden figure, and vendettas are not considered good *ton*. I don't want revenge. I don't even want the Laughing Princess any more. I just want to go home."

"Very well, mistress. Padji will see to it himself." He turned and stalked towards his horse.

"No!"

"You cannot prevent me, mistress," he said stubbornly. "Padji has his own vengeance to seek. Twice the fiend—a man half my size—has tricked me, to my shame. Once he used my mistress's signal. This time, my beloved's own voice. My own mixture—a secret worth ten rajahs' treasures—he stole from me and used to make me sleep. For these offences, he will pay."

=19=

To ACCOMPANY PADJI was madness, Amanda knew. The Laughing Princess was simply not that important, and an intelligent, mature woman would merely pity these misguided men. To seek revenge was beneath her.

On the other hand, the Falcon had used her unforgivably. From the start, she'd thrust aside the evidence against him, and blindly believed in Mr. Brentick. He'd known, and deliberately toyed with her feelings, callously exploited her trust. He'd spent five long months seducing her, led her to the brink of ruin—and he never even wanted her. Getting the statue wasn't enough. He'd wanted personal revenge, and so he'd humiliated her. How he must have laughed at his besotted employer.

Amanda took up the pile of clothes, stomped to the bushes, and quickly changed into the shabby smock and breeches. At least they fit relatively well, and she'd be far more comfortable travelling in this garb than in her narrow-skirted kerseymere frock.

Within hours she discovered the value not only of her attire but of a youth spent riding endlessly through the moorland. Roderick had made a sturdy horsewoman of her. Consequently, the pace Padji set, though wearying, was not beyond her endurance.

At every fork and crossroads, Padji stopped, dismounted, and studied the alternate routes, though he seemed sure of the way to go. Amanda guessed these pauses were more for her and the horses' benefit than his. In any case, when she questioned him, all she got was some incomprehensible piece of Oriental logic.

Dark had already fallen when they came within sight of a large inn. Padji reined in his horse.

"That is the place, mistress," he said in Hindustani, though there was no one to overhear. "Large and busy, with many people hurrying about. The man who employs the thief is noble and wealthy. He will not wish to make the exchange in a low place, where thieves and ruffians abound. This abode offers privacy and safety."

"I should think they'd feel safer a great deal farther from York," Amanda answered. "He must at least allow for the possibility you're after him."

"Nay, beloved. The Falcon will wish to be rid of the statue as quickly as possible."

"In that case, maybe he's already rid of it."

Padji shook his head. "I know the roads and the inns, mistress. Many times have I travelled these ways by night. Were I the thief, this site would I choose. But you do not understand. You know only the part of his mind he has shown you. Padji has used these many long weeks to study the part which is hidden."

She turned in the saddle to glare at him. "Many weeks? Do you mean to tell me you knew all along? You knew and never told me? A seducer, you called him. Why the devil couldn't you tell me he was the Falcon?"

"I adore you, my golden-eyed one, and your wisdom fills me with rapturous admiration. But you are a very bad liar. The instant you knew his secret, he must see it in your countenance. Too dangerous," Padji concluded.

"Too dangerous? More dangerous than this? You might have thrown him out on his ear the first day he arrived. Gad, you might have dispatched him while we were still on board ship. You knew then, didn't you?" Amanda accused. "You've known from the start."

"Mistress, this is not the time for lengthy converse. The villains are in our hands at last. Later we may talk."

"I'm not moving another damned inch," she snapped. "I knew there was more to it. I *knew* it. The whole curst lot of you have been using me. And here am I, like a fool, letting you use me again. What the devil is wrong with me?" She wheeled her mount round. "I'm going home, and if you don't come with me, I'll turn you over to the constables. I will. I swear it."

"Nay, mistress," Padji said quietly. He pulled his horse round to block her retreat. "The Falcon left you alone by the road to weep. Must that shape his last vision of you? How many scores of women do you think the fiend has abandoned to their tears? What reason has he to remember you among so many others? He's left his mark on you, beloved. Will you not mark him as well? Shall I merely kill him? Or shall *we two* make him pay, painfully, for his treachery?"

The large, richly furnished chamber was a place of luxurious repose. A fire blazed in the grate. A decanter of wine stood on the small table before it, between two sumptuous armchairs that invited weary travellers to bask in comfort and warmth.

Two weary travellers occupied the room at present, but neither seemed inclined to succumb to the beckoning languor of their surroundings.

Jessup paced the room, muttering crossly to himself. His master stood at the window, his hands tightly clasped behind him.

"Damn fool way to go about it," Jessup grumbled. "Half the day in York. The Indian could have caught up with you before she ever got to the bank, and then where'd we be?"

"He didn't and we're here, just as I promised. I had to give you time to get to Hedgrave, didn't I?"

"Aye, I got to him all right. He was at the tavern, waitin', and not likin' the waitin'—nor me much, when it come to that. And there I was, tellin' him you'd got it, when there was no knowin' for sure you had. He didn't like my harin' off ahead of him, neither, I'll tell you."

"From the moment she decided to go to the bank, the statue was as good as in my hands," Philip said tightly.

"As good ain't good enough. You was half an hour late."

"Our farewells took a bit longer than I'd planned." Philip closed his eyes.

Did you have to make me love you, too?

Don't.

I want you, too.

Don't.

He turned away from the window.

"You look like a bleedin' popinjay," said Jessup.

Philip glanced down at his costume: midnight-blue velvet coat and silver satin breeches. Relatively subdued attire for a pink of the ton. Still, the yellow satin waistcoat, upon which brilliant birds of paradise paraded, was all the most flamboyant fop could wish. Admiring oneself, unfortunately, proved hazardous. Even the slight bending of his head drove his shirt points into his jaw.

"Yes," he calmly agreed. "A precious peacock, am I not? I wanted to go out in a blaze of glory. After tonight, the Falcon retires."

"About bloomin' time. Your relations is drivin' me to drink. I swear that's near been the worst of this whole stinkin' business—runnin' back and forth 'twixt that addlepated ol' carcass in London and them vipers in Derbyshire. Five blessed months tryin' to keep 'em all quiet. You better keep a sharp eye out for that lot, guv. Now they've found out what a nabob you are, they're like to bleed you dry."

"I'm aware of your labours, soldier. Believe me, I do not underestimate the enormity of your sacrifice." Philip took up his eyeglass and inspected it. "That is why I've decided the entire reward will be yours."

Jessup stopped pacing so abruptly that he nearly toppled over backwards. "What? You gone clean mad?"

"The witch poisoned you, Jessup. No money on earth

can repay what you've endured on my account."

"Now, guv, we been over this a hundred times. You tole me time and again to be careful what I ate and where I got it from. It weren't—"

"This isn't a debate, soldier. I made up my mind long ago." Philip screwed the glass into his eye. "Now, only tell me what a pretty fellow I am, and we shall mince down to await his lordship."

"Oh, you're a pretty sight, all right," Jessup said grimly. " 'Cept I wouldn't look in the mirror if I was you. Might bust a gut, laughin'."

Philip felt no desire to gaze at his reflection. He knew what he'd see: a fool and a fraud. He'd discard the costume soon enough. Himself he could not discard so easily.

He took up the figure he'd so neatly wrapped after the last, careful inspection. She remained intact, this prodigious costly lady, smooth and beautiful as ever. How radiantly she'd smiled at him. How serene lay the tiny, perfect hands upon her swollen belly. And how the sight of her had sickened him.

He was sick of all of it—this curst piece of wood, Lord Hedgrave's obsession . . . but most of all, the Falcon was sick to death of himself.

I want you, too.

What could he have said?

I love you, Amanda.

Oh, aye. Then told her who he was, what he was?

He'd gone mad for a moment when, holding her, he'd thought he need not take the statue after all. He'd lie, tell Hedgrave it had been stolen again—better yet, claim it was all a mistake. The thing was still in India, he'd say. But Hedgrave would learn the truth, and set some other—even less scrupulous—after her. Or the marquess would hunt her down himself. In any case, it was too late. The time for honesty had come and gone a year ago on the ship, and the time since was all fraud and betrayal.

She'd have forgiven you, his conscience spoke.

Perhaps, the Falcon answered, *but I'd have despised her for it.*

Jessup stood by the door, his square, stolid face sunk in gloom as he gazed at his master. "You comin'?" he asked. "Or you goin' to stand there glowerin' all night?"

Philip flicked an imaginary speck of lint from his sleeve. "I'm coming," he said.

A short time later, an elegant equipage clattered into the inn's courtyard, and a host of obsequious minions hastened eagerly to tend to it.

No one noticed the two figures standing in the shadows.

"You see?" Padji whispered in Hindustani.

The carriage steps were let down, the door opened, and Amanda beheld a tall, lean, somberly attired figure emerge. As the man turned to speak to his coachman, the lamplight revealed a proud, handsome profile. The hair beneath the gleaming beaver was light.

"Are you sure it's he?" she asked softly.

Padji grinned, and pulled her towards the stables.

Lord Hedgrave had arrived with half a dozen outriders, and a public conveyance followed minutes later. Thus, most of the stablemen had hurried out to the inn yard. The two remaining within the stable made the mistake of objecting to Padji's entrance before they'd acquired reinforcements. He knocked one unconscious with a careless swipe of his hand. The other he threw against the wall. He quickly bound the unconscious men and dragged them into an empty stall.

"Guard the door," he ordered. "If anyone comes, divert them. I want but a moment. When you hear me cry out, run quickly, as I told you."

Amanda nodded. Clenching her teeth to stop their chattering, she moved to the doors. She had to strain to hear anything above her thundering heartbeats. To steady herself, she fixed her mind on counting out the passing seconds. She'd just reached two hundred when Padji's voice rang out, and she dashed through the door and round to the side of the stables.

The first startled whinny swelled into a cacophony of shrieks and crashes. The stablemen rushed towards the noise, then swiftly scattered as a herd of terrified horses thundered down upon them. The crowded courtyard erupted into chaos. Cursing coachmen leapt to control their panicked teams. Screaming passengers ran every which way, tripping over baggage and each other. Grooms darted among the flailing hooves, some to drag guests to safety, others to capture the maddened animals.

The uproar without rapidly alerted those within, and in minutes the inn emptied most of its human contents into the courtyard's pandemonium.

Under cover of the tumult, Amanda and Padji easily slipped unheeded into the enormous hostelry.

The sprawling inn was a nightmarish maze of corridors, yet Padji never hesitated. He headed straight past the public dining room and down a passage to the left. There, to Amanda's consternation, stood a tall servant, wielding a pistol. He shouted a warning. Padji never paused. He caught the man by the shoulder and flung him against the wall. The servant subsided into a heap.

They turned into another hallway, where another armed guard waited. Padji flung him out of his path with a negligent motion that belied the strength of his arm. So it continued endlessly.

Time and again, Amanda watched one careless blow throw a man several feet, to crash into walls or timbers, and sink, unconscious, to the floor. As she skirted the bodies, she fervently hoped Padji had not broken their skulls. She had small time for pity or anxiety, however. She could only follow blindly, and pretend it wasn't happening. Always another turning, another guard, another hall beyond. Would it never end?

"It's a warren," she gasped as she sidestepped yet another sad heap of unconscious human. "How the devil do you expect to find—"

"Hist, mistress." Padji stopped short, and hauled her back round the corner they'd just turned.

She heard footsteps hurrying towards them.

"Who's there?" a voice called. "What the devil's up? What's all that racket?"

"Dear God," she whispered. "It's Mr. Wringle."

Padji nodded. "Quick, mistress. Go out to him, and draw him back this way."

She stared at her servant in horror.

"Do it." He pushed her forward.

Amanda crushed her hat down low over her forehead and, limbs shaking, rounded the corner once more.

"You there!" Wringle called. "Where you think you be goin'? This here area's private."

Amanda staggered back a pace. "Bloody hell," she croaked in a fair imitation of a drunken groom. "Where's the demmed privy?"

"Ain't no privy this way." Wringle stomped closer, his eyes narrowed. "How'd you get so far, anyhow? Didn't the others tell you—" He paused and peered suspiciously at her. "You ain't no lad," he growled as he reached for her arm.

Amanda jerked away and darted back the way she'd come. She rounded the corner, then jumped clear in the nick of time. Padji charged, caught Wringle, and with one graceful sweep of his hand, knocked him unconscious.

Within the cozy parlour, two men faced each other across a linen-draped table. If they were aware of the riot out of doors, they gave no sign. At any rate, a host of armed and well-trained men stood between them and external distractions. Lord Hedgrave had paid handsomely for both privacy and security. It was not his business to worry, but that of the men he'd paid. At the moment, only one concern appeared to possess him.

"It's a wooden statue," he said, gazing with displeasure at the Laughing Princess. "This is not what I requested."

"The Falcon had but one opportunity to study the rani's residence," Philip said. "He'd made a careful study of her character, though, previously. He knew she must have hidden it very cleverly, or she'd not have managed to keep it so long."

Lord Hedgrave glanced at the figure briefly, then at Philip, more consideringly.

"Many curious objects adorned her chambers," Philip continued. "This one the Falcon found most fascinating of all." He took up the statue and lightly caressed it. "He'd seen similar figures before, many times. Usually, however, such talismans are crudely carved and quite small, because they're meant to be worn. This I think you'd agree would make a most uncomfortable pendant."

"I see," said Lord Hedgrave.

Philip took out his knife.

"I presume the man already checked," the marquess said.

"That was neither necessary nor advisable."

The knife dug delicately into one of the drapery folds that lay beneath the figure's tiny hands. A curved sliver of wood broke away. Philip repeated the operation at the fold beneath the belly, and removed another narrow crescent of wood. Then he lifted away the curved piece representing the belly itself. Within the statue lay a mound of shimmering white.

"Good God," the marquess breathed.

Philip took out the great, tear-shaped pearl and held it up to the light. "The Tear of Joy," he said. "Perfect, isn't it? The faintest tinge of rose. Lovely colour, and quite flawless. Some would say this was a pearl beyond price. Certainly it has cost some of us dearly." He held the pearl out to the marquess. "I ought to warn you it's cursed," he added with a mocking smile.

A small smile of satisfaction began to curve Lord Hedgrave's stern mouth as he reached for the pearl. Then Philip felt a rush of air at his back and saw the marquess's countenance freeze, even as his hand did, while the colour swiftly drained from his face.

A familiar warning chill sliced down Philip's neck. He whirled round . . . to find himself staring down the barrel of a pistol.

At the other end, holding with two steady hands, stood Miss Cavencourt. Behind her, also pointing a pistol, stood a grinning Padji.

"The knife," said Miss Cavencourt.

Philip carefully set his knife upon the table.

"The pearl," she said.

His gaze locked with glittering gold. Hard. Merciless. In that moment, he knew she'd not hesitate to kill him.

She put out one hand. Without a word, without releasing his gaze, he dropped the pearl into it.

"No!" the marquess screamed. He shot round the table and lunged at Amanda, who quickly retreated. In the same instant, Philip caught a flash of metal, as Padji cracked his weapon against Lord Hedgrave's skull. The marquess sank to the floor.

It had all happened in a heartbeat, and even as she'd backed away, Miss Cavencourt's pistol remained trained on Philip. He'd not moved a muscle.

"He'd better not be dead," she warned Padji in a hard, quiet voice. "I told you not to kill him."

"He lives, mistress. It was but a little tap. In a short while, he wakes, and I give him something to drink. Then he will not wish to pursue the matter, I think. A little poison," he explained reassuringly to Philip. "It will not kill him, for my mistress tells me that would be unwise. He is a great prince, and his death would cause some annoying outcry." He paused briefly. "A mere thief, however, is another matter, is it not, mistress?"

Miss Cavencourt shrugged and lowered her pistol. She coolly stepped past Philip and collected the pieces of the mutilated Laughing Princess. The Indian's gun was pointed straight at Philip's head. The Falcon stood motionless. Only his eyes followed her. Despise her? How could he have dared? She was magnificent.

Miss Cavencourt did not spare him another glance. Statue and pearl cradled safely in her hands, she slipped from the room as quietly as she'd entered.

Good-bye, darling.

Philip turned his gaze to the Indian. Padji pushed the door closed with his foot.

"You must not trouble your heart, Falcon," he said. "You brought your master what he wanted. The object simply slipped from your hands. Such things happen."

"You're going to kill me," Philip said.

Padji nodded sadly. "It is my *dharma.*"

"I pray you will not trouble your tender heart over that," Philip answered calmly. "I'm not afraid to die."

"Nay, only afraid to live, O Falcon. Such a fool you are. Like this one." Padji nudged the marquess's inert body with his foot. "He thinks the pearl is what he wants. A fool."

"I see we English are all fools, where you and the rani are concerned," Philip said. "This was all some sort of elaborate trap, wasn't it? Miss Cavencourt was simply the means to get you here, and you were to be the instrument of revenge. Yet you say you're not going to kill him."

"So it is. He must live. His fate is not yet unfolded."

"And what of Amanda? Or doesn't anyone care what becomes of her?" Philip scowled. "Evidently not. You and the rani left her to my tender mercies, didn't you?"

"Merely a painful education," said Padji amiably. "Her heart was too trusting. She is wiser now. Be at ease, Falcon. The rani will look after her daughter."

"She's no kin to that witch," Philip coldly returned.

Padji came away from the door. "You are clever, yet you are blind as well. It is the rani's own blood runs in the veins of the mistress you betrayed. Her mother's grandmother and the grandmother of the Rani Simhi were sisters."

"No," Philip said, aghast. "Amanda is not—"

"Her mother was weak, and so her heartless world destroyed her. They despised her for her tainted blood. It will not be the same with the daughter. The rani will see to it. Now, take up your blade," Padji politely invited. "I prefer not to kill you in cold blood."

Not the rani's kin. That was impossible. Yet what did it matter, after all?

Philip reached for his knife, though he knew the exercise was futile. He would die, of course. Without the element of surprise, he stood no chance against Padji.

As the Falcon's fingers closed about the handle, the room, and the moment, swept away in a rush of images. The ship . . . soft hands cool upon his burning face . . . a full moon gleaming above and the gentle splash of waves below . . . the stories . . . the scent . . . patchouli. Amanda, shrieking with laughter in the snow . . . careening crazily about the ice, her hands trustingly clasped in his. Amanda in his arms, her mouth ripe and soft, opening to his . . . her body, slim and sensuous, curving into his touch . . . gone . . . slipped through his hands.

He took up the knife and met Padji's enigmatic gaze.

"Please," the Falcon said, though there was no pleading in his cool, quiet voice. "Tell her I love her."

=20=

LORD DANBRIDGE LOOKED up from his letter as the door opened and his caller entered.

"You took your time about it," said his lordship.

"Press of business," the visitor answered. The door closed silently behind him.

Lord Danbridge rose from his chair and crossed the room to shake his guest's hand. "Well, I'm glad to see you—though you have left me a pretty mess to untangle."

"Be thankful it wasn't the one I had to untangle for myself. Two grieving—or is it greedy?—widows, one hysterical solicitor, and one marquess promising to stick his spoon in the wall. Not to mention my loyal servant, who has spent the last month working endless variations on the theme of 'I told you so.' Bloody insolent devil he is. I ought to have packed him off years ago," Lord Felkoner complained.

"Hedgrave has recovered, I understand."

"Physically, yes. Padji treated him to one of his milder poisons. I rather wish the Indian had exercised less restraint. I've had all I can do to keep his lordship quiet in Derbyshire. Now he's well, he refuses to be quiet any longer. If I won't go after them—which I assured him I wouldn't—he'll do it himself, he says. I brought him with me because he wants watching, and because I'd hoped you might be able to reason with him."

Lord Danbridge shook his head sadly. "Ah, my lad, it's

a bad business. I never should have brought you into it."
He moved away and gestured to a chair. " 'My lad,' indeed," he muttered. "Still thinking of you as the wild young man I met all those years ago. It's 'my lord' now—and I don't mind saying I'm glad for you, Philip."

Viscount Felkoner accepted the offered chair. His host dropped into the seat opposite.

"How did you get out of it alive, by the way?" Danbridge asked.

"Simple enough. The Indian didn't kill me. Don't ask me why. He is as inscrutable as he is immense. I woke to a thundering headache and the melodious sounds of his lordship, Marquess of Hedgrave, retching into the carpet."

"Poor Dickie," Lord Danbridge murmured. "Dashed hothead, too, just like you, and just as stubborn. Never expected to inherit either, you know. Three older brothers in the way in his case. That's why he went to India. Got into scrapes, too, but earned his fortune, just as he'd planned. Hadn't planned for the woman, though. One never does. Of course, you couldn't understand. I daresay she's well past her prime now. Then . . . ah, Philip. A wildcat she was, the most beautiful wildcat I've ever laid eyes on."

He smiled nostalgically into the empty grate. "Too fiery and dangerous for my tastes. Even her husband was afraid of her. Not Dickie. She was just what he wanted. He never cared for safe women—safe anything, for that matter. I think he craved trouble the way some men crave drink, or opium."

Philip stirred restlessly in his chair.

"Well, you don't want to listen to me maundering on about the old days," his host said more briskly.

"I gathered you had a reason for sending for me."

"Yes." Lord Danbridge leaned forward slightly. "I'm aware Dickie's back on this hobby-horse of his. He's written to Miss Cavencourt, you see. She showed me the letter herself—"

Philip tensed. "You've seen her?"

"Oh, I've seen her," came the rueful answer. "Whirled in like all heaven's avenging angels, and gave me what for. Don't know how she tied me to the business."

"Padji," said Philip. "He knows everything."

"In any case, she told me to warn 'his deranged lordship'—those were her exact words—that if he or his hired villains came within five miles of her, she'd take her story to the papers."

Philip bit back a smile. "I imagine she'll express herself equally vividly to his lordship."

"No. She said she would not attempt to communicate with him because he was a prime candidate for Bedlam who ought to be kept under permanent restraint for the safety of the nation. She'd come to me, she said, because she assumed I had some modicum of sense. It is my delightful responsibility to inform Dickie that if he doesn't steer clear, she'll bring down a whopping scandal on his benighted head. I think she'll do it, too."

"She will."

"Which means, I'm afraid, that your illustrious name must be dragged in the mud as well. Not that she mentioned you by name," Lord Danbridge added. "I guessed she hadn't made the connexion."

"She rarely reads the papers," Philip answered. "Besides, we've kept the details quiet. Philip Astonley, very recently returned from the East, has succeeded to the title of Viscount Felkoner. Few would connect that fellow with the Falcon." He paused, his hands tightening on the chair arms. "She didn't mention the Falcon?"

" 'Hired criminals. The lowest sort of thieves and thugs.' The Falcon never came up by name, no."

"I see. Where is she now?"

Lord Danbridge looked at him. "You needn't worry Hedgrave will find her. She's—"

"Is she still in London?" Philip demanded.

217

"Heavens, no. She came to me because she was intending to return to India, she said, and didn't want to be pestered with any more of Dickie's 'minions.' "

Philip shot up from his chair. "No. She wouldn't. Dammit, man, when did you see her?"

"Near a fortnight ago. I wrote you immediately after." Danbridge struggled up from his chair. "What in blazes is this about?"

Lord Felkoner turned away from his mentor's sharp scrutiny and headed for the door. "A woman," he muttered. "A woman, devil take her." He slammed out.

Midafternoon found the new Lord Felkoner dashing wildly about the Gravesend docks, collaring sailors and dockworkers. In his wake trailed an exhausted and increasingly exasperated Jessup.

At length, the servant caught up with his master, and grabbed his aristocratic arm. "They ain't lyin' to you, guv," he shouted. "The bloody ship's gone. It's been gone near a week, and her with it. You're actin' like a bleedin' lunatic."

Philip shook him off. "There are other ships. She's only a few days' lead. We might catch up at Lisbon."

"*We*?" Jessup repeated. "You ain't gettin' me on no more ships. No thanks, your almighty lordship. I ain't packin' for you because it's a damn fool thing to do, and I ain't goin' with you, because that's crazier still. You set foot in India and you're a dead man, and I don't plan to watch you die or die alongside of you." He saluted smartly, then turned on his heel and stomped off.

Jessup's aching feet and empty stomach took him as far as the nearest chophouse.

He entered, fell into the first vacant chair, planted his elbows on the table, and bellowed for service.

A moment later, a shadow fell upon the table.

"Is that you, Mr. Wringle, making such a dreadful roar? Cross, are you? Well, that's what comes of not taking proper care of yourself, ain't it?"

Jessup lifted startled eyes to the vision standing by his shoulder. Then he blinked. Twice. "Bella, my lass, that ain't you?" he whispered incredulously.

"Who is it, then, I'd like to know?" she answered pertly.

"What're you doin' here?" he asked.

Bella pointed to a corner where an auburn-haired woman of middle age dined with a grey-haired fellow in captain's garb. "Cap'n Blayton wrote her he was coming, and she took me along to meet him. Weren't proper, she said, for a lady to come alone. I don't think she'll be a widow much longer," the maid confided in lower tones.

"But you here still, and your mistress gone? Why ain't you with her?"

"I had enough of them heathens," Bella said firmly. "Anyways, that little Jane was just begging to go, though what good she'll do my poor Miss Amanda, I couldn't say. That child don't know a comb from a coal scuttle. But she learns quick enough, and she'll do on the ship, I expect, and there'll be plenty of proper maids in Calcutta. Mr. Roderick—that is, his lordship—he'll see to it. And if he don't, why that wicked old woman—"

"Ah, my lass, never mind 'em," said Jessup as he took her hand and pressed it to his cheek. "Only come sit by me, do, and let me look in them snappin' black eyes o' yourn, sweetheart. I missed you somethin' fierce, I did."

Lord Felkoner was arguing heatedly with an exhausted sea captain when another gentleman noiselessly entered the shipping office.

"I'll pay you double. Triple," the viscount shouted. "I'll buy the damned ship."

"My lord, it isn't mine to sell," the captain said patiently. "Besides, we've only just come. The cargo's not unloaded.

If you please, there are several other—"

"They've *all* just come, dammit. Isn't there one curst vessel—"

"Felkoner," a quiet, firm voice interrupted.

Philip turned. "My lord," he said stiffly.

"Another voyage East, I take it? Calcutta perhaps?"

"It's none of your damned business, *my lord*."

"I'm afraid it is," his lordship answered. He nodded towards the door. "Come along, my boy."

Philip's eyes blazed and his posture grew rigid. "I'm not your damned boy, my lord. Furthermore—"

"Oh, be quiet, Felkoner. And do mind your language. You set a bad example for the seamen. Now come along."

"I'm not your hired help any longer. Find someone else—" A pistol flashed into view and Philip's sentence dangled unfinished.

"My lord," the alarmed captain began.

"Now you just look out the window, captain," Lord Hedgrave politely suggested. "You are an intelligent fellow. You've seen and heard nothing."

He gestured at the door with the pistol and Philip obediently moved in that direction.

"Don't try anything foolish, my lad," the marquess softly advised. "There's not a trick you know I didn't learn years ago, while you were still crawling about in skirts." He paused briefly before adding, "Though for the life of me I couldn't say which of us is the greater fool."

=== 21 ===

TWO SARI-CLAD WOMEN stood at the carved vetiver entryway. In the moonlight, the garden was a wonderland of silver and shadow. The flowers' voluptuous fragrance drifted to them on a light, warm breeze.

"Anumati's night," said the rani. "The time is fitting to unfold my tale."

"You've kept me waiting long enough," Amanda said. Nearly a month I've been here."

"Nearly a month here, five months upon the ship, and still you weep." The rani turned away from the entry. "We must find a lover to dry your tears."

"I have had quite enough of love, thank you." Amanda followed the princess back into the chamber. "It offers precious little rapture to compensate for the madness."

"That is because you did not take him into your bed," the rani calmly returned. "But it is useless to speak to you of these matters. You have confused notions of sin."

As they sank onto the cushions, the princess signalled to a servant, who brought in the hookah. With another signal, all the servants vanished.

The two cousins smoked quietly for a while, the only sound in the room the bubble of the pipe.

"I lied to you," the rani said at last. "I am an excellent liar. The skill has many times saved my life. At other times, it brought me what I wanted. Tonight, however, I shall try not to lie very much."

Amanda laughed. "Why, thank you, *Mother*."

"Ah, I am a dreadful mother, but it cannot be helped." the princess said with a shrug. "Here is some truth: My husband gave Richard Whitestone the pearl in reward for taking me away. It is true the Englishman later abandoned me. I only failed to mention that I pursued him to Bombay. There, through means I will not tire you by describing, Padji and I tricked him and stole the pearl. My lover did not discover the theft until he was well upon the sea."

"You stole it for revenge. That's understandable."

The Indian woman nodded. "He loved me. He had not intended this, but it happened. This I know, just as I know he would have remained with me, but for an accident of Fate. He was the youngest of four sons. Shortly before he fulfilled his bargain with my husband, my English lover learned a fire had consumed his family home, and killed all his near kin at once. Thus he gained a great title he'd never dreamed would be his."

"Now I understand," Amanda said, her voice tinged with bitterness. "That's why he left you. He'd not want a pack of half-breeds to carry on his illustrious name."

"Certainly he would not. You saw how your mother was treated—and she merely a part Indian. I understood his reasons and saw his wisdom. Nonetheless, all his reasons and wisdom were blindness and folly. He married a noble English lady and they lived, loveless, as other noble couples do. I learned of it and rejoiced, just as I rejoiced when their union bore no fruit. No sons, no daughters. Richard Whitestone threw away a great love . . . and ended with nothing."

"That," said Amanda, "is just as he deserves."

"So I reminded him. I made the pearl the symbol of his folly. Each year, on the anniversary of the theft, he received a letter from me. I taunted him cruelly. He is stubborn, proud, and hot-tempered. To provoke him has never been difficult."

"No wonder he became so obsessed with the pearl."

Amanda gazed thoughtfully at the mouthpiece in her hand. "Yet it wasn't the pearl he wanted, was it?"

"No, but to believe so was far less humiliating to such a man than to admit the truth."

Amanda looked up to meet the rani's dark, liquid gaze. "Why did you give it to me?" she asked.

Her cousin sighed. "A complicated story. Lord Hedgrave has agents throughout India. For years, however, I found it easy enough to remain inaccessible. I waited until his wife was dead. Then I came to Calcutta, and awaited the approach of his pawns. Naturally, their clumsy attempts failed. To behold the Lioness is not to capture her. Eventually, I thought, the marquess must come himself, as I'd countless times dared him to do."

"But he didn't. He sent the—that thief."

"When I first came to Calcutta, the Falcon was unknown. Within a few short years, all India spoke of him. By that time, I had met you, and discovered a heart like mine beat in your breast. Like mine," the rani added with a smile, "were my heart not quite so black with sin. A lioness lives within you, nonetheless."

"I'm no lioness. I haven't a fraction of your wisdom or experience. Why give it to me?" Amanda demanded. "You knew how naive I was—and how unscrupulous *he* was. You were a match for him. I wasn't. Didn't you care what happened to me? Did you *want* Hedgrave to get the pearl?"

The princess reached out to take Amanda's hand. "I knew you would never let him have it," she said quietly. "Never. You know that as well, Amanda."

"I don't know anything like it, and I can't believe you could be so reckless as to rely on me. You didn't have to. You could have relied on yourself. Why did you have to make a perfectly simple matter so devilish complicated?" Amanda disengaged her hand and took up her neglected pipe. "This is no explanation at all," she grumbled. "I might have expected it." She inhaled deeply of the lightly scented smoke.

"There is more," said her cousin imperturbably. "I shall—" She stopped and listened. "Someone comes."

Amanda, too, heard footsteps in the hall beyond. She looked up.

Padji's immense form filled the doorway. "If you please, mistress," he said with every appearance of disgust. "Visitors."

Amanda tensed. "Roderick," she whispered. "He's found out I'm here."

The rani shook her head. "At this late hour?" she answered Padji reprovingly. "Send them away."

Amanda relaxed and brought the comforting pipe to her mouth again.

Padji did not move.

"If you please, mistress, they are mad," he said. "One holds a knife to my back. The other a pistol."

The smoke she'd just inhaled caught in Amanda's windpipe, choking her. Coughing and gasping, she watched through streaming eyes as Padji grudgingly moved aside and two men entered the room. Two tall, fair-haired men.

Amanda wiped her eyes, but that didn't help. She was hallucinating. What in blazes was in the pipe?

One of the men was hurrying towards her. No.

"Amanda," he said. "My love, I—" He halted midstride, his eyes riveted upon the rani.

Dazedly, Amanda looked at her cousin. The princess held a pistol, which was pointed straight at him.

"Back, Falcon," said the princess. "Your elderly friend will put away his weapon or I shall drive a bullet through your black heart."

She met Amanda's startled gaze and smiled. "Men," she said. "Just like children. They never think."

Lord Hedgrave—for that was the "elderly friend"—handed Padji his pistol. "Let him be, Nalini," the marquess said quietly. "Your quarrel is with me."

"Is it?" the princess answered haughtily without looking

at him. "I have no quarrels with feeble old men."

The marquess laughed. "Wicked girl."

"I am no longer a girl, Richard Whitestone."

"Perhaps not. Yet wicked you are."

The rani threw him a careless glance. She lay the pistol down.

The Falcon took a cautious step towards Amanda. She glared at him. "Go to the devil," she said.

"Ah, Miss Cavencourt," said the marquess. "I didn't know you at first. No wonder my travelling companion behaved so heedlessly." He turned to the rani. "When I first made the lady's acquaintance, she wore a smock and breeches," he explained. "The sari is a deal more becoming. Don't you agree, my lord?" he asked the Falcon.

Midnight-blue eyes bored into Amanda. "Yes," he answered hoarsely.

"Go to hell," she said. Her heart pounded so she thought the room must thunder with it. "You sicken me."

"If my beloved ones so wish it," Padji offered, "I shall cut out the dogs' hearts."

"Perhaps later," the rani said. "Go away, Padji."

Padji left.

"You as well, child," the princess continued. "Take your Falcon into the garden. I would speak privately with this pitiful old man."

"So you *will* speak to me, Nalini?" Lord Hedgrave asked as he crossed the room to her. "After all these years, and all my crimes?"

She shrugged. "Perhaps we shall speak. Perhaps I shall poison you. Who knows?"

Lord Hedgrave dropped gracefully onto the cushions beside her.

The Falcon held out his hand to Amanda. "Take me to the garden," he said softly.

The woman he followed outside was the goddess he'[.]

dreamed of for eighteen long months. She wore a sari of gold, but the moonlight transformed it to liquid silver, shimmering in sensuous curves about her slim form. Her long, dark hair fell in rippling waves upon her shoulders and back. The sari draped gracefully to conceal one arm. Her other lay bare and smooth, but for the small sleeve of her brocade *choli*. Thin gold bangles tinkled as she moved, and behind her trailed the faint scent of patchouli.

She led him down a path thick with flowers and shrubs, then on to the ornamental pool at the garden's heart. There she stood, her exotic countenance shut against him, her stance cool and straight. Unwelcoming. Unyielding.

He'd been mad to come. Where would he find the magic words to unlock the barrier his folly had built between them?

"Amanda," he began.

"I don't even know your name," she said with chilly politeness. "Your *real* name."

Remorse smote him in a swelling ache.

"It's Philip," he said. "Philip Andrew Astonley." He hesitated, then continued doggedly. "Viscount Felkoner. Of Felkonwood, Derbyshire."

"So that was you," she said, her tones expressionless. "Mrs. Gales showed me the piece in the *Gazette*. I should have realised. Felkoner—Falcon. I collect you chose that particular pseudonym to spite your father. The article said you lost two brothers. My condolences."

He didn't want polite condolences. He didn't want polite anything. He wanted to pull her into his arms and make her love him again, make her eyes fill with trust and tenderness once more. How had he thought he could live without that, without her?

"None of my predecessors will be greatly missed," he said stiffly. "A pity, because my father at least would have appreciated the irony. He was so certain I'd be the first to go. Not through natural causes, of course," he added, unable to keep the bitterness from his voice. "The gallows, perhaps, or some equally sordid conclusion."

"There's time yet to prove him right." She stared fixedly at the water. "You tempt Fate by coming here."

"I had no choice." He took a step nearer. She moved two paces back. His hands clenched at his sides.

"I wanted to come after you," he said miserably. "I wanted to come right away, but I didn't dare leave his confounded lordship out of my sight for an instant. How he found a chance to write you, I'll never know. If I'd caught him at it, I'd have broken both his arms myself."

She didn't respond.

"Dammit, why didn't you let Padji kill us both?" he demanded. "There were no witnesses, and—"

"Padji explained that," she said. "It is bad *ton* to murder a peer of the realm."

"Indeed? Well, it's perfectly good form to kill a thief. He meant to kill me. I saw it in his eyes. But he didn't. Why?" he asked. "Was that your doing?"

She shot him a brief, scornful glance. "You can thank yourself. It was your last maudlin speech changed his mind. Really, I had not imagined even you could sink so low. Not that it worked quite the way you intended. Oh, he believed you, amazingly enough, but he didn't spare you out of pity. He decided a lifetime burning in the fires of unrequited love was a more fitting punishment."

Hot shame swept his face. That was her opinion of him. She thought his dying words merely some pathetic attempt to save his own skin. As though he'd have begged for mercy, when all he'd wanted then was to be put out of his misery. She couldn't know how wisely Padji had judged.

"Padji knew exactly what he was doing," he admitted, his face flaming again. "He knew. *She* knew," he added, nodding towards the palace. "How, I can't say. She's not quite human, is she? But I've had time enough to reflect, and I could swear they knew I'd want you the moment I met you. You were meant to be my undoing, Amanda."

That earned him another disbelieving glance.

"You were," he went on determinedly. "You undid me utterly. I couldn't understand how I could be so careless. How I could misjudge, time and again. I, the Falcon. After you stole back the statue—the first time—I spent weeks in London trying to discover where you'd gone. Weeks. The Falcon should have solved that in a few hours."

"You'd never been on that end of a robbery before. I daresay the shock addled your wits." She moved several steps away.

He followed. "Do you really believe that was all? While I was in London, trying to track you down, I learned I'd inherited. All my life my father tried to crush me, as though I were some unspeakable vermin polluting his family. Suddenly, I found myself lord of all he'd denied me: his castle, his vast acres, his money—all mine. Yet the very day I got the happy news, I headed for Yorkshire."

Her face turned sharply to him, her eyes lit with incredulity. "You knew—before you came—and you travelled all the way to Kirkby Glenham—and worked as my *servant*? What the devil is wrong with you?"

"You," he said.

She refused to understand. "It was the damned pearl," she muttered. "It's definitely cursed. It makes men *insane*."

"It's nothing to do with the dratted pearl," he snapped. "The Tear of Joy was a convenient excuse, I admit. It made you a professional problem, and I thought I could solve you as easily as all the others. Yet the truth was always there. I locked it away in the dark, but couldn't stifle it. It never stopped trying to break out."

"There's no truth in you," she said coldly. "I stopped believing in you the instant I realised who you were. I don't know what your game is now, and I don't care. I won't play." She moved past him, and headed back the way they'd come.

Philip stood a moment while despair warred with need. He'd journeyed all this way, spent months on another curst ship. This time he'd travelled without her, and the way had

228

been long and lonely indeed. He would *not* go back to his great, empty tomb of a house without her. If he could not return with her, he'd not return at all.

She'd walked away with cool dignity, unhurried. The Falcon darted after her, and caught her from behind. His hand covered her mouth before she could cry out, while his other arm dragged her back against him. Swiftly he pulled her into a narrow path sheltered by tall shrubs.

She fought him, just as she had that night so long ago, and her blows were no gentler now.

"Stop it," he growled. "Drat you, *stop* it."

She slammed her heel against his shin.

"Damnation," he muttered.

Her teeth caught at his hand. He yanked it away. She had scarcely an instant to draw breath for a scream before his knife was out and resting lightly upon her throat. She stilled.

"That's better," he said. "Now *listen* to me, damn you."

"Bastard," she breathed.

"I love you," he said. "I've loved you from the moment you jammed your elbow into my belly. I loved you that night in Calcutta and after, on the ship. I loved you after you stole back your sandalwood princess, even while I hated you and wanted to strangle you. I loved you the whole time in Yorkshire while I plotted to get it back. And I loved you when you held a gun to my heart and stole the pearl and your princess away again."

She made a slight movement. He pulled his arm more tightly against her waist, to mould the length of her back firmly to him. She gasped, but subsided against him.

"I have *always* loved you," he continued angrily. "I can't help that I've behaved like an unscrupulous, dishonourable, obstinate swine the whole time, because that's what I am. Damn it, Amanda, can't you understand? You understand *everything*."

"I understand," she answered breathlessly. "I just wasn't sure you did. Will you please put away the knife? It makes me nervous."

"If I put it away, *I'll* be nervous."

"You? The Falcon? You're not afraid of anything."

He sighed. "Except closets. And you. I'm scared to death of you, Amanda. I'm terrified you'll say No."

"To what?" He heard laughter in her voice.

His eyes narrowed. She was a deal too like her cousin, he decided as he took the blade away and let it fall to the ground. He turned her to face him, then gathered her close. She didn't struggle. Why should she? She knew he'd never hurt her. She knew why he'd come. She'd been waiting for him, waiting to get even. The little she-cat had tormented him . . . deliberately. Yet she'd forgiven him, and that was all that mattered.

"I want a wife," he said. "A Lady Falcon to come with me to Derbyshire to make the great, lonely aerie I've inherited a home. And fill it with disobedient, insolent, deceitful, thieving little brats."

"*My* children," she loftily informed him, "will not be bratty little thieves."

"Why not? Their father's a thief. Their mother as well."

She shook her head. "I refuse to live in a menagerie of wild beasts. I have books to write. I need order and peace. Quiet, angelic children. And a very good secretary."

"I'm an excellent secretary," he pointed out, "nearly as good as I am a thief."

Slowly she raised trusting golden eyes to him, and his heart ached with tenderness.

"The thief is a dreadful man," she said. "But the secretary is a superior being. I can't finish my book without him. I've tried, Mr. Brentick. It's no good."

"I'm not Mr. Brentick."

"You're everybody to me, Falcon. All the world. My tassel-gentle," she added softly. Her hand slid up his chest, then farther up, to stroke his cheek.

He turned his face to kiss her palm. He'd never been

gentle with her before, it seemed. He meant to, this time, but the scent of her skin sapped his reason. Silk rustled under his hands, and beneath it moved a warm, beckoning body. He pulled her closer and hungrily captured her mouth. He tasted sweet fruit and smoke. That was she. Light and shadow. Innocence and sin. Joy and madness.

The taste of her raced through his veins like sweet, hot honey. The more he drank of her, the more he burned with thirst. A long moment after, he broke away to rest his cheek against hers. "I want you," he said thickly. "*Now*. You can come willingly . . . or I'll steal you."

He heard her low, throaty chuckle. "The Falcon must do what he does best," she murmured.

He grinned. Then he swept her up in his arms, and carried her deep into the shadows.

In the carved vetiver doorway, a man and a woman stood. The man's arm circled the woman's shoulders. Her dark head rested serenely upon his breast.

"I'll have to put a stop to it," Lord Hedgrave said. "He can't ravish Lord Cavencourt's sister in the garden."

"Indeed, he cannot," the Lioness agreed composedly. "My cousin will not permit this. She will merely torment him and send him away. And he will return for more torment. Men," she said with a sigh. "Like children."

He smiled. "Women," he returned. "Like devils. Perhaps I was wrong to bring him with me."

"He would have come regardless."

"Yes, and I didn't trust him alone in his state. Not a vessel was to be had that day. If I hadn't taken him in hand and quieted him down, I daresay the poor devil would have *rowed* to Calcutta."

"He left it late enough," the princess said.

"What was he to do, with a half-dead peer on his hands? Though I rather suspect he remained with me primarily to keep me from dashing off after his darling," the marquess added with a chuckle.

"Perhaps his heart understood your fate was linked with his. In any case, he has found the jewel his heart sought. Her love will fill his life with joy."

"But a thief, Nalini?" he teased. "Don't you think you might have done better by her?"

"He was for her," came the confident answer. "It was meant to be. I saw it in his eyes, just as I saw through his false garb. Tall, strong, and passionate, as I had promised her." She glanced up at her long-lost lover. "Like you."

"Ah, yes, me. A feeble old man. I wonder why you bothered."

The rani shrugged. "Young lovers are tiresome. So hasty."

He laughed. "Well, you are in luck, my wicked love." He turned and drew her into his embrace. "This decrepit old fellow is devilish slow."

"Then we shall love but once," the princess softly answered. "Once, but very, very slowly . . . through all the time remaining until we die. And then . . . "

"And then?" he breathed against her lips.

"And then I shall find you in your next life and plague you again."

Avon Regency Romance

Kasey Michaels

THE CHAOTIC MISS CRISPINO
76300-1/$3.99 US/$4.99 Can

THE DUBIOUS MISS DALRYMPLE
89908-6/$2.95 US/$3.50 Can

Loretta Chase

THE ENGLISH WITCH
70660-1/$2.95 US/$3.50 Can

ISABELLA
70597-4/$2.95 US/$3.95 Can

KNAVES' WAGER
71363-2/$3.95 US/$4.95 Can

THE SANDALWOOD PRINCESS
71455-8/$3.99 US/$4.99 Can

THE VISCOUNT VAGABOND
70836-1/$2.95 US/$3.50 Can

Jo Beverley

THE STANFORTH SECRETS
71438-8/$3.99 US/$4.99 Can

Coming Soon

THE STOLEN BRIDE by *Jo Beverley*

Avon Romances—
the best in exceptional authors and unforgettable novels!

HIGHLAND MOON Judith E. French
76104-1/$4.50 US/$5.50 Can

SCOUNDREL'S CAPTIVE JoAnn DeLazzari
76420-2/$4.50 US/$5.50 Can

FIRE LILY Deborah Camp
76394-X/$4.50 US/$5.50 Can

SURRENDER IN SCARLET Patricia Camden
76262-5/$4.50 US/$5.50 Can

TIGER DANCE Jillian Hunter
76095-9/$4.50 US/$5.50 Can

LOVE ME WITH FURY Cara Miles
76450-4/$4.50 US/$5.50 Can

DIAMONDS AND DREAMS Rebecca Paisley
76564-0/$4.50 US/$5.50 Can

WILD CARD BRIDE Joy Tucker
76445-8/$4.50 US/$5.50 Can

ROGUE'S MISTRESS Eugenia Riley
76474-1/$4.50 US/$5.50 Can

CONQUEROR'S KISS Hannah Howell
76503-9/$4.50 US/$5.50 Can